Journey

Jae Watson

Legend Press

Independent Book Publisher

Legend Press Ltd
13a Northwold Road, London, N16 7HL
info@legendpress.co.uk
www.legendpress.co.uk
www.myspace.com/legendpress

Contents © Jae Watson 2007

British Library Catologuing in Publication Data available.

ISBN 978-0-9551032-4-7

*All characters, other than those clearly in the public domain, and
place names, other than those well-established such as town and
cities, are fictitious and any resemblance is purely coincidental.*

Set in Times
Printed by Gutenberg Press, Malta

Cover designed by Gudrun Jobst
www.yellowoftheegg.co.uk

Independent Book Publisher

Part 1

Chapter 1

'We must travel in the direction of our fear' John Berryman, *A Point of Age*[1]

There are journeys that take us miles from home, broadening our minds, widening our horizons, and then there are journeys that take us into lost or undiscovered regions of ourselves, into the landscape of the mind and the contours of the soul. The choices we make along the way, as well as the chance encounters, all have a part in sculpting our internal geography; the process, as I was about to discover, can be both painful and terrifying.

My journey with Sara Fitzgerald began in the restless autumn following the terrorist attacks, when London was awash with fear, blinking and trembling in the path of a brakeless truck. It was one of my reasons for leaving the city, although not the only one. As for Sara, I had no idea at the start of our journey why she chose to go travelling at that particular point in her life, but then there were many things about Sara I didn't yet know.

I suppose we could have been any two friends – twenty-something, looking for adventure, following in the well-worn path of the gap-year traveller. But that wasn't to be. Things happened, things that would draw me into a journey of discovery and self-discovery; things that would irrevocably split my life in two.

3

Sara and I arrived in Delhi after two months of travelling and an eighteen-hour journey from Sunauli – a sleepy village straddling the Indian-Nepal border. It was a wearying journey with too many stops. At each station the train was greeted by a frenzied scramble: vendors pushed freshly-made omelettes and bhajias through window grilles, or climbed on board to turn the carriage into a culinary circus. Wiry men, with large metal urns swinging from their necks, glided through the carriages crying out, "chai, chai garam," in gravelled tenors. We finished each meal with this sweet concoction, spiced with ginger and cardamom, and then hurled the rough ceramic cups out of the window to smash on the tracks below. My keen sense of responsibility, inherited from my father, wouldn't allow me to do this at first and I hoarded little bags of rubbish while searching in vain for waste bins. I eventually gave up. I still drew the line at plastic, a curse on India's landscape, but anything remotely edible I handed over to nature and to the herds of brown pigs, which happily devoured everything from yesterday's newspaper to rotten vegetables and human faeces.

After tea, a carnival of beggars paraded through the carriage. First, a man bereft of his legs, swinging gracefully on his arms, then a blind man whose misted eyes danced subversively in their sockets, and finally a girl of perhaps five or six who cleaned the carriage with a twig brush before opening her hand in our faces like a grubby lotus flower. I gave the girl fifty rupees because she had actually done something useful and then, as always, battled with my conscience. I bet everyone gave the child money and never the legless man. I imagined him swinging home rupee-less to his expectant family.

"Hey, Marianne, I could kill for a beer and a cigarette." Sara interrupted my thoughts.

I shot her a look that said keep your voice down; the family sitting opposite were Muslim and I didn't want to offend. They had been kind to us on the journey, pushing vegetable pakoras and over-ripe oranges into our laps while plying us with questions about our lives in England.

4

"Is it true that many men and women live together without ever getting married?"

"Is it always foggy in London?"…

Sara didn't notice my look; her head was buried in the *Hindustan Times*. Every now and then she read a snippet out loud. *"'An inter-caste marriage took a riotous turn in Gonda on Wednesday night when over a dozen people went on the rampage, attacking Mr Manoj Damodar Naik with stones, wooden sticks – dandas – slaps, fist blows and threatened him with dire consequences. The victim said that his inter-caste marriage had fuelled the trouble.'* I've been to a few weddings like that."

I let out a small laugh but continued to stare out of the window. I was in awe of this vast country, which could spring delights and horrors like a grinning Jack-in-the-box and I loved travelling by train; it was a good opportunity to rest from the frenetic pace, to gather my thoughts. I liked the sense of moving forward at great speed yet taking up only a narrow space in the landscape, slicing through small strips of life, without the need to interact.

"Oh God, Mari!" Sara exclaimed a few minutes later. *"'A family of eleven were wiped out by a tanker in a road mishap in Delhi. According to police reports, the driver of the tanker, Mr P. Nallayyan, was delivering dry chillies when he lost control of the vehicle and rammed it into the family, who lived on the roadside. They were all killed instantly.'* I don't think the word 'mishap' quite does the story justice, do you?"

Sara's voice drifted through my thoughts, making little impact on my emotions. We heard stories like this on a daily basis and to my shame I was quickly growing numb to some of the horrors of life in India. Besides, I had horrors of my own to deal with. I fixed my eyes on the patchwork poverty of the rural scenery, made innocuous by the barrier of window grilles, until the sun melted into the deep folds of the night.

Before midnight we prepared for sleep. There was a three-tier sleeping system, with two sets of bunks in each carriage. We always made for the top bunks, away from curious stares.

They weren't exactly comfortable although the firm leather was preferable to the budget hotel beds I had tossed and turned in over previous months. I quickly learned that you rarely find silence in India: jumbled words drift through the night to tangle with fragmented dreams; holy cows, ribs and hip-bones pushing through undernourished flesh, brush against walls and pound the earth in their endless search for food.

When I couldn't sleep I thought about my travels – the people I'd met, the places I'd seen – but mostly I thought about Nathaniel. It was nearly three months since he had ended our relationship – coldly, inexplicably – and I was still reeling from the blow, still no closer to understanding why. He haunted my dreams and sometimes, in the deepest part of the night, I was certain he was thinking of me at the exact moment I was thinking of him, that we were connected by an invisible thread stretching between the continents. I believed it would only be a matter of time before he made contact. My certainty usually evaporated in the uncompromising heat of the morning sun.

*****

It was a scorching day at the end of October when we arrived at New Delhi Station. I sensed a bristling tension in the city that I hadn't felt anywhere else. The choking heat was a shock to my system after the piercingly fresh air of the Himalayas, where we had just spent ten wonderful days trekking. A soft, thick dust – stirred up by a terrifying number of motorbikes, cars and auto-rickshaws – caught in our throats and covered everything in a grey shroud.

We booked into a hotel in Paharganj, a seedy but enthralling part of the city littered with cheap accommodation.

"I don't want to hang around here for too long." Sara was brushing her hair in a small mirror, which hung over a cracked sink. She pulled it into a ponytail using a silk headscarf, the way she usually wore it during the day – denying admirers the sight of its full glory until nightfall.

"Me neither. I think we should catch that train to Agra tomorrow evening." I nudged her along so I could find a space to brush my own hair, which was inferior in length and lustre to Sara's treacle cascade but not bad by ordinary standards. Nathaniel had once described it as "warm honey", but then he used to love everything about me.

I had been told at my school in Shrewsbury, in that unequivocal way boys have of categorising girls, that I was of above-average attractiveness. However, London, where I went to university, was full of beautiful people and 'average' took on a different meaning. Sara was definitely above average; I imagined she was often startled by the beauty of her own reflection.

I think it was Simone Weil who said that a beautiful woman, on seeing herself in the mirror, knows, 'This is I'; an ugly woman knows with equal certainty, 'This is not I'.

I was happiest with my reflection when I caught it off-guard, when I saw it as I imagined Nathaniel used to – unselfconscious, happy; that was when I knew I was seeing *myself*. Nathaniel had always been quick to tell me I was beautiful and everyone needs to hear those words from time to time. I don't remember hearing them from my mother, who left when I was three years old, and the words didn't sit easily with my gentle father – they were too bold for him. It takes courage to speak them out loud. Perhaps that's why my mother abandoned him – abandoned us.

That evening Sara and I had a basic thali in one of the vibrant cafés of the Paharganj and then, exhausted, we crashed out for the night. The following day we visited the Jama Masjid Mosque, the largest in India, and then browsed in the Chandni Chowk Bazaar for a couple of hours before returning to our hotel. I still couldn't shake off the sense of unease I was experiencing and, despite the wonders on offer in Delhi, I couldn't wait to leave.

At dusk, we left the hotel to make our way back to New Delhi Station, where we planned to catch a train to Agra. We were late because Sara couldn't find her stash of cannabis and wouldn't leave without it.

"We're going to miss the train!" I repeated at frequent intervals, sharp irritation rising in my voice. The thought of spending another night in Delhi was unappealing. Sara eventually found her supply, but we then had to run with our heavy backpacks on if we were to stand any chance of catching the train.

Lights were beginning to twinkle as we approached the marketplace, which was still bustling with hoards of people shopping for the approaching Diwali and Eid celebrations. The sound of many voices chatting and haggling merged into an excited chorus; small children, bored with shopping, tugged at their mother's saris, while the fluid eyes of older children darted about like swallows in anticipation of the coming events.

It was as we reached the market stalls that the bomb went off. We were no more than fifty metres from the centre of the blast and we dropped instantly to our stomachs with our faces buried in the dust. My rucksack rammed into the back of my neck, making it difficult to raise my head, but I could see masses of screaming people and the unearthly sight of bodies falling in slow motion from the sky; a shower of blood drenched the earth.

"Oh god!", "Oh shit" was all we said for seconds, maybe minutes.

Sara jumped up before I did, threw off her backpack and ran towards the chaos. I followed more slowly, with a sickening terror that quivered in my heart. I could only think that there might be another blast. I remembered hearing of those who had escaped the London tube attacks only to jump on the fated bus.

I could smell blood, hot and bitter, and the thick stench of fear, which I had never believed could be so tangible; I saw the faces of people who thought the world was at an end, eyes impossibly big, mouths gaping at the horror. Some people ran about frantically, fingers pulling at their own hair; others were paralysed, frozen into the ground, as if cursed by the Queen of Narnia. I wanted to run, run and keep running. My heart pounded with the force of adrenalin; my limbs twitched with the desire for flight. But then something else kicked in; it came from another part of me, above and beyond my instinct – the desire not to be a coward, the need to run towards my fear. It wasn't heroism; it was survival.

As I reached the crowd I lost sight of Sara. I stared into the centre of the mayhem; people were wailing and tugging at the arms of loved ones who lay so obviously dead, all life blasted from their bodies.

I realised how little I could do, how useless I was. Then I saw a child of perhaps three or four standing alone, frozen next to the body of a woman, presumably her mother. There was a small pool of blood forming around the woman's head.

I picked the child up; her shabby skirt was drenched in urine. I held her close to me, kissing her tangled hair, telling her it would be ok. Her fragile body offered me as much comfort as I hope I offered her.

We both stared in hopeless horror at the mother. Judging from her clothes she was poor – a beggar, probably an 'Untouchable', not even worthy of belonging to a caste. We had been told never to give money to these women, who begged, child in arms; they would only spend it on alcohol; it would never benefit the child. Occasionally I gave them food if I had any to spare.

"Mata!" the child said, as if uttering her first word; she pointed limply towards her mother. Then, as if this single word had the potency of a spell, the woman's body twitched into life, first an arm, then a leg. She pushed herself up into a seated position and rubbed her head; the flow of blood was now drying into a scarlet mask on one side of her face. She looked around, dazed, and saw me with her child. Without speaking, she struggled to a standing position and shuffled towards me, as if obeying deeply primitive instincts. She moved slowly, zombie-like, arms stretched before her. A large gold ring through her nose emphasised the fragility of her tiny frame.

"You must see a doctor," I said, "you're injured."

She didn't speak but gestured again for the child. Reluctantly,

I handed the little girl to her. I felt exposed, as if giving up my battle shield.

"Please, let me take you to the hospital," I continued, partly feeling the need to be of use, partly wanting an excuse to leave the Dantesque scene, but it was obvious the woman didn't understand. She hardly seemed aware of the bloody carnage around her, as if it was only to be expected along with the daily grind of hunger and hopelessness that marked her life. Her eyes looked dead; nothing could harm her, not even the terrorist's bomb.

She held out one hand to me in what looked like an automatic gesture – she probably did it in her sleep. It was a quick movement, hand out and then into the mouth, miming the act of eating. She did this three times. I pulled out a five-hundred rupee note from my money belt and placed it in her hand.

"Buy food!" I said. "Please, buy food." I mimicked her own earlier actions and then pointed at the child's stomach.

She nodded, without surprise, without gratitude, and walked away. The child waved her tiny, dusty hand at me as if we were saying goodbye after a day at the seaside.

Then the police were swarming around the scene, shouting, pushing us back.

"Get away, get away, you must go to your homes."

I saw Sara and went to her. I noticed she had blood on her hands and a little on her forehead, like smudges made by the priest on Ash Wednesday. She looked wild, her hair flowing loose about her shoulders. We instinctively put our arms around each other, but we didn't move or speak. We seemed drawn to the scene like pins to a magnet. We should have been part of it; we should have been there those few crucial minutes earlier. If we had, we would have been caught in the centre of the blast. To leave the scene would surely be to leave our destiny.

We did eventually return to the hotel, where our room was still vacant. When we examined our backpacks they were splattered with thick clots of blood, which we scrubbed off vigorously before washing the unspeakable evidence from our own bodies.

I rang my dad to let him know I was ok; I didn't tell him just how close we had been to the centre of the blast. To my knowledge Sara didn't contact anyone. We were both subdued and when we did talk we could only speak about the incident, in disbelieving tones.

"Were we really there? Did it really happen?"

I asked Sara what she had done when we were apart.

"Not much," she replied.

I pushed her to tell me about the blood on her hands and she admitted, almost with embarrassment, that she'd tried to help a man with a wounded arm, before being shooed away by police.

"Talk about out of the frying pan into the fire," I said, thinking about one of my reasons for leaving London. Sara smiled, a Mona Lisa smile, as if there was more meaning to my comment than I knew. Despite how shaken we were, neither of us suggested going home and we both agreed that we wanted to continue our travels as planned.

We soon learned that there had in fact been three blasts that day. Ours had been the first at 5.40pm, followed by one in Sarojini Nagar, another crowded market in the south of Delhi, and the third on a bus in Govindpuri to the south-east. We tried to find out more detailed information but there was a great deal of confusion and idle speculation in the streets.

That night I dreamed about the child and her mother, the lack of emotion in their faces, the resignation in their eyes. It had scared me as much as the sight of the bloodied corpses.

Over the next two days we avidly read local newspapers and discovered that sixteen people had died in the Paharganj explosion and forty-three in Sarojini Nagar. Many more were injured.

Police Commissioner KK Paul said that explosives in Paharganj were planted either in a motorcycle or a rickshaw, while in Sarojini Nagar it was thought a pressure cooker had been placed near a gas cylinder. Reports said that the explosions were intended to cause maximum damage in places frequented by people from all religions.

Prime Minister Manmohan Singh said, "These are dastardly acts of terrorism. We are resolute in our commitment to fight terrorism in all forms." He added that ten people had been detained in connection with the bombings.

Security officials commented that they could not rule out the involvement of Lashkar-e-Toiba, a radical Muslim group fighting for the self-determination of Kashmir.

Some observers believed that militants might have been trying to scupper improving relations between Pakistan and India. Pakistan condemned the explosions as 'Criminal acts of terrorism'.

As police sifted through the charred debris for clues, a group calling itself Inqilabi Muhaz (IIM) telephoned news organisations to claim it had carried out the explosion to further its ends in Kashmir. However, no organisation of that name appeared to be known by police or to experienced observers in Kashmir.

As we read and re-read accounts of the blasts and spoke to locals as well as other travellers, we slowly began to organise the horrors in our minds. I knew already that the scenes would never leave me; they were as much part of my life now as a childhood trip to the zoo or memories of my graduation day.

It was Tuesday before we could book seats again on the train to Agra, and that evening we retraced our steps to New Delhi Station at an almost identical time, passing the devastation on our way. As we reached the station entrance a man ran towards us, holding one arm in the air, eyes wild and zealous. I cried out and braced myself for flight, thinking he was either a terrorist or a maniac, but as he drew closer I recognised Sara's headscarf tied like a militant band, or perhaps a lover's memento, around his arm.

"Madam, you saved my life!" he cried. I thought he was about to fall at Sara's feet but he just bowed several times.

"They told me in the hospital that your prompt actions saved me from certain death. How can I thank you? What can I do?"

Sara looked uncomfortable.

"Nothing, you can do nothing. I'm just glad you're alive."

"There must be something," he persisted.

"Just keep on living. Look, I'm sorry, we have a train to catch." She held his hand briefly but was already moving away from him into the station.

"Sara! For God's sake!" I said, grabbing her arm. "You did an amazing thing; why are you so embarrassed by it?"

She slowed her pace. "I only tied a sodding scarf around his arm. What else could I do? Watch him die?"

Not for the first time, I was struck by how little I knew Sara, by how little any of us know each other. Another person's mind is a Pandora's box without a key. It is hard to imagine that anyone else thinks as we do – the madness of never ceasing thought, the trivial snippets that childishly play in our heads and surprise us with their absurdity, remnants of nursery rhymes from childhood or inane songs that go round in our minds on a never-ending loop. This along with the fear of what others might think and a nagging self-criticism.

We imagine that other people have a purity of thought and clarity of purpose that we lack. For example, I imagined that on the day of the bombings, Sara saw a man with an injured arm and, without any other thought to distract her from her purpose, ran to him, ripped the scarf from her head and firmly tied it around his arm, just above the point of injury. In reality, perhaps she considered running from the scene, or leaving the man until someone came along better qualified to deal with his injuries. Perhaps she even worried about ruining her clothes with the ineffaceable mark of his blood.

And what about the bombers setting out to complete their tasks, striding towards their day's deadly work? Apart from running through instructions in their minds, remembering the details of the plan, perhaps the first bomber is wishing he'd had a pee before leaving home, his bladder throbbing with discomfort. The second meanwhile may be seething about a row he'd had with a friend the previous night, although the friendship had probably run its course. He turns the friend's caustic words over in his mind, wishing he'd come up with the fantastic put-down, with its right blend of sarcasm and wit, which has just formed perfectly in his mind. Perhaps the third bomber is realising, with a cold fear – unlike the scorching terror he is about to inflict – that he never meant to get in this deep. He knows he's the weakest link in an otherwise solid chain, but he can't pull out; he fears the impact of failure more than the consequences of honesty.

Of course I didn't share any of these musings with Sara. We climbed aboard the train for Agra, alone with our jumbled thoughts, each a perfectly sealed casket.

Chapter 2

I met Sara in unusual circumstances. We had both graduated from London University, but I studied English Literature while she read Law; I lived north, she lived south. It was unlikely our paths would have crossed in the normal course of events.

The first thing that struck me about Sara was her voice. I later learned that her father was from Galway; this accounted for the soft lilt that combined with a harder English tone to produce something clear and melodic. I heard her voice before I saw her, speaking with calm.

"You don't understand!" The voice came from an open sash window in a house in Islington. It was a summer's day, the sort of day when the heat droops over everything like a dusty blanket, choking the air and muting the light. There was no breeze to disperse the fumes spewed out by a legion of cars; London was sipping a deadly cocktail. In only a matter of days, terrorists would devastate the Underground and create a climate of fear, which would run like an icy seam through the heart of the city.

I don't know why, but I stopped. I was on my way to a friend's place – one of the few people I knew in London with a garden. It's a mixed area; one minute you're walking past grand Georgian houses set around elegant squares, gardens bursting with roses and hollyhocks, but turn a corner and the place is teeming with flats and bed-sits, abandoned fridges littering the pavements and weeds pushing though concrete drives. The area I was now passing through definitely belonged to the first category.

Then the voice changed in tone; it was louder and tight with tension.

"It's the only thing I want from you!" It was still a strong voice with no hint of victim in it but I sensed the frayed edges of panic. I imagined the girl must be standing close to the window, which meant she was some distance from the door and perhaps in a vulnerable position – although vulnerable is not a word I have since used to describe Sara.

There was no one else in the square, which is unusual in London at anytime but the stagnant heat seemed to have driven people indoors, or into the welcome shade of gardens. I found it difficult to assess the situation. Did I need to worry? Was it any of my business? Then I heard a thud and a scream.

I looked around again, hoping to get help, but there was still no one in sight. You hear stories about members of the public intervening in fights, helping victims of attack – in the streets, on buses – and ending up injured or, worse still, dead. Most people didn't bother anymore. I'm not sure why I did.

I cautiously opened the little iron-gate and climbed through a mass of pink roses, which released their scent around me, so that I could look through the low sash window into the house. I saw an elegant room, pale green and cream, decorated in a style sympathetic to the period of the house. I noticed a baby grand piano in one corner, on top of which was a simple vase containing the same pink roses, probably plucked from the garden that morning. On the floor I saw a girl bending over a fair-haired man, who was lying awkwardly. He looked to be unconscious or even dead.

I couldn't see the girl's face since a dark shaft of hair covered it. I didn't say anything at first; she didn't look to be in immediate danger and I felt detached, as if I was watching a scene in a murder mystery play. I remember thinking how striking a vignette it was – a perfect room with two beautiful figures, she bending over him so that her hair swept his apparently lifeless groin.

I could see her dilemma. The door appeared to open inwards

and the bulk of his body blocked it. He was a tall man, over six-foot and well-built. She looked fragile in comparison. If she attempted to move him, which would be difficult on a carpeted floor, he might come round and harm her. She seemed to be checking he was ok, but then she stood up and tried to drag him away from the entrance, pulling at his arm with little success.

"Move you bastard!" she said. I was concerned she was in a state of shock and it was at that point I decided to speak.

"Are you alright?" I asked. My voice came out small and shaky. She let go of, or rather dropped, his arm and turned to me. Her face was beautiful: creamy skin, dark blue eyes, full lips parted so that she had the expression of a child caught eating strawberries saved for afternoon tea.

"Who are you?" she asked, in an accusing tone.

"Marianne," I said apologetically. "I heard you scream; I thought you might need help."

She lowered her head and seemed to consider my offer for a few seconds. She then came over to the window.

"Look," she spoke calmly, "I met this guy in a bar." She nodded towards him. "I didn't realise he was a nutter; he tried to rape me."

I must admit, despite my shock at her allegation, I did wonder what the girl was doing going home with a complete stranger; it seemed very irresponsible.

"I really need to get my things from upstairs," she continued, "my purse and stuff. Could you help me move him?" I was surprised by the request; we weren't talking about a box of books or a log in the road. It was a man who, at the very least, was unconscious.

"Don't you think you should call an ambulance…and the police? If he tried to rape you-"

"No!" she was emphatic, glancing quickly behind her. "I'll do that once I get my stuff. It's too complicated." She put her hand on my arm through the window.

"Please Marianne, if he comes round he'll kill me. I need to get my things, quickly!"

"Ok," I said, already drawn into Sara's fine silver web. "Just help me through the window."

Together, we dragged the man into the centre of the room; I flinched when I saw blood on his temple. We stepped into the hallway and closed the door.

"How did he fall?" I asked, still trying to piece things together. "He's a big man!"

"He tripped on the rug, banged his head." She was distracted. "Look, I'll only be a minute; wait for me here." She flew up the staircase.

The reality of the situation then hit me; I felt sick; my body shook. I moved towards the front door ready for flight if I heard the slightest noise coming from the room. I leaned against a silk-papered wall, closing my fingers around my mobile phone. I decided that, if it came to it, the girl would have to fend for herself.

I noticed several rosewood-framed photographs in the hallway, showing portraits of individuals or family groups. The fair-haired man appeared in most of them, usually towering above a small woman with well-cut auburn hair, and two grinning children.

I know you can't tell everything about a person's character from a photograph, but I thought the man looked kind. He had a tanned, freckled face and fair lashes, which framed striking blue eyes. He was probably only in his mid-thirties but he had deep lines etched around his eyes, which I imagined were caused by smiling and squinting into the Riviera sun.

I doubted the words of the girl and thought about calling the police but, at that moment, Sara came leaping down the stairs with a bag over one shoulder. Her face was transparent.

"Thanks so much for waiting, Marianne; I don't know what I would have done without you."

She left the front door slightly ajar and we stepped outside where the heat closed around us once more. She was taller than I'd thought, less fragile. She wore a diaphanous green top and low-waisted jeans; her hair trailed darkly over her shoulders.

"I called an ambulance from upstairs; they won't be long. I need to get away from here."

"But..."

"Let's go and get a drink, hey?" Her long fingers fumbled with a packet of cigarettes. "I'm shaking all over." She managed to extract one and light it, offering me another in the process. I refused – I don't smoke but had a sudden urge to accept one, to be included in Sara's drama. I felt a sense of intimacy with her, as if we had been friends for a long time. I later realised she had this effect on everyone. In that moment my life, my plans, didn't seem to matter; she had seduced me away from my path and onto her own.

Perhaps, with hindsight, I am making it all sound too dramatic, or maybe I am trying to excuse my questionable behaviour but, at first, I saw Sara as a victim, someone who needed my help. I had been reading tons of feminist literature as research for a freelance article I was working on; I was steeped in the likes of Virginia Woolf, Kate Chopin and Toni Morrison. Sara's story fitted in with my thinking.

I was also a bit fed-up with my life at the time; some of my closest friends had left London after graduating, while others were firmly rooted in smart careers that demanded all of their attention. In contrast, I seemed to have lost my direction altogether.

After graduating, I applied for a place on a reputable journalism course but, despite a good degree, I had been turned down with a brief letter advising me to 'get some life experience and try again'. I was deeply disappointed; it ruined my neat five-year plan: complete the course, get a good job in journalism and write novels from a sunny garden-flat. Instead, for three years, I had been doing whatever scraps of – usually mind-numbing – work were thrown to me by an agency that only cared about creaming off their slice of my earnings, and I was still living in a dilapidated flat in Finsbury Park. In my spare time I wrote and tried to catch the attention of newspapers and magazines with my articles. I applied again for the journalism course and for a second time I was rejected. As a result, I was feeling less than content.

There was something else as well, something harder to explain. London seemed a city gripped by fear; it was a nebulous kind of fear that infiltrated everything. It prowled the streets and darkened the Underground; it froze solid in our hearts. It wasn't just about the threat of terror attacks – although of course that was a major factor – it was also about the reported rise in violent crime, the abuse and murder of children, war and rumours of war. Whether real or imagined, nowhere appeared safe, not our public transport system, our streets, not even our hospitals and schools. The planet itself seemed to be in revolt, with an eruption of earthquakes, floods and tidal waves as well as unpredictable climatic change. The British press reported it all with a kind of sick glee, feasting on one disaster after another. It seemed irresponsible to me and I started to become disillusioned with my chosen profession.

Young people were blamed for binge drinking and drug taking, for not caring enough about anything, but it seemed more likely that we were made inert by the sense that we were powerless to do anything. The response for many was to drink, dance and be merry, for tomorrow we might die.

The only really positive thing in my life that summer had been Nathaniel. We'd talked several times about moving in together and Nathaniel was more than ready to do it immediately, but I stalled on the decision.

I had met Nathaniel in my first term, my first week, at university. He was in the final year of a psychology degree. He stood out immediately from the frenetic crowd of new students who were desperately trying to be noticed, scrambling to sign up for fresher activities. Not because he was physically striking, although he possessed a cool, classic beauty with his discerning blue eyes, fine determined nose and wheat-blond hair that looked like it was being permanently redesigned by the wind (it was the only thing about him that lacked control). Not because he was trying to be cool either, although he was cool, but because he wasn't trying to be anything. He was the eye of the hurricane, the calm amid the frenzy.

I asked him for directions to a place he was already going and we went there together. By the time we arrived I knew I could love him. We discovered we were in the same hall of residence and made arrangements to meet for a drink later that week.

I had never expected to fall in love while so young and while my angsty friends were still enjoying one dramatic sexual encounter after another. They were cynical about my relationship with Nathaniel, saying things like, "It will never last," and, "Why don't you play the field?" The problem was that I really did believe (back then) that Nathaniel was *the one*, although I felt like a freak of nature for believing such a thing in the hedonistic, quick-fix world of university.

I always seemed to have one foot rooted in the past, in a time when love happened like a lightening strike, suddenly, unexpectedly, and burned forever in the heart of the bewildered love-struck. My heroines were not the fickle, fluffy creatures of 21st Century chick-lit but the dark and dangerous creations of sexually-suppressed Victorian England.

However, I was also scared of grown-up commitment and a little embarrassed by the thought of settling down at the tender age of twenty-four – although my parents and grandparents had been deeply entrenched in married life by then. In consequence I pulled away from Nathaniel, leaving us both wounded and confused.

"Yeah sure!" I said to Sara. "I just need to call my friend to tell her I'll be late."

I didn't make it to my friend's place that day. Sara and I went for a coffee on Upper Street and then caught a tube from Angel to Soho where we drank in various bars until two in the morning. We talked a lot, mainly about inconsequential things and mainly about people Sara knew. She painted a vivid picture of her world, her wealthy friends and their antics: Sebastian, supposedly in hiding from the Russian mafia, staying with his English cousins in Kensington, always pissed on vodka and recounting outlandish tales; Maddie, a bipolar lawyer who was hilariously indiscreet about her celebrity clients when high, but so difficult to be around when low that even her pet poodle jumped to its death from the third-floor balcony...

Sara had a way of talking about people and about events that made me feel she was disclosing a slightly wicked secret and that she had chosen me to disclose it to. She was a child opening a door to a magical world, one hand to her lips telling me to shush, the other ushering me in. I could just about see a tantalising strip of her world. In comparison my own world seemed flat and monochrome and I longed to step inside with her.

In Sara's presence I didn't exactly forget the events that had taken place earlier that evening – the freckled man, the blood on his temple – it was more that they lost their horror; they became part of the drama that was Sara's world, smoothed into normality by her hypnotic voice.

I hadn't drunk so much in ages and when I miraculously found my way home and onto my bed, I fell into an unsatisfying sleep, splintered by dreams. It was only the next morning, when I was curled up on my sofa sipping coffee, that I thought again about the freckled man and hoped that Sara really had called an ambulance. For all I knew, two grinning children had skipped into their sunny lounge the previous day to discover their father's stiff and bloodied corpse.

Chapter 3

'Man has places in his heart which do not yet exist, and into them enters suffering in order that they may have existence.'
Leon Bloy, *The Pilgrim of the Absolute* [2]

We arrived in Agra tired and irritable, still trying to make sense of our horrific experience in Delhi. Sara had been subdued on the train journey and seemed eager to throw off her backpack as soon as possible. We managed to find a clean, cheap hotel with a wonderful view of the Taj Mahal from the rooftop. We were content to sit up there for the evening, bathing our faces in the mellow orange glow of the falling sun.

The hotel owner, Rajpal, came up to join us. We told him about our near miss and he offered us sympathy as well as grass, which we readily accepted. I wanted to forget, at least for a while, the scenes I had witnessed.

"It's good stuff," he said, "from Nepal." He stayed with us to share the spliff and to talk for a while. He was a Sikh man, tall and very attractive. He asked us numerous questions about our lives in England, but we were more interested in finding out about his life and the Sikh culture.

He described the beliefs of his ancestors and their crusade for dharmayudha (righteousness). "Sikhism had its roots in protest," he said. "It was a reaction against the caste system and the menial drudgery of the Dalits…untouchables. It aimed to fuse the best of Islam and Hinduism."

"And what's this?" Sara asked, fingering the steel bangle on

Rajpal's right wrist.

"It's a Karra." He looked directly into Sara's eyes, which at that moment appeared large and child-like. "It symbolises fearlessness and strength."

I thought I noticed something passing between them – a moment.

"Indian people seem so much happier than Westerners, despite their relative poverty," I said.

Raj threw his head back and laughed, revealing strong, white teeth.

"What's so funny?"

"It just reminds me of my father. He used to tell me stories when I was a child about the Westerners who flocked here in the 1960s searching for peace, wisdom and whatever else. My father's business happened to be on what became known as the 'Hippy Trail' and he became very rich by local standards, almost overnight. Suddenly he was able to afford all the things these flower children were running here to escape." He laughed again, perhaps at the joyful irony of it all. I felt naïve for making such a simplistic comment and had the sense, as I often did, of being outside of something.

"What was your father's business?" Sara asked.

"Incense, brass, cheap jewellery; you know, everyday sorts of things. They couldn't get enough of it; they looked to my father as if he were imbued with some great wisdom – he was a very striking man, especially in his turban. "*Money is the root of all evil*," they would say as they handed over their rupees. My father would smile and nod, wisely. "The most misquoted line in the Bible," he said to the family later. "The *love* of money is the root of evil, not money itself. It is a very costly misquote." He chuckled as he counted his day's earnings. "But they can afford it."

"He just didn't understand. "Why don't they look to their own prophet? He's not such a bad chap." My father was a big fan of Jesus. "They come here clutching every single holy book to their chests except for the Bible, as if they're ashamed of it," he used to say."

"I guess people just get bored with their own culture and religion," I replied. "You know, dusty churches, old ladies in hats. Eastern stuff seems more…exotic, somehow."

"Well, I'll let you into a little secret." Raj leaned forward, his eyes glittering. "People are just as likely to be unhappy here in India as you lot are in your English castles. They live with the same fears as you: the fear of other races; the fear of other religions; the fear of anyone who isn't from the same town, the same street; the fear of anyone who isn't like their family; the fear of anyone who isn't like themselves."

I noticed Sara looking intently at Raj as he spoke, an almost religious fervour in her eyes.

"Look at the current situation," he continued in mellifluous tones. "Muslims and Hindus killing each other, Sunnis fighting Shi'ites, neighbour against neighbour. See what you have just witnessed in Delhi. Where does it all end? When one miserable man is left standing and what is the point of that? I tell you, you have as much chance of finding happiness in your own backyard as you do in an Ashram in India, with all its mantras, incense and jangling bells; they are just aids, not answers."

"Oh great," I said, "so what's the point?"

"The point is…if there is a point…given half a chance many Indians would choose a Western lifestyle, even though it wouldn't make them any happier. We could all swap lives with each other like a never-ending game of musical chairs but it wouldn't bring us happiness."

"So what does bring happiness?"

"See, there you go again!" Raj wagged his finger at me. "I haven't got all the answers, you know. I'm not a guru; I'm not even a very good Sikh. I just get on with my life, like everyone else. All I know is that I have spoken with a lot of people on this rooftop, from every culture and nationality. It doesn't matter where they're from, who they are – some have the secret, some don't."

Raj rose from his seat. "Anyway, it's late and we have to be up early."

The following morning Raj escorted us to the Taj Mahal to see the great mausoleum by sunrise. "Before all the tourists arrive," he had suggested. We had a wonderful day and found Raj to be a knowledgeable and entertaining guide. That night he cooked us a delicious Punjabi meal, which we ate with him on the rooftop, continuing our philosophical discussions until two in the morning. I then went to bed, leaving Sara and Raj alone.

I woke up at six and Sara still wasn't in her bed. I guessed something had happened between them and I went back to sleep. I slept until ten and awoke again to find Sara's bed untouched. I showered and dressed, ready for a day in Agra. I assumed Sara would be on the rooftop, or having breakfast locally, but she was nowhere to be found. We had planned to go to Agra Fort that day and the following day to explore Fatehpur Sikri, a ghostly city which, according to the *Lonely Planet*[3], was a 'Striking legacy of Mughal history and a good example of Hindu and Muslim combined architecture'.

I left a note for Sara in the hotel room and one with the receptionist, who told me he had no idea of Sara's whereabouts. I said I was going to a nearby café for breakfast, if she wished to join me, or otherwise I would meet her back at the hotel in an hour.

I didn't see Sara all of that day and not until late that night. Neither could I find Rajpal and had to assume they had gone somewhere together. I eventually made my own way to Agra Fort but, despite the impressiveness of the 16th Century sandstone edifice and the beauty of the pearl mosque within its walls, I was too pissed off with Sara to really appreciate it.

Sara and I had planned our twelve-month trip on a wet Saturday afternoon in a Camden café. We had agreed on several issues but, most importantly, we had agreed never to abandon each other for a man, or to break pre-made arrangements on our journey. This didn't mean we wouldn't enjoy the odd fling or one-night-stand, in fact we knew this was likely to happen and that it would add sparkle to the journey. But, in reality, I was grieving for Nathaniel and didn't want another serious relationship. Sara had plenty of opportunity but seemed content with the odd flirtation. In other words, the agreement worked very well until Agra.

When Sara returned at midnight I was sitting on the rooftop reading *The Tibetan Book of Living and Dying* by Sogyal Rinpoche[4]. It was a bit hard going and my thoughts were all over the place.

'When I first came to the West,' said Rinpoche, *'I was shocked by the contrast between the attitudes to death I had been brought up with and those I now found...Western society has no real understanding of death or what happens in death or after death...According to the wisdom of Buddha, we can actually use our lives to prepare for death...In the Buddhist approach, life and death are seen as one whole, where death is the beginning of another chapter of life. Death is a mirror in which the entire meaning of life is reflected... we find the whole of life and death presented together as a series of constantly changing transitional realities known as bardos...bardos are occurring continuously throughout life and death and are junctures when the possibility of liberation, or enlightenment, is heightened...'*

What would I do if Sara didn't turn up at all, I had thought, not because she had been abducted or murdered – for some reason this didn't cross my mind – but rather because she had found a new adventure, a better adventure than the old one?

'The bardos are particularly powerful opportunities for liberation because there are certain moments that are much more powerful than others and much more charged with potential, when whatever you do has a crucial and far reaching effect...'

Perhaps I would return to England, try to persuade Nathaniel to come back to me. I still couldn't believe that his love had vanished.

'I think of a bardo as being like a moment when you step towards the edge of a precipice...'

But I couldn't return; it would have seemed like failure. It would also mean stepping back into pain and uncertainty. Anyway, I thought painfully, it was likely that Nathaniel had already begun a new life with someone else.

'...such a moment, for example, is when a master introduces a disciple to the essential, original, and innermost nature of his or her mind.'

What on earth was going on in Nathaniel's mind? I wished I had known. Or Sara's for that matter; her mind was increasingly a mystery to me.

'The greatest and most charged of these moments, however, is the moment of death.'

"Wow, what a day!" Sara seemed to fly onto the roof and land in front of me like some Hindu goddess. Her hair was dishevelled and she had dark circles under her strangely illumined eyes. I didn't speak.

"You should go to Fatehpur Sikri; it's so amazing and really vast."

I think I must have looked disbelieving. Not only had she been out all day without letting me know, she had visited the place we had both planned to see the following day. In fact, I had read the description to her on the train coming to Agra and said how much I wanted to see it. My mind began to work overtime; what sort of bitch was she? She was either cruel or very stupid to think I wouldn't be angry and Sara was far from stupid. She pulled a chair up next to mine.

"Look, I'm sorry Mari. It would have been really nice to go together but it was just such a good opportunity and you were asleep. I didn't want to disturb you."

"What the fuck do you mean disturb me? You didn't think about me; you wanted to go with Raj, so you did, without giving me a second thought. That's what you do, Sara; you're selfish."

For a second she looked genuinely shocked; I might even have seen a small gasp of hurt in her eyes. "I'm really, really sorry Marianne. Look, we can go again tomorrow. It's impossible to see it all in one day anyway."

"Sara, don't you understand? You can't just break arrangements without letting me know…we agreed." I fought back tears. "I didn't know where the hell you were; I was worried you'd been murdered or abducted." I know this was a lie but I was trying to find a way of driving the message home to her.

"But I left you a note. Didn't you get it?"

This knocked me into silence. I had searched the room, asked at the hotel reception – there was nothing.

"I didn't see one. Where?"

"I put it on your bed."

"But why on earth did you put it there? I probably kicked it off in my sleep."

"I'm sorry." She looked slightly perplexed. I didn't know whether to feel even more angry or relieved. She had thought about me but she had still broken our arrangement.

"Look Sara," I rose from my chair, feeling confused. "I'm knackered; we can talk in the morning. Maybe it's better if we go our separate ways for a while."

I didn't really want that to happen but I did want to punish her in some way and it was very hard to make Sara feel repentant about anything. I left her on the rooftop and went to our room. I found the note under my bed, written in Sara's elegant script:

Dear Mari,

It's six a.m. I've just spent an amazing night with Raj (you should definitely do it with a Sikh). He has to go to Fatepur Sikri on business. He wants me to go too and said we could see the ruins while we're there. I don't want to wake you at this ridiculous hour but I'm too high to go to sleep.

I'm really, really sorry; I know we had an arrangement but

I'll make it up to you, I promise – I really like this guy. Have a lovely day without me – I'm sure you're sick of me by now anyway! Don't worry if you want to go to Agra Fort; I'm not that bothered. I'll be back tonight to tell you all the gory details!

Love you
Sara x

I sat on my bed and read the note three times. Against my will, the anger evaporated. If I had seen it that morning I might have felt mildly pissed off but I would have understood and been determined to enjoy a day alone.

I suddenly felt ashamed at how I'd spoken to Sara. She had rarely done anything to hurt me, but I had a kind of nagging premonition that one day she would. This seemed to shadow my opinion of her, inform my decisions. It was as if, at the very core of me, I didn't trust her, yet I had no real reason not to. I considered going back up to the roof to apologise but a less forgiving, less gracious part of me wouldn't; I still wanted her to feel remorse.

I climbed into bed and stared at the ceiling. Strips of orange light, cast through wooden window shutters, made a blurred pattern on the uneven plasterwork. A ceiling fan groaned as it turned, perhaps tired of its pointless journey, each blade cutting mercilessly through the orange light, sending a welcome waft of air onto my shamed face. This was maybe the point of its existence.

I could hear the voices of locals outside speaking quickly, urgently. I tried to imagine what they were saying, what could be so important. Then I heard a high-pitched frantic bark, one of the many feral dogs that roamed in packs through the streets of every town in India, ganging up on weaker dogs or worrying the cows. Several others joined in to form a ragged chorus.

I wished I had seen the note that morning. How on earth did it fall from the bed and slip underneath? When I really thought about it, it seemed unlikely. The beds were basic structures, wooden slats with a thin mattress on top. The note was under the very middle of the bed – if it had been anywhere else I would have seen it.

Fresh doubts crowded my mind. Perhaps Sara had only placed the note there on her return, to cover her tracks before joining me on the rooftop? My mind wouldn't rest from its suspicious workings. When Sara climbed into her bed an hour later I pretended to be asleep.

Chapter 4

Despite little sleep I was awake early and took my book up to the rooftop. It was two more hours before Ṣara joined me and she looked annoyingly refreshed.

"Hi!" she said brightly. "I'm starving. Let's go and grab some breakfast?" She was good at putting things behind her, like yesterday's newspaper.

"Can we talk first?" I asked, suppressing my irritation. "I need to clear some things up."

"Yes, sure." She settled back into the seat and pulled her feet up onto the chair, using her knees as a surface on which to roll a cigarette. I felt like a teacher reprimanding a challenging student. It made me feel old and serious.

"What time did you leave the note?" I tried to keep my voice level and free of accusation. Her expression didn't change; she was focused on the job in hand.

"About six," she replied. "Why?"

"It's just that I woke up about that time and didn't see you, or the note."

"Maybe it was earlier or perhaps I woke you when I closed the door going out. I know the sun was just coming up." She expertly brought the filter paper together around the tobacco and rolled it between her fingers to form a smooth cylinder. She licked the paper with one swift motion and then rolled it again to seal it. She inserted a makeshift roach, banged the cigarette twice on her knee and placed it between her lips before striking a match to light it. She then gave me her full attention.

"Look Marianne," she said, furrowing her brow. "You seem really pissed off with me. I've been thinking, like you said, maybe it would be a good idea to split up for a while; we could meet in Jaipur in a few days."

I felt the rejection like a thump in the gut. It didn't matter that I'd made the suggestion in the first place, in my imagination Sara was jumping at the chance to get away from me, and who could blame her? Yet, I felt we should be sticking together, supporting each other after Delhi.

"Sara," I said, feeling desperation rise to my throat. "I really don't want to do that. I was just pissed off because I hadn't seen the note. I'm sorry!"

"It's ok," she said. I was thrown by her eyes, which were unusually soft and transparent. "But I'd really like to chill out here for a few days, spend a bit of time with Raj. When we meet up again we'll have loads to talk about."

I knew it was useless to try to change her mind. She might even have decided this plan with Raj the day before. I had simply played into their hands.

"Ok," I said curtly. "I'll find out about buses and leave tomorrow."

The rest of the day was disjointed. I felt homesick and missed Nathaniel painfully. I thought about flying home but knew it would be cowardly. Once again I imagined what I would be doing if, on that soggy September day, my heart disintegrating with the loss of love, I had never agreed to go travelling with Sara Fitzgerald. I envisaged the straightforward life I could have been leading with Nathaniel, doing the ordinary things that couples do. It then seemed such an enticing life in its ordinariness. I wanted it back so desperately that I wept for it, as if weeping could ever bring it back.

I wrote several pages of self-pitying prose in my diary and spent too much money on sweet, milky coffee and coconut cakes in places that catered for package tourists and which Sara and I usually went to lengths to avoid.

I exchanged my book for something I thought would be lighter in both weight and content, entitled *The Celestine Prophecy – An Adventure*[5]. Tired of walking around the polluted streets of Agra and exploring Kinari Chowk, the local market, I found another café and settled down to read, aiming to make one cup of coffee last as long as possible.

The book started innocuously enough; it was a relief to enter a different world, find respite from my own miserable thoughts. It read like an adventure story – the disappearance of an ancient Peruvian manuscript containing important insights for humankind, a journey to the Andes and the rainforests of Peru, a bit of intrigue and sexual frisson. Then the tone changed.

'For half a century now, a new consciousness has been entering the human world, a new awareness that can only be called transcendent; spiritual...It begins with heightened perception of how our lives move forward. We notice these chance events that occur at just the right moment and bring forth just the right individuals, to suddenly send our lives in a new important direction.'

One of the characters talked about a 'profound restlessness' that we feel when we are beginning to glimpse an alternative kind of experience; moments in our lives that feel different, more intense and inspiring – those 'bardos' again. This was a new concept for me, yet I had read similar things in two unrelated books. It must be coincidence, I thought. I was in a land where spiritual concepts are as prevalent as mosquitoes; some are bound to collide.

'We know that life is really about a spiritual unfolding that is personal and enchanting – an unfolding that no science or philosophy or religion has yet fully clarified...once we do understand what is happening...human society will take a quantum leap into a whole new way of life.'

The two main characters were having a conversation over dinner. The female character *'wrinkled her nose and giggled'* – she was already annoying me – before telling her dinner partner about the 'First Insight'. ' *"This occurs," she explained, "when*

we become conscious of the coincidence in our lives…we sense
again, as in childhood, that there is another side of life that we
have yet to discover, some other process operating behind the
scenes.'"

"Crap!" I exclaimed aloud, throwing the book onto the table
and squeezing my eyes closed to hold in the tears, "Absolute
crap!"

*****

I had never felt quite so alone as when I stood at the bus
station in Agra, clutching my backpack and bottle of water. The
earliest bus I had been able to book to Jaipur was two o'clock
the following day and somehow I managed to avoid Sara until
then.

I decided to pay a bit extra for what was described as
a 'Super Deluxe Tourist Bus', as opposed to the ramshackle
vehicles we normally used, sharing seats with chickens and
wiry-legged men. We drew a lot of attention as white Western
women and I wasn't in the mood for attracting any kind of
attention. I was told the journey would take six hours and I
hoped, being a tourist bus, it would arrive closer to the
advertised time than usual, allowing me to find accommodation
before dark.

I arrived at Idgah bus station at one-forty-five. Three buses
were parked in the dusty square: a large white one, which had
the words 'Sharma Tours' across the side in smart red and green
letters, and '*air con*' written in smaller letters beneath; a square-
nosed blue bus which wouldn't have been out of place in 1955;
and a ramshackle mini-bus. I assumed the large white bus was
the one on which I would be travelling.

There was already a group of Israelis waiting. They sat on
their backpacks, easy with themselves – many of them, I
learned, had come straight out of national service back home.
Their bodies looked strong and lean, and their hair had grown
long and knotty. Army uniforms had been exchanged for the

brightly coloured uniform of the traveller.

At two-thirty there was still no movement around any of the buses and I realised it was going to be the same old story. No one else seemed perturbed but I was anxious to start my journey, if I was going to make it at all.

At three o'clock, two boys carried rusted buckets of water across the square to the large white bus and made lethargic sweeping movements over the vehicle with dirty rags. I thought it was a good sign but nothing else happened. Half-an-hour later, in total exasperation, I marched to the office to ask when the bus would be leaving. Two rotund men looked me up and down with wary eyes.

"We're waiting for the driver," one of them said unconvincingly.

"Ok, which bus are we on?" I asked sharply.

They exchanged some words in Hindi and then the same man pointed to the blue bus.

"But I thought it was the tourist bus, the white one?" I said weakly, knowing I was powerless to change anything. He shrugged.

I left the office, tossing my hair back while their laughs prodded my back like the fingers of a school bully. Tears pushed at the back of my eyes. I bit my hand to stop the flow and walked over to the blue bus so that my face couldn't be seen. At least there was some tread on the tyres. I remembered a previous bus journey Sara and I had endured during a five-hour storm; torrential rain had lashed the windows and the windscreen wipers had failed to work. But it hadn't stopped the driver overtaking on precarious bends or listening to frenetic Hindi music while chattering with his friends. They had all stood around him at the front of the bus as if they were enjoying a night out at the local club.

We had been told that drivers are expected to make long journeys back-to-back and the only way they can stay awake is to take large quantities of speed, causing them to laugh and chatter all night. I had scribbled a hasty Will in the back of a notepad and emotional messages for loved ones. Sara had laughed at me but we both vowed to travel by train in future. Interestingly, we hadn't demanded to get off the bus and at times I even felt a kind of numb acceptance about my fate.

"Madam, you are on *that* bus!" a melodious voice sang behind me. I turned to see an elderly man nodding towards the minibus, standing in all its dilapidated glory.

"No, I'm not," I said firmly. "I paid for a tourist bus."

"That *is* the tourist bus," he said. "It is a very good bus."

"It's not; it's a crap bus." The tears were now brutalising the backs of my eyes. "Where's the manager?"

"He's away." The man's expression didn't change; he had a serene, patient look that said, "Why do Westerners make such a fuss about everything? Surely one bus is much like another, as long as it gets you to your destination."

"The bus is already two hours late." My tears were now flowing unashamedly. "And you are conning us with this heap of crap." I wanted to hurt the man, make him feel bad.

"Where is your honour?" I demanded. "You are without honour." It sounded so antiquated, like a bad line from a Bollywood movie. Sara and I laughed about it later, but at the time I felt they were the right words to stab at this man's serene heart.

"Sir," he said, "there are not enough passengers for the big bus, but I promise you will get to your destination on this vehicle."

"And where is that?" I asked. "Hell? And don't call me Sir."

I climbed onto the minibus feeling like a lamb to the slaughter. I settled for a seat near the back. The window was veiled in dust so that the world outside shimmered like a sepia photograph. Other passengers climbed on, seemingly in good spirits.

"It's always the same," an Israeli guy said as he passed. "You have to laugh."

I didn't want to laugh and at that moment I didn't want to be in India. I desperately wanted to be in London on a wet Saturday afternoon, jumping off the 73 bus to meet Nathaniel.

We would drink warm, frothy lattes and read about the world from a safe distance; maybe we would catch a movie or meet Sue and James for drinks. I didn't want to be so intimately involved in this vast, shifting world, sticky with life, clotted thick with humanity, battering at my senses with its noisy death and blistered life, always in my face like a demanding child, pulling my hair, forcing me to look. I wanted *my* life back, whole, smooth and clean.

The bus pulled away just after four o'clock, the time the next bus had been due to leave. Or rather it was pushed away as, not surprisingly, the battery was flat.

I was at least grateful that I didn't have anyone sitting next to me; in fact the seat next to mine was the only empty one on the bus and I imagined that my negative vibes had put people off. I hid my face in my book, hoping to distract my mind from misery, to become lost in someone else's story. Then there was a loud banging on the window.

"Wait!" someone shouted. The bus slowed and a guy jumped on, loaded with a well-worn backpack.

"Close thing!" He spoke to the whole bus, his eyes bright with humour. The mood of the bus seemed to lift and several people laughed or made comments in return. I felt irritated by the late arrival as he moved down and sat next to me, imagining that he was the sort of person who had the knack of turning up just on time for everything.

Chapter 5

I have heard it said that most travellers are running away from something, whether from failure, heartbreak or something far more sinister. At the start of my journey I probably would have said I was leaving behind the pain of my ended relationship with Nathaniel, as well as rejection from the journalism course and a general sense of unease about the state of affairs in London. However, as time went on, I recognised that there were deeper, more entrenched issues in my life.

I also began to wonder if Sara had something to run from. I questioned why she should leave London at the start of a promising career in law and I couldn't forget the incident with the freckled man. I had never had a satisfactory explanation from Sara as to what had happened that day. In fact, it was only when we arrived in Thailand on the very first leg of our journey that it dawned on me that I hardly knew Sara at all. We had thrown our backpacks onto the sandy floor of a tiny beach hut in the sticky heat of our first night on Ko Pha Ngan and strangeness settled about us like an unwelcome cloud.

I tiptoed around Sara for the first few days; she seemed oblivious to my discomfort and in contrast appeared totally at ease. I felt my ordinariness in contrast to what I perceived to be Sara's sparkle and wondered if I'd made the right choice in coming away with her; not because I didn't want Sara's company but because I was concerned that, before too long, she wouldn't want mine.

Two weeks after arriving, we had our first row; it shattered the honeymoon politeness of our friendship. We lay in hammocks outside the quaint but basic beach hut; it was a perfect blue evening with the scent of the South China Sea mingling with coconut and lemongrass. Massive Attack were weaving their spell from Sara's ipod, we had drunk several Tiger Beers and we were pretty chilled.

It was also my birthday – I had just turned twenty-five and the quarter-century mark had freaked me out. I worried about my non-existent career and my future without Nathaniel. Sara and I, not for the first time, were having a conversation about relationships. I always felt slightly embarrassed about my lack of experience with men. Sara had slept with more men than she could remember and was neither proud nor ashamed to admit it.

"I suppose our parents' generation would be considered loose for sleeping around," I said.

"Yeah, but those values were imposed by men to make sure they weren't forking out for someone else's offspring." Sara stretched in her hammock like an insouciant cat.

"I don't have a clue what my mother's views were on sex and relationships," I said, "and my dad just avoided the subject."

"Aren't you ever curious to know more about your mum, Mari? I'd be like, who the hell is she!"

I was surprised by the question. Sara and I had shared very little about our families up to that point. The reluctance existed on both sides; although I had been led largely by Sara, who was usually dismissive of my questions.

"Not really," I began tentatively. "Dad and I have managed fine without her."

"How old were you when she left?"

I felt the familiar sense of unease rise in my belly – a strange brew of shame, loss and anger.

"Three." The number dried in my mouth, thick with a significance I didn't understand.

"God! What a bitch." Sara's words hung limply in the air for a few seconds, impotent because they had no real target.

My father rarely talked about my mother after she left. We only had one photograph, which he kept in a drawer; it showed a pretty, young woman in a red bikini, sitting on a beach in South Wales. My father had taken the shot from above and my mother filled the whole frame with only a glimpse of sand and the striped beach towel beneath her. A tiny strip of the sea was pushed tantalisingly into one corner of the frame.

She seemed too big for the photograph, as if she might burst out of it at any moment. She was laughing, what looked to be a vivacious, natural laugh, her face and smooth cleavage rising towards the camera. Despite my frequent interrogations, Dad said he couldn't remember what she was laughing about.

I studied the photograph obsessively after she left, perhaps trying to find clues to a puzzle I couldn't solve. I hadn't looked at it for years now; it seemed to have nothing to do with me anymore.

"Where did she go?" Sara asked.

I was reluctant to continue. It felt like dangerous ground riddled with landmines, ground I had rarely stepped upon.

"The only thing my dad told me was that she went to join the women at Greenham Common." I laughed nervously; for some reason I felt embarrassed by this. For years I had thought Greenham Common was this mythical place, a kind of Neverland for mothers who didn't want their children.

"Wow, Greenham Common, that's cool!" Sara said. "No one gets that passionate about stuff anymore."

"Apparently she was an ardent feminist, always banging on about equality." This was a phrase I had overheard my paternal grandmother use in disparaging tones after my mother left. I also heard them describe her as a 'staunch Catholic' and 'riddled with guilt'. That didn't stop her from 'living in sin', they added. These disjointed phrases haunted my childhood.

"But equality is such a redundant fight," said Sara. "Why don't women just realise it?" She shifted in the hammock so that it rocked unevenly and she took a long swig of beer. I sensed she was rising to a heated debate. I wasn't sure I

41

was in the mood.

"There was never a question of whether women are equal to men; you might as well ask if purple is equal to red or a carrot equal to a potato. It's a nonsensical question."

"I guess it's more about equal rights than innate equality." I wasn't sure if I was defending my mother's position or my own.

"Yeah, but most women don't believe that; they're always mouthing off about being equal instead of just claiming it, living it. Some of our generation are the worst. Look at the Britney brigade, going on about girl power but dressing like tarts, always scheming to catch a man and then moaning about how badly he treats her. They haven't got a clue about female power or about what issues still need to be fought. They've just mistaken self-interest for sisterhood. It's like we've slipped back fifty years…"

On another occasion I might have taken the bit of this discussion. I enjoyed our varied and often heated debates but I felt Sara had opened something up with her original question and I wanted to use the opportunity to find out more about her, perhaps get onto a deeper level in our friendship.

"What about your mum? You've never said much about her."

"Oh, she's a bitch as well. Do you fancy a birthday spliff?" Sara held up a plastic bag containing rich, green ganja. She waved it in the air like a goody-bag at a child's party. I would normally have let this go but I felt I'd been led along a dark and rocky path, only to be abandoned at the end of it.

"You always do that."

"Do what?" Her face was transparent.

"Get me to open up and then you change the subject when it comes to you."

"Do I? I'm sorry. I didn't think you wanted to talk about it anymore." She looked so genuinely surprised by my reaction that I felt silly to pursue it. However, fuelled by alcohol and a build-up of resentment, I continued.

"Yeah, but you ask me something that forces me to open up, then you come out with some flippant or dismissive comment when I return the question." I knew I wasn't explaining myself well and I wasn't sure if I even had a good case but I desperately wanted Sara to see how she behaved and I was driven on by a punitive urge.

"Marianne, you could have just said you didn't want to talk about it; I would have respected that." As usual she made absolute logical sense, but it still missed the point.

"I know Sara, but don't you see, the question itself has an effect on me. One minute we're talking about blokes and books and unimportant things and then you ask a question that puts me in a totally different head space." Sara looked puzzled and I knew she didn't get it. It made me want to push more.

"If I ask you difficult questions, say about your childhood or something, doesn't it bother you?"

"You can ask me any question you like, it's cool; I don't have to answer it." She rubbed the ganja between her fingers to loosen it, removing any hard seeds, and then scattered it evenly along the cigarette papers. "I think you let things get to you too much Mari; chill out and take a bit more responsibility for yourself."

"What the hell does that mean? I do take responsibility."

"I just mean that you don't have to be hurt by everything…"

"Ok. I want to know what happened that day in Islington." I pushed myself up in my hammock; I could feel my face burning with exasperation. "What *really* happened?"

I probably put more emphasis on the word 'really' than intended, revealing my doubt about Sara's version of events.

"I told you what happened, Marianne," she said firmly, implying there was no room for further discussion. Her face was as immovable as alabaster.

"Yes, but it didn't fit together. What were you doing in his house if you'd only just met the guy?"

"He seemed nice; I fancied him," she replied matter-of-factly.

"Yeah, but he was obviously married with kids…the photos."

"Look Marianne, it doesn't matter; it was a long time ago." She talked as if it were years rather than months. She pushed her head back into the hammock and took the first drag of the spliff, looking up into the darkening sky where tiny stars were making their first glittering appearance.

"But the guy was lying on the floor," I persisted. "There was blood on his head. Didn't the police question you?" Sara was unresponsive. She took several more drags, blowing the smoke away from me, dismissing the air around her with each slow exhale. The sweet smell of ganja perfumed the warm breeze. She seemed to be looking beyond the stars to something much more distant. Eventually she turned to face me.

"I made an anonymous call; I didn't want to get involved."

I felt angered by her response. It was so typical of her, I thought, so careless not to take responsibility.

"But you *were* involved," I said harshly. "For all you know, the poor bloke might have been dead. Weren't you in the least bit concerned?" Something in me wanted to drive Sara to an expression of feeling.

"Poor bloke!" she said, swinging her legs over the side of the hammock. "The poor bloke tried to rape me, something I know you've never believed." I caught Sara in a rare moment of exposure, her face gaunt and pained. I felt terrible.

"Sara, I'm sorry." I reached out to hold her hand but she pulled it away.

"Marianne, I think we should spend tomorrow apart; we're getting on each other's nerves." She slipped out of the hammock and walked across the beach towards the sea. Her left hand moved up to her face and I imagined she was wiping away a rebellious tear. I was gutted. Partly because I felt guilty for hurting her but also because she had indicated I was getting on her nerves.

I think I always expected that one day Sara would exit my life as suddenly as she'd entered it – although in reality it was I who had entered her life. On that smouldering summer's day when I climbed through the sash window in Islington, I broke into another world, Sara's world. I left behind several friends and possibly even lost Nathaniel, in a round about way, because of my friendship with Sara. Yet still she felt like a transitory part of my life. I always imagined that one day she would walk through a door, gently close it behind her and never return. I suppose she did in a way, but not in the way I had expected.

Chapter 6

'Thought is a man in his wholeness, wholly attending.'
DH Lawrence, *Thought*[6]

"Sorry." The guy smiled as he reached the seat next to me.
"You've got a travelling companion."

He had a heavy accent; I thought Spanish – dark hair, two
days' growth of stubble, unnervingly dark eyes and full lips.

"Miguel," he said, holding out his hand after finding a place
for his backpack.

"Marianne," I replied, taking his hand, deciding it wasn't
worth being rude and resigning myself to his presence. There
was a lot of resignation in India.

I returned to my book. There were no reading lights on the
bus and soon we would be travelling in darkness, except for
the garish red fairy-lights that decked a statue of Ganesh, the
elephant-headed god, at the front of the bus.

It wasn't until I finished the final words and closed the book
that Miguel spoke. His voice led me back to reality like a
mother gently waking a child from a deep sleep.

"You were lost in the story, really deeply lost, like you
wanted to be in the pages."

I realised it was true. "Yes, it was very interesting."

"What was it about?" He seemed actually very interested.

"Well, I suppose it's about the awareness of coincidence in
our lives, as well as the energy we all have…which we compete
over. It says that's what eventually leads to the breakdown of

most relationships."

"I guess that's true, and what else?"

"Well, it says we can learn to use this energy through love to feed each other as well as the planet. It says the world is now ready to receive a spiritual message after centuries of creating material security. I don't really know what to make of it."

"I guess it's like waking up," said Miguel.

"What do you mean?" I asked, fascinated by his eyes.

"Well, we're all asleep, totally asleep, living in a kind of hell on earth. We need someone to wake us up so we can really live."

"But I feel like I am awake, especially in India; it kind of shakes you up."

"Yes, but are you really awake? Think about a child of two or three; they are so fully alive, so exquisitely aware. They are not afraid to love, not afraid of the future or ashamed of the past; they play, explore and can be happy without hang-ups or inhibitions; they do exactly what they want, live totally in the moment." Miguel's face was delightfully expressive, his Spanish mouth struggling to form English words.

"Then we learn, from our parents, from society, that it is unacceptable to live like that; we take on social constructs and duties, we put ourselves in prisons. We have to keep up the facade so that people will like us; we lie all the time."

"I don't think that's true," I replied. I considered myself to be a very honest person.

"But you're lying now, Marianne." Miguel locked my eyes into his, seemingly unaware or unconcerned by the other passengers around us. "Think about it; we tell lies about how we feel, why we're angry, what we want. We do all sorts of devious things to get our own way and invent sophisticated reasons for why we do it."

I felt ruffled, caught out by this unexpected challenge. "But we can't live like two-year-old children all our lives; the world would be in chaos."

"No, you're right, we can't. We have all lost our innocence.

We are adults with adult responsibilities, but we can change our programmes, our patterns."

"What do you mean 'patterns?'" I felt myself being willingly drawn into his words.

"I mean the rigid way our minds work. We constantly tell ourselves what we can and can't do. We are all insane; we have voices in our heads telling us to do things, talking us out of doing other things, limiting us, stifling us." I found I could relate to this.

"These patterns form over time, until we don't even realise they're there. We never question them; we just do what we have always done, even if it is harmful to us."

Miguel turned, so that he faced me square on and his body inadvertently blocked my escape route. Instead of feeling trapped, I felt contained and safe. His face was beautifully animated – hopeful.

"Just imagine what it would be like, Marianne, if we changed the pattern, chose to live free from guilt and shame and duty, free from the past; imagine what it would be like if we stepped out of the prison, a new creature, happy, childlike and joyful."

I felt my defences rise as Miguel mentioned 'the past'. Something inside me reached out to cling onto Nathaniel, to claw him back to me.

"Isn't it a bit of a cliché to say 'let go of the past'? I feel like I can hold onto the past and still live in the present."

"How can you travel on a ship if you still have one foot on the shore? You shouldn't be afraid. I don't believe the past will disappear if you let go of it; it just won't hold you back. Carrying the past makes it too heavy to live in the present."

The idea of letting go of Nathaniel was so physically painful that I couldn't bear to think about it. I was already scared that I would forget what he looked like. I frequently took out his increasingly battered photograph from a pocket in my backpack to remind myself of every angle, every curve of his face.

I wrapped my arms about my chest and looked out of the hopelessly grimy window. A group of children in dusty clothes waved at me, mischief and excitement played on their faces. I gave a small wave back; I didn't want to disappoint them.

"Marianne," Miguel persisted. "How can you do something you don't know, if you keep doing what you do know? I say take a risk and enjoy life. You shouldn't attach yourself to people, to things, to events because you are afraid to live."

These words seemed to come from inside my own head rather than via my ears. I wondered whether Miguel had even spoken them. I felt angry and for a second wished he wasn't there. I turned on him.

"You don't know me, Miguel; you haven't got a clue what is going on with me!"

"I'm sorry, I don't know you Marianne, but I know myself and we are all the same; we are all connected. Einstein said we experience ourselves, our thoughts and feelings as something separated from the rest, a kind of optical delusion of consciousness. This is like a prison, restricting us and our affection to a few people nearest to us. I believe we can only free ourselves from this prison by widening our circle of compassion to embrace all living creatures and the whole of nature. And there is no limit to the love and compassion we have."

I was slightly taken aback by this outpouring from someone I had just met but at the same time fascinated by his passion and apparent clarity.

The bus pulled up alongside a brightly-lit canteen. Miguel and I got out to stretch our legs and were immediately surrounded by vendors and beggars thrusting hands in our faces. After a month in India I had become quite rude and dismissive. It was difficult to deal with the in-your-face poverty and endless begging. Most travellers developed techniques to ignore the approaches, never making eye contact or engaging in conversation. Miguel didn't hand out money but seemed able to maintain his openness, smiling and chatting with everyone while still being firm. I was impressed by his show of respect for others.

We returned to the bus with cups of sweet, milky chai.

"So why do you think *you're* so awake while the rest of us are asleep?" We were on the move again and sipping our chai in the seductive intimacy of the bus.

"I'm awake in this moment, but there is always the danger I will fall asleep again; that's why I need other people, people who are also awake to keep reminding me to stay awake. We all need each other."

I studied Miguel's face; he did look awake, really awake. I remembered seeing a beggar in Delhi with cataracts in his eyes; he was blinded by a misty film that looked like water in the moment before it turns to ice. Perhaps everybody's eyes freeze over eventually, the impact of age and bitterness. Miguel's eyes were clearer than any adults I had seen, fluid, like warm treacle.

"I think it's so simple Marianne; happiness is so simple." Miguel touched my hand and I wanted to cry; I felt the sudden need to bury my face in his chest and sob. I bit my lip.

"No, it's not!" I spat. "It's fucking impossible."

"It's not impossible. *You* choose to be hurt by people; you choose to be offended; you choose to be unhappy."

I thought of the terrorist attacks in Delhi, the fear and terrible pain inflicted on so many people. I thought about Sara, her seeming invincibility, while I felt constantly irritated and angry, and I thought of how coldly Nathaniel had ended our relationship.

"If people do hurtful things," I snapped, "then they hurt us."

"No, Marianne, the things people do are not done personally against us. People act in a certain way because of their own programmes; we can choose to be hurt by it or not to be hurt. We should have control over our own minds – we are not victims."

"I can't accept that." I replied. "We're not robots either; we *are* affected by other people. I am a product of my upbringing, the inadequacies of my parents."

"Don't blame other people for your condition Marianne, especially your parents. They are just obeying their own programmes, like you."

I felt ashamed for bringing my father into it; he was a lovely, kind person, a little fearful of life but that was understandable. My mother abandoned both of us and he never got over it. Dad had always been there for me, to support me unconditionally through exams, disappointments and traumas. But my mother, she was a different story; she was selfish.

"How can you say that? You can't know everybody's story."

"No, I don't, but that doesn't change the facts. Blaming others for our failings will not change anything; taking responsibility for our actions will. Did you know, Marianne, scientists have discovered that when we are angry the chemicals released stay in our body for up to three months? If we are in a state of chronic anger then we are living with the presence of toxic chemicals in our body – eventually they will poison us. Marianne, for your own sake, don't blame other people; whatever they have done it's not about you, it is about them."

"Maybe you're right." I hung my head. "I do blame other people, all the time." I felt this as a revelation. How many times had I blamed my dad for not being more proactive, Nathaniel for not always being the way I wanted him to be, my mother for not loving me enough to stay around and Sara for just being who she was.

As Miguel spoke I felt sudden clarity, my eyes opening. In a flash of something that I imagined to be enlightenment I saw clearly that I had been projecting onto Sara my feelings about my mother; I always expected that one day she would abandon me as well. Because of this I could not allow myself to trust her. It was the same with Nathaniel. But then he had abandoned me, hadn't he?

"Though don't wallow in self-blame either." Miguel's words were harsh but there was love and humour dancing in his eyes. "I believe we create our own reality Marianne; your word is law in *your* universe. If you can only see that you will have limitless power. As Marianne Williamson said in *Return to Love*[7], 'Our deepest fear is not that we are inadequate; our deepest fear is that we are powerful beyond measure. It is our light, not our darkness that most frightens us.'"

We continued to talk, cocooned in the sticky heat, oblivious to those around us. I relaxed into Miguel, unafraid of physical contact. He was warm, pliable and smelled of sweat and fresh spices. He seemed at home in his own body without being overly conscious of its beauty. I took pleasure in watching his lips move around words as if they were creating succulent fruit with every new syllable. I loved him. I don't know where it came from but I loved him, his humanness, his godlikeness, the working of his hands as he talked.

I wanted to take his hand, stop its movement so that I could trace the curve of each finger down into the fleshy web and up into the next – his heart which beat inside him, the hairs which sprouted from his body and formed a soft triangle beneath his arms and around his penis. I felt a child-like curiosity – almost absent of sexuality – about his penis. Was it the colour of his arm, coffee and cream, was it large or small, was it stirring now as he spoke to me, or soft with sleep? I was fascinated by his every movement. It suddenly seemed impossible that we could move, breathe and walk on our own. What kept us going?

I didn't want the journey to end. I was experiencing joy, pure and unadulterated, drug-free joy. But it did end. The bus pulled up in a shabby street in Jaipur and we all piled out.

Chapter 7

"I know a good hotel if you have nowhere to stay." Miguel was pulling his backpack on.

"Yes, that'd be great; it's later than I thought." We jumped into a rickshaw and after a fifteen-minute journey, arrived at the Vishnu Hotel. It was large and formed a quadrangle around a garden. There were about thirty travellers of many nationalities sitting in the garden, drinking, eating, talking; I liked the place instantly.

"Do you want to share a room?" Miguel asked. "It'd be cheaper."

"Yes," seemed the obvious answer; I didn't see any reason not to. We checked in and dumped our bags in a simple, twin-bedded room. We then went into the garden to grab some beers and sat on the grass with a group of other travellers.

They were a mix of Europeans, Americans and Kiwis; most looked like they'd been travelling for some time. They had a relaxed, slightly grimy glow about them: colourful, lived-in clothes picked up on their travels; sun-blanched hair tied up in cotton or hemp bandannas; piercings on various parts of their anatomy; and cheap ethnic jewellery collected from market stalls around the world. I guess I looked the same.

A French girl represented all that I thought was cool about travellers: perfect skin, glazed but not scorched by the sun, and a neat figure on which Indian-cotton hung well. She lay on her side, stretched out, at ease with the world, so that a golden swathe of waist was revealed. It was adorned with a tasteful, black Celtic-knot tattoo that circled her belly button, where there was a discreet silver piercing in the centre. I thought she looked a bit smug, too cool, and I felt my defences rise. I didn't want to share Miguel with anyone; I just wanted to be lost in conversation with him again.

However, I soon found myself enjoying the scene and I felt connected to people in a way I didn't think I had felt before. My mind seemed breathtakingly clear, my body energised. It was a bit like an amphetamine trip but there was no sickness in my stomach and none of the edginess that accompanies the chemical high. I felt very calm and for once I felt I knew who I was, not in relation to anyone else – to Nathaniel or Sara, my dad or my friends – I existed alone as a sentient being but I didn't feel alone; I felt connected to everyone around me.

I didn't join in the conversation straight away, as I normally would, waiting to have my say, to share my travelling stories, make myself sound interesting. I observed the others, watching their faces, listening to their words. I noticed their beauty, their insecurity and saw myself in them.

I then shifted into another mental state, even more heightened and aware; I stripped away their clothes, piercings and body paint, their hair and skin – the things we judge others by, the things that make us choose whether or not to like them, whether to accept them into our tribe. I stripped away their flesh, bones, marrow and any remaining atoms, until they were just spirit; we were *all* spirit, confined in our own little prisons, desperately trying to express ourselves, to be liked and accepted. I felt both exhilarated by what I was experiencing and slightly disturbed. It crossed my mind that I was having a breakdown.

In my first summer vacation at university, I did some work experience with a local newspaper. They asked me to write a piece on a man who had won the lottery and subsequently suffered a nervous breakdown. I interviewed him in a psychiatric unit where he was convalescing. It was an alien environment to me and I felt a mixture of fascination and repulsion as I walked past a litter of broken people. The man had been a respected teacher and told me he'd had a breakdown two years earlier. He described the exact moment when he felt his mind disintegrate, like an overcooked chestnut.

There was still a fragility about him, as if every nerve, synapse and tendon was stretched, ready to snap. I felt fear; I was looking at a raw, stripped-down human being and I knew that it could be any one of us – it could be me. However, the man described his experience in totally negative terms. He felt fragmentation, mental agony, fear, while my feelings were exhilaration, love and clarity.

In the still-warm early hours Miguel and I went back to our room; we pushed our beds together and made love. It felt like the natural conclusion to all that had gone before. I felt physically closer to Miguel than I had to anyone, including Nathaniel.

First we lay together, naked, very still, face-to-face, so that as much of our flesh was in contact as possible. Before anything else I wanted his lips, the lips that had given me so many succulent words, words that had fed my starving soul.

I spent a long time on his lips, ignoring other aches. I had the power to stop the words that seemed to pour from him as if it was his burden to share them with the world. I stilled them, gave his mouth another purpose.

Then I couldn't ignore the call of my flesh and the pressing of his. I wrapped my legs around his waist and my arms around his back and pulled him as close as possible. I turned him onto his back and sat where I could feel the urgent pulse of his penis between my legs. I pushed his hands above his head so that he was vulnerable, exposed, and then pressed his arms into the pillow, forcing his body into a Modigliani recline.

I kissed the mound of his chest, his ribs, exposed by the cruciform stretch of his arms. Next the forbidden hollows of his armpits with their tangle of hair and intoxicating scent. With my lips I travelled up the tender skin of his inner arms – as silk-soft as a girl's – until I reached his neck, to me the most vulnerable part of a man's body, sinews stretched in willing pain, Christ in agony on the cross. I breathed in the flesh, sensing the warm blood coursing just below the surface.

I kissed his almond eyelids, feeling the tender flutter of eyelashes beneath my lips. Then I buried my face in his coconut-scented curls.

I could feel his penis, hard and restless beneath me, and I could ignore it no longer. I slid his hardness inside my aching softness and sat up so that I swallowed him deep inside me, and so that I could still see the beauty of his face.

His eyes terrified me with their honesty, their happiness; I almost turned away but I forced myself to hold his gaze. Then I saw his lips open, hovering on the edge of words; I fell forwards and locked my mouth onto his again, stilling his voice.

We moved very slowly for a long time; I'm not sure how long, minutes melted into immeasurable pleasure. No words, just breath and heartbeat and skin, the sense that this communion was all that mattered – an intimacy so mundane, so sacred.

At first I was alert in all of my senses, feeling how much my body had missed the rapture of physical closeness, the soft friction of skin on skin, the smell of excited flesh. As we moved towards the same moment of oblivion, giving of ourselves, taking what we needed, I thought how exposed we are in love-making. In the same moment we are at our most vulnerable and our most focused.

Then, in the final moment there is nothing, no sound, no smell, no sight; all of our senses rush together along a narrowing tunnel, towards one point of piercing, ecstatic light.

We awoke early, still entwined, our bodies glowing in the intensifying heat. I had never been able to sleep like that with Nathaniel; I had always claimed my own space. It made me realise that, despite my love for Nathaniel, I had often withheld myself from him, both physically and emotionally. This thought saddened me; I wished I could make things right.

Miguel and I spent the day together exploring the Pink City

– although it would be better described as dusty orange – with its frenzy of camel carts and glittering bazaars. The Pink City is built on a grid pattern with various streets or quarters allocated to different professions – silversmiths, potters, weavers, etc.

I paid a tailor in Surajpol Bizarre to make me a skirt from a rich indigo fabric. Miguel then helped me choose some silver earrings, which we haggled down to half their original price, and I bought him a leather band for his wrist, which had a Buddhist symbol scratched into it. I also bought a simple silver necklace for Sara.

We came across a man with a magnificent moustache and a candy-bright turban. He sat in the lotus position on a dusty cloth, dwarfed by a fully-grown male elephant. The elephant was tied to a tree by a thin stretch of frayed rope. Also tied to the tree, by a more substantial, metal chain, was a baby elephant.

"Why does the baby have such a strong chain while the big elephant only has a thin rope?" I asked the man.

"Well, madam," the man's head tilted engagingly from side-to-side, "the big elephant no longer needs a strong chain; he is an obedient fellow and knows where he must be; he will not stray. The baby elephant is still learning the rules."

"That's a bit like us," commented Miguel as we walked away. "We explore all the time when we're children; our curiosity is endless, but society puts strong chains on our curiosity. By the time we're adults we put them on ourselves."

I felt I was walking on air the whole day and I liked the feeling; I was still me but a lighter, more transparent me. Miguel had helped me to see a few things about myself, but I knew that my enlightenment wasn't directly about him or about being in his presence; it was within me, within my grasp at any time.

Miguel left Jaipur that evening to visit a friend in the nearby village of Dausa. Before he left, he asked if he could take *The Celestine Prophecy* in exchange for one of his books – *The Four Agreements* by Don Miguel Ruiz[9].

I was sad to say goodbye; I felt that, despite our connection, I probably wouldn't see Miguel again, that we had taken what we needed from each other. In fact, we didn't even exchange email addresses and it was strangely liberating to walk away from someone with whom I had been so intimate and not make empty promises about staying in touch. In the bigger scheme of things, I suppose we would always stay connected in some sense or other.

I found an internet café and emailed Sara. I was looking forward to seeing her again, to sharing my new self with her. The row didn't seem to matter anymore; I was determined to live in the moment. In a round about way our row had led me to Miguel, and to one of those 'bardos,' even though I'd gone there kicking and screaming.

I was also looking forward to moving on to Varanasi. I had heard many stories about the holy city from other travellers and, in my new state of enlightenment, it held a strong fascination for me.

Unfortunately, my transformation was far from complete and I had a lot more kicking and screaming to do along the way.

Chapter 8

'Direct your eyesight inward and you'll find a thousand regions in your mind yet undiscovered. Travel them, and be expert in home Cosmography.' Henry David Thoreau[8]

"So what does the 'Holy Bible' say about Varanasi?" Sara was taking the piss, as usual, out of my reliance on the *Lonely Planet*. She was reclining on her bunk and looked totally at ease as she did in any setting, no matter how foreign. I was sitting cramped and cross-legged on the opposite bunk after another long and restless night on a train. However, my tiredness was counteracted by an unusual amount of excitement about seeing Varanasi; I had built the place up as my own kind of personal Mecca, somewhere I could perhaps find a few more answers.

Sara met me in Jaipur three days after Miguel left; we had enjoyed a long evening of catching up, our differences in Agra already seemed far behind us. Surprisingly, she didn't take the piss out of my experiences with Miguel, although I didn't tell her absolutely everything – I found the sex easier to talk about than my less carnal experiences.

Sara had acquired a bit of serenity herself during her time with Rajpal. She seemed gentler, as if her personality was in soft focus. I don't think she told me the full story either, but I could see that her feelings for Raj ran deep and she said she hoped to meet up with him again soon. I had never heard her talk so tenderly about a man; she was usually dismissive of the male sex, as if men weren't worth bothering with. It was different with Raj; her eyes illuminated when she mentioned his name. She talked about him with respect; she even wore his karra on her right wrist and I noticed that she often caressed it, as if conjuring up his memory. I guessed that the Delhi bomb had had a similar impact on Sara as it had on me. It kind of blasted away our defences so that a small shaft of light could pass through. I was momentarily opened up to other possibilities. The difficulty was in staying open.

"It sounds amazing," I said, ignoring her jibe. "*Varanasi, the city of Shiva, on the banks of the sacred Ganges is one of the holiest places in India. Hindu pilgrims come to bathe in the waters, a ritual which washes away sin.*"

There was a sudden spark in Sara's eyes. "I wonder what it's like to have all your sin washed away. Do you think you'd feel all light and floaty?"

I thought back to my childhood as a Roman Catholic; infused with fantasies of miracles and martyrdom I'd naturally gravitated towards religiosity, until I'd been seduced by adolescent interests. I'd spent hours staring at plaster statues positioned like mute guards around the school, waiting to catch us out in our childish sin. Perhaps I'd hoped for a sign, a nod or a wink when no one else was looking, some proof that God cared. I offered my inadequate sins to a priest in the confessional each week and worked my way to forgiveness around a string of rosary beads.

"I don't know," I said. "I kind of went off the rails when I was sixteen."

"Oh yeah, Mari, you're more *on the rails* than anyone else I know." Sara's legs were now dangling over the edge of the bunk. "In fact, you're a bit of a prude." A small smile played on her insouciant lips.

"Bitch!" I threw a sarong at her that I had borrowed the night before; she caught it and stuffed it into her already bulging backpack.

"Carry on reading!" She was like a child demanding a bedtime story.

I obeyed. "*The city is an auspicious place to die, since expiring here offers Moksha – liberation from the cycle of birth and death. It's a magical city where the most intimate rituals of life and death take place in public on the city's famous ghats.*"

"Yeah," Sara said, "Hindus burn their dead on the ghats in public. I like that, no bullshit, just burn them and scatter them in the river."

"Oh no, I don't want to burn." I shuddered at the thought. "I'd rather rot in private in the earth."

"You weirdo! You've read too many sodding Bronte novels." Sara smoothed moisturiser with careless efficiency over her face and hands. "Carry on!"

"*In the past the city has been known as Kashi and Benares, but its present name is a restoration of an ancient one meaning 'the city between two rivers.'* Apparently, Mark Twain said Varanasi is '*...older than history, older than tradition, older even than legend and looks twice as old as all of them put together.*'"

"Oh yeah," Sara yawned, "what about accommodation?" I felt irritated by how quickly she lost interest. It was as if she promised to swim in the sea with you but always turned around before it got too deep. I swallowed my irritation, trying to maintain my newly centred-self.

"*One of the best ways to get your bearings in Varanasi is to remember the position of the ghats...the alleyways of the old city can be disorientating, but the hotels are well signposted.*' Wow! It has been unofficially estimated that two or three travellers go missing in Varanasi every few months."

"They'll probably crawl out of some opium den in ten years' time with these huge grins on their faces," Sara laughed.

"Yeah, well as long as it's not us."

"I don't know; I can imagine worse fates."

"Anyway," I continued, not wishing to pursue this line of

thought, "it says the old city is the place to find budget hotels, if you don't mind living in cramped conditions – it's the most atmospheric."

"I guess that's where we'll be staying then," said Sara, popping shut the clasps on her backpack. "Cheap, cramped and atmospheric – what more could a girl want?"

The last three hours were the worst; they dragged interminably and we were relieved to finally stretch out of the train at Varanasi Junction. It was getting dark by the time we reached the old town and we still had to find a room.

"Jump in, very good hotel, very cheap." A scrum of auto-rickshaw drivers crowded around us jostling for precious business; we ignored their pleas and pushed our way through. We knew they were looking for commission from hotels, which invariably belonged to family members and we'd end up paying the difference.

By now we had the knack of finding the right area and the best value hotel but Varanasi was different, everything seemed awkward. It didn't help that there were frequent power-cuts, which darkened the narrow streets and blanked out hotel windows. Most places were full and I felt a little shot of panic.

After some time we remembered that the five-day Kartik Poornima or Diwali celebrations were commencing that weekend – with three-hundred-and-thirty-million Hindu gods, at the last count – and with most festivals governed by the phases of the moon, it was difficult to keep track of exactly when they would take place. Crowds of people had already descended on the city making it almost impossible to find decent accommodation.

We eventually returned to the Avaneesh Hotel, one of the first places we'd seen and rejected on the grounds that it looked particularly dilapidated and only offered squat toilets. It was in Godaulia, on the edge of the old city and lost in a dark tangle of streets. The owner, a rotund man, who looked as neglected as his hotel, smirked as we entered the lobby for a second time.

"Passports!" he demanded. The smirk dissolved into a scowl, which looked much more at home on his inhospitable face. Sara threw her passport towards him and he shoved a large key across the desk.

"You are lucky; there is only one room left." His voice came out like the growl of a wary dog. "Wait here while I find someone to clear it out."

My heart sank at these words but we waited, rooted to the spot by weariness and resignation. I noticed a yellowing sign behind the desk: *'Your hotel manager is Mr Sultan. He is happy to help. No smokes, drinks or noise anywhere in hotel.'*

"The room is ready," a boy announced ten minutes later. Mr Sultan didn't waste any more words on us but nodded in our general direction, signalling us to go.

It was an attic room and the only guest room on the third floor, although the word 'guest' is putting it a little too strongly. It smelled as if all the odours of the hotel had risen up to find a final resting place there. We assumed it wasn't used very often.

We flung open the windows to encourage any stray breeze to visit, before lying fully clothed on the narrow beds. I stared wearily at the naked light-bulb, which hung crookedly from the ceiling, until another power-cut plunged us into semi-darkness with just the vague glow of candlelight outside. We could hear the faint, plaintive cries of holy men calling followers to prayer.

For a while we were both lost in our own thoughts. I had the strange sense that Varanasi had claimed us for herself; I thought I saw it in the water-stained patterns on the ceiling, smelled it in the chalky dampness of the walls, but I could do no more to change it than I could change my own past.

"Let's go and grab something to eat?" Sara suggested when the light eventually flickered back on.

"Sounds good to me." I pushed myself up from the bed, a realisation of hunger overcoming my desire to sleep.

"God, this is a dodgy joint!" Sara loosened her hair from its tie so that it fell like silk around her shoulders. "And I don't trust that Mr Sultan one bit."

"I don't think he likes us much either." I splashed tepid water onto my face in an attempt to wake up and to remove the grime of the long train journey from my skin.

By torchlight we found our way to a restaurant overlooking the Ganges, or the Ganga as it is known by locals. The light from a thousand candles and lanterns played on the waters and the aroma of spices joined with the scent of candle smoke and the sour breath of the river to form a heady perfume.

As usual we had chosen a traveller-friendly haven; we had little choice on a tight budget. Hindi music weaved seductively through the dense murmur of conversation – voices from every part of the globe. We ordered food and drank Kingfisher Beer served from a teapot – alcohol is officially banned in the old town of Varanasi, as it is in other holy cities. After dinner we met two other backpackers, Bert and Sam, and we walked down to the river where we sat beneath colourful lanterns lit for Diwali. Sam turned on his MP3 player and we were accompanied by gentle Hindustani music. "It's a really cool disc, man." Sam relaxed into the ghat step. "Bismillah Khan is frigging ninety-years-old and still hangs out in Varanasi." Bert rolled a spliff and we talked.

Conversation becomes an art form when you're travelling; there's nothing else to distract you. It isn't about *doing* anymore – doing your job, doing the chores, doing up your home – none of that matters; it's about *being* and how well or how interestingly you manage that. It is both liberating and terrifying; many travellers crack under the pressure.

Bert and Sam were Americans; they had been travelling for two years and told us they had spent several months in Vietnam, Thailand and Cambodia before busing through Malaysia to Singapore, where they had caught a flight to Mumbai. They were on their way to Nepal via Gorakhpur to trek in the Anapurna mountain range, something Sara and I had already done.

Despite the length of time they had been travelling, Bert and Sam still had a relatively clean-scrubbed look. Some of the long-term travellers we came across along the old hippy trail had come to India in the 60s or 70s and never left; they had just disappeared from their lives back home. Many had become psychotic with the constant use of cannabis or LSD, while others appeared to have found a rare kind of peace. I imagined they never fully integrated with the locals but would find it impossible to settle back into the increasingly materialistic West. They looked lean and haunted with knotty hair and dust-brown skin. Their clothes were ethnic and well-worn – unlike the short-termers who rapidly disposed of their costumes at the end of their travels to return to city offices.

I suppose Bert and Sam were attractive in a self-conscious, West Coast way; college boys let loose on the world, sun-bleached surfer hair, even tans – you get the picture. Neither of them could take their eyes off Sara.

"Cool place," said Bert, rocking frenetically on the step. "Have you seen those fucking burning ghats, man?" Bert's arms were attempting to illustrate the awesomeness of what he'd seen, but they punched the air in an unruly fashion like a puppet on speed.

"Seems a bit voyeuristic to me." Sara took a long draw on the spliff before passing it on. Bert's arms deflated back to his side and Sam came to life.

"Yeah, yeah, I know what you mean." He took several short, greedy drags and then held the spliff high in the air, as if trying to get the attention of a schoolteacher. "I felt, like disrespectful, man, but I couldn't stop looking."

There was something parodic about Bert and Sam, which I couldn't quite place; the more stoned I became the more I had to resist the urge to giggle at their slick double-act.

"Well, I'm going to look," I said defiantly. "If you burn your dead in public it's meant to be seen. Anyway, how was Cambodia? I wish we'd had time to get there."

"Crazy!" Bert's arms flew into the air again. "We like

crossed the border from Poipet in Thailand and got a ride in a pick-up truck along this diabolical hundred-k road to Siem Reap. I'm not bullshitting; there were sixteen of us in this truck with sixteen backpacks. The road was like full of potholes from mine blasts in the days of the Khmer Rouge. After six hours my ass was raw."

"Yeah," Sam interjected smoothly – they had obviously recounted this tale a number of times before. "The week before we got there, these pirates tied up a bunch of travellers and held guns to their heads."

"Yeah, but Angkor Wat was cool," continued Bert, "all these awesome temples."

"Do you have any more of that grass?" Sara asked. "We're getting low."

"Sure man," said Bert, fumbling in his bag. "We got some charas from these guys in Delhi who'd been up to Manali; it's good stuff."

The conversation moved on to comparing the quality of cannabis we'd sampled on our travels. This subject was beginning to bore me. I smoked it as a kind of social inclusion policy rather than as an enthusiast. I could go for weeks, months, and not miss it whereas lately it was rare to see Sara without a spliff in her hand. I took the opportunity to visit the toilet, which I hoped would be slightly less basic than the one in our hotel.

When I returned, Bert looked even more animated than before, while Sara was sitting back in a relaxed fashion with one leg pulled up to her chest. She was fixing another joint. She did it quickly, elegantly, creating a smooth, compact cylinder that always burned evenly.

"...How can you say that after what they've done to your country?" Bert rocked forward so violently I thought he might fall off the step. "I think they're the biggest threat to the modern world, man."

I guessed they were talking about terrorists as this subject was on everyone's lips. It was a subject I really didn't want to get into after our experience in Delhi. I was still having nightmares about it.

"I totally disagree," said Sara, twirling a strand of hair around an index finger. "*You* see them as a threat 'cos you're all so bloody insular. I mean you're two of what like only thirty per cent of Americans who have passports. You see everything from outside as a threat, like a virus trying to get into your plastic bubble; that's why you destroy anything that doesn't speak your language."

"So, you're saying *we're* like the biggest threat to the world, man?" Sam looked wounded, as if he was being personally attacked.

"Yeah, one of them, but I think the biggest threat to us in Britain is our own culture; it's turning on us like a fucking Pit Bull. Chavs are breeding more than anyone else; we'll soon be outnumbered."

"What do you mean by 'chavs'?" Sam looked puzzled.

"Council Housing, Aggressive, Vulgar," I supplied. "White trash to you."

"Not necessarily," said Sara. "It's not about class; it's about attitude. Chavs have infiltrated everything from music to TV; in fact all of modern culture, and they're so fucking aggressive."

"Well maybe they've got something to be aggressive about." I said. "Poor housing, unemployment, poverty, while Tony Blair spends the country's money ballsing up Iraq."

"It's got nothing to do with money either." Sara sounded irritated. She exhaled a steady stream of smoke. "There are plenty of rich chavs about. As I said 'chavdom' is a state of mind, an attitude. Chavs have no sense of their place in history or of the bigger picture; they exist in this self-seeking, materialistic void; they are totally vacuous. Everything they do is for their own ends."

"You could say the same about terrorists," replied Bert.

"No! They believe in something; that's why they're such a threat to us. We're so soft that anything with a point threatens to burst us. But, actually, I think terrorists have done us a favour; they've made us face our fears, see what's important, or…more accurately, what's not."

Bert was sucking furiously on the spliff; the whites of his eyes were turning marbled red. "Sure, man, I hate our President, he's a frigging madman, but you're saying you'd go have a coffee with the bastards who blew up your city as well as mine, killing thousands of people... including guys I knew?"

"Really!" I was curious to know more. I thought about sharing our near-miss with Bert and Sam. Perhaps the re-telling of the story with people who understood might have helped me to make sense of it, but Sara wouldn't let go of her point.

"At least you'd get a decent conversation out of them." She stubbed the spliff-end hard onto the ghat step." Put it this way," Sara was on a roll, "I'd rather spend the night with a so-called terrorist than with a chav. I bet the sex would be better."

I was uncomfortable with the direction of the conversation. I felt Sara was tossing a hot coal into the air just to see if anyone would catch it. She knew I found the subject emotive; I wasn't sure she even believed what she was saying. There was a fragility, a disintegration in Sara's face that I had never seen before and I was becoming concerned. She was smoking and drinking furiously.

"People who believe in things are much more passionate," she ploughed on, "and passion makes for better sex."

"It doesn't make what they do right," said Sam.

"Did I say anything about right or wrong?" Frustration skated across Sara's perfectly symmetrical features. "I'm not talking about right or wrong. I'm just saying they're more interesting. If you put a couple of Islamic extremists in the *Big Brother* house it might be worth watching." She giggled, perhaps at the bizarre image forming in her mind. "I bet you wouldn't get the mind-numbing crap that comes out of the mouths of chavs."

"I just don't see how you can condone terrorists," Bert's voice cracked, heavy with emotion.

"You're assuming I condone them 'cos I find them less threatening than chavs. I just think we've all been lulled into this false sense of *insecurity*. We're a lost generation in an atomised culture."

"What do you mean?" Sam looked even more puzzled.

Sara laughed loudly, slightly maniacally. "I don't know what the fuck I mean," she said. "I'm too bloody stoned."

It suddenly seemed that Bert, Sam and I were the water and Sara the spoon. With very little physical motion she had stirred us up into a frenetic swirl and then withdrawn to watch the ensuing turbulence. After an uncomfortable pause, we moved onto safer ground and our voices drifted out into the velvet night.

We eventually said goodbye to Bert and Sam, although I had the feeling we would see them again; they had Sara's scent. I already detected desperation in Bert's eyes and, while he didn't know whether to love Sara or fear her, like Edmund in Narnia, he knew he wanted more and more of the delicious Turkish Delight.

Chapter 9

We decided to give Varanasi a chance by daylight, having formed a somewhat negative opinion of the city the previous evening. First, we had a leisurely breakfast of mango porridge and chai. Neither of us had slept well; the beds were less comfortable than usual and we had been woken by strange noises in the night. In consequence we were tired and irritable.

I had never been anywhere before like Varanasi, even in India. Trying to describe it is a challenge as its effect goes beyond words. I guess Medieval England would be a good comparison, with modern technology thrown in. A snarl of switchback lanes, known as galis, were crammed with market stalls selling silk brocades made on nearby looms, as well as jewellery, rugs and brass-work. Pigs vie with cows for scraps of food and children carry baskets on their heads overflowing with cow-dung, which splashes in the pathway of crawling babies. In places, the stench is an assault to the sensitive Western nose – that peculiar mix of human waste, dust, kerosene and motorbike fuel – and is only made bearable by the masking scents of sandalwood, jasmine and lotus flower, which are burned in incense sticks on every street.

In contrast, slotted between market stalls, like a glaring anachronism, you find a neon-lit internet café, full of gap-year travellers – still wired to the West – sending exaggerated tales of adventure to anxious parents and jealous friends.

The Ganges slides lethargically past it all and pilgrims gather each day to bathe in the water, perform puja to the rising sun or build funeral pyres. More mundanely, locals sell bread and flowers or have their daily shit and shave. On festival days the riverbank is thick with a colourful swathe of humanity and that is how it looked as Sara and I descended Dasaswamedha Ghat to the edge of the river.

I had bad stomach cramps and was happy to settle on the steps of the ghat to watch the festival. Larger than life, garishly coloured statues of gods and goddesses, manifestations of the great uncreated Brahman – Hanuman and Devi, Ganesh and Saraswati – were draped in marigold garlands by a group of loin-clothed men, before being immersed in the Ganges. A goddess – milky white and expressionless – was placed respectfully on a boat and sent floating down the river. Hundreds of people gathered to watch – women in bright saris, children with magic in their eyes and travellers like us. I was transfixed.

After half-an-hour, I turned to find that Sara was asleep. My initial feeling was one of irritation. Firstly, because she was missing the action, but also her sleeping meant I had to stay with her until she woke up and I couldn't sleep myself for fear that we would be stripped of our valuables. It wasn't that I actually wanted to leave the ghats or that I *could* sleep, it was the principle. I checked myself. I had come to realise while travelling that I often did things out of a sense of duty rather than because I wanted to do them. This was a hang-up Sara didn't share and while I was sometimes irritated by her ability to do exactly what she wanted when she wanted, I also envied this quality in her.

Sara only slept for half-an-hour and then stretched up with a contented smile.

"That was nice," she said. "I was so knackered."

"Me too." I was unable to shake irritation from my voice.

"Why don't you have a sleep now?" she said, smoothing her hair.

It was so simple. She wasn't selfish exactly, she thought about me, cared about me, but there was just a natural order in our relationship; she got what she needed first.

"I don't know how you can sleep out here," I said. "It's so

bloody noisy."

She smiled and looked towards the river, seemingly unaffected by my tone. I pushed on.

"God, I'm going to be knackered by tonight." I couldn't seem to stop; I laboured the point until I felt angry at my own pettiness. I remembered my conversations with Miguel in Jaipur, the insights I'd had about myself and my rigid programming, and yet here I was already slipping back into old patterns. Why did it have to be so hard?

"I've got an idea!" She turned to me, her eyes sparkling like a schoolgirl up to no good. There was always an adventure waiting around the corner for Sara.

"Go on," I said, not sure if I had the energy for one of her ideas.

"Bert and Sam said you can buy pure amphetamine in a pharmacy here – that'd keep us awake."

"I'm not sure I want to be *that* much awake." My voice was still flat and cool.

Sara's expression didn't change; she was already planning her mission.

*****

Our last experimentation with drugs had taken place in Pushkar, Rajasthan, where we had spent a few days before coming to Varanasi. Pushkar is a travellers' haven with masses of cheap hotels and cafés. Temples are set like jewels around a beautiful lotus-shaped lake and Sadhus, smeared with ash, sit in solitary meditation on the edge of the water, searching for spiritual enlightenment. Each evening travellers gather around the lake to eat, play drums and juggle fire as the sun falls behind the hills. The main street in Pushkar, better described as a dusty lane, is crammed with shops selling cheap hippy clothes, Rajasthani fabrics and intricately embroidered throws and cushion covers.

We booked into a half-decent hotel and exchanged our books

at a second-hand shop. I had decided at the start of our travels to read literature that was either set in the country we were currently visiting or that had a spiritual bent. I had a romantic notion of totally immersing myself in local culture and opening my mind to different philosophies. We spent hours reading and drinking Limca – a sweet lemon drink – by the lake. It was a lovely time, free of the stress of dealing with crazy bureaucracy and train delays. I felt very close to Sara in those few days; it was as if a sweet calm had settled over us after the storm of Delhi.

We strolled through the small town, allowing ourselves to be drawn into makeshift shops. At twilight shopkeepers lit kerosene lamps, which caused silk rugs to shimmer with intense colour. They served us chai in small glasses and we sat cross-legged on the floor, sipping the sweet concoction in shadowed intimacy while beautiful boys unrolled rug after rug for our benefit. They flirted gently as they traced the patterns with supple fingers. We were willingly hypnotised by them.

Each evening we strolled along the main drag, passing a boy of about sixteen who called out, "café, chai, bhang lassi," like a haunting mantra. We discovered, from other travellers, that bhang lassi was the usual yoghurt drink laced with bhang, a derivative of marijuana.

"Let's get one tonight," said Sara. "It'll be fun!"

That evening we bought a small bhang lassi each and drank it like milkshake in the café. Half-an-hour later we felt no different and dismissed it as a waste of money.

There was a small travelling theatre in town performing a Hindu drama, with all parts played by boys and men like in early Shakespeare productions. We didn't understand a word but it was a novel experience to see boys in lavish costume giggling as they recited words of love to each other.

Another half-hour went by before I felt anything, then it was as if my eyes and ears opened fully for the first time so that every sound was sharply focused; I was sure I could understand the chattering of a group of Rajasthani women sitting thirty metres away. I looked at Sara, her pupils were dilated and she looked amazingly beautiful. We laughed spontaneously and then couldn't stop.

"Wow!" she said. "I'm rushing."

"Me too!"

We didn't sleep at all that night. Our minds raced, chasing bizarre concepts, separating and coming back together; it was as if we shared the same thoughts. We explored Pushkar seeing everything in a new light. Camels were the most hilarious things ever created and when we bumped into a man with an ornately dressed cow, which danced to the music of his pipe, we laughed until we cried. Time was distorted and skipped about so that we didn't know if we'd spent an hour or five minutes staring at the weird branches of a Banyan tree reaching towards the lake.

Sara's cynicism seemed temporarily dissolved by the powerful potion and she held my hand, swinging it like a schoolgirl, while she sang *So long, Marianne*. It became the theme-tune to that night.

"It was my dad's favourite song; he loved Leonard Cohen. He used to sing it to my mum; the old bitch didn't deserve it. How come you were called Marianne?" she asked.

"Apparently my mother chose it…after Marianne Faithful."

Sara continued to sing, her words flowing out like a steady but slightly garbled stream.

As the sun came up, we retreated to the hotel room and clung to our beds, which swayed like flying carpets. We eventually fell asleep around seven and slept until midday. We giggled whenever we recalled that night.

"Oh go on!" said Sara. "I'm going to get some anyway; you might as well join me."

"I don't mind coming with you." My curiosity was growing stronger than my resistance. "I'll decide later if I take it."

We found the pharmacy after an hour's search and it was surprisingly easy to buy the amphetamine. It came in a small ampoule of clear liquid at only seventy rupees. We bought one each and stuffed them into our money belts.

I suppose I knew I would take the amphetamine. I had vowed before leaving London that I would try to overcome my natural reserve and grab whatever experience came my way. This was partly a reaction to the unexpected breakdown of my relationship with Nathaniel, which had left me emotionally devastated, angry and 'devil may care' about life, or so I thought. A lot of what I did felt like an act of revenge against life, God, whatever. Every time I felt scared or uncertain about doing something, I decided that it was the very thing I should do, no matter how crazy. I overcame a few phobias in the process and gave myself a lot of nightmares.

We drank down the bitter liquid at six o'clock that evening. After half-an-hour it kicked in and our tiredness and irritability disappeared. The Kartik Poornima celebrations were underway and as it grew dark the ghats sparkled with a thousand earthen lamps, candles, incense and flowers festooned the doorways of shops and homes. When we arrived at Manikarnika Ghat we realised a funeral ceremony was about to take place. A procession was weaving through the streets of the old town towards the river. Several men – either sons of the deceased or doms (outcastes fulfilling their dharma) – carried a bamboo stretcher bearing the body. Other family members dressed in white carried flowers and shimmering candles; the procession was accompanied by the sound of drums, pipes and solemn chants. On the ghat ready to receive the corpse was a large pile of wood.

We found a place to watch the ceremony from above so that we were looking down on the proceedings. The body was first dipped in the sacred Ganges and then placed carefully on the woodpile. More wood was added until the body was buried and then the pyre lit. The flames took some time to gather strength but once they did the wood burned so fiercely that the mourners had to take several steps back. The sheet soon burned off to expose more resilient flesh; one leg poked out inelegantly from the pyre. I felt sad for the leg and for the person to whom it belonged.

"It's so beautiful," said Sara. The flames burned behind her eyes. I don't think I had ever seen her look so peaceful; perhaps it was the effect of the drugs.

We had been watching the proceedings for some time when a small Indian man approached us with an angry expression.

"You are very bad," he said, pointing into our faces. I felt confused, scared. What he was saying didn't make sense; there were plenty of other observers to the scene and he hadn't approached them. I thought he could detect the drugs in our eyes.

"What the hell are you talking about?" Sara demanded, her face suddenly hard and closed.

"I saw you taking photographs, you bad ladies; you are very disrespectful."

"How could we take photographs when we have no fucking cameras?" Sara held her hands up to show their freedom from any such appendage. The man, probably sensing he would get nowhere with Sara, turned his attention to me.

"It was this lady I saw." He pointed jaggedly in my face. "She took a photograph; she has no respect." My hands automatically tightened around my money belt, where I kept my mobile phone with its inbuilt camera, although I'd had no intention of using it. I had left my main camera in the hotel safe. I was also acutely aware of the empty amphetamine ampoule sitting accusingly next to my phone. The man's eyes dropped to the bag.

"You see, madam, you have a camera; you must come with me to the police station; it is a grave offence." I thought of the tourists who had gone missing and fear tugged at my heart.

"We're not moving," said Sara defiantly. "If you want to call the police, you're welcome."

"Ok," said the man, moving his head furiously from side-to-side. "I will."

He walked away. I would have been inclined to move

swiftly on at that point; I had witnessed enough and wasn't in the mood for conflict. The amphetamine was making my heart pound wildly and I felt nauseous. Sara turned to watch the funeral again, smiling as if she'd enjoyed the confrontation.

"Shall we go?" I said. "I've had enough." I tried to keep my voice steady but images of *Midnight Express* filled my mind and us languishing in a filthy prison.

"No!" She was emphatic. "He was just trying it on. Anyway, this is where I want to be."

I think I hated her for a moment. Then, in less than five minutes, the little man returned with a not-so-little police officer. Even Sara looked surprised.

"You have been seen to take photographs of the funeral, madam," said the police officer. "It is very bad; you must come with me."

I looked around frantically trying to gain the attention of fellow voyeurs, but the crowd seemed oblivious to what was taking place or they chose to ignore it. The chaotic sound of the pipes plus the affect of amphetamine were pushing me towards blind panic.

The policeman held out his hand to grab me; I pulled away.

"Get off me," I said.

"Leave her alone and piss off." Sara slapped his arm. The policeman's face stiffened.

"Look!" I said, trying to calm things down. "There has been a mistake. We have not been taking photographs. We respect your religion." I sounded feeble, even to myself. However, the policeman's face softened a little.

"If you come over here with me, perhaps we can sort it out." He pointed to a narrow alleyway to the right of the ghat.

Sara and I looked at each other and I think it crossed both of our minds at the same time that we were victims of a scam. The policeman – if he was in fact a policeman – was after rupees, not justice.

"Let's go," Sara shouted. We ran from the river towards the old town, entering the labyrinthine streets; the footsteps of the policeman and his accomplice banged behind us and I heard one of them shout, "Be sure, we will get you". Sara laughed as she ran and I couldn't help doing the same, although for me it was the laughter of hysteria. Ragged children grabbed at our skirts, oblivious to the panic in our eyes; the Hitchcockian screech of caged birds and garbled Hindi crashed off buildings so that the noise multiplied into a wild cacophony.

We took random turns into side streets bumping into lethargic cows or whining scooters transporting mum, dad and two children as well as the family dog. At one point we thought we had lost our pursuers, only to almost bump into them as we turned a bend. Eventually we found ourselves down by the ghats.

"Oh God," I said, gulping in air, "how did we get back here?"

"Let's stop," replied Sara. "We seem to have lost them."

We forced ourselves to calm down and slowly traced a route back to the hotel, constantly looking over our shoulders as we went. We collapsed on our beds, shaken and sober.

"Varanasi is not agreeing with me," I stated. "Shall we leave tomorrow?"

"It might be wise," said Sara, already rolling a cigarette with steady hands.

If we had left the next morning the story might have been different. Perhaps I would have completed the journey, returned to London to settle back into an ordinary life, but Varanasi wouldn't let us go. The ancient Mother seemed to have a purpose, which neither of us could escape.

Jae Watson

Chapter 10

The next day, Sara fell ill and was confined to bed for several days. It was unusual to see her laid so low; she looked helpless and I noticed how thin she had become. When I commented on it she told me to take a good look at myself in the mirror. We had both lost a great deal of weight, probably a result of a largely vegan diet, drinking loads of water and eating very few sugary products. Our bodies had adjusted to small quantities of food and we walked every day, sometimes over long distances with heavy backpacks. I was probably fitter and healthier than I had ever been.

We weren't sure what caused Sara's illness but we guessed she had probably caught a bug of some description, an almost inevitable part of travelling in India. She was extremely weak and had bad stomach pains; it meant we were forced to stay in Varanasi for longer than intended.

I did venture out, but stayed close to the hotel, afraid of bumping into our pursuers. I returned at frequent intervals to look after Sara and to give her fresh water – the only thing she could keep down.

I remembered what Miguel had said about falling asleep and I decided, since there was little else to occupy my time while Sara was ill, I would read the book he had given me and try to recapture what I had felt in Jaipur. I didn't want to spend my days in the sick room with Sara – she slept most of the time anyway – and the hotel lobby wasn't conducive to relaxation; it was more like a gaoler's office, bare and grey, with the ever-present Mr Sultan sitting like a sloppy Buddha in one corner. Instead, I found a café close to the hotel with a roof terrace and planted myself there, with my book and a glass of chai.

'*The Toltec of southern Mexico were women and men of knowledge; they were allegedly scientists and artists who formed a society to explore and conserve ancient spiritual knowledge and practice. Three-thousand years ago a man, who lived near a city surrounded by mountains, dreamed that he saw his own body sleeping; he went outside and looked up at the millions of stars and heard his own voice say, "I am made of light; I am made of stars." He realised that stars don't create light but that they are made of light; that everything is made of light and that everything that exists is one living being, the force of the Supreme Creator. Matter is a mirror that reflects light and creates images of that light – billions of manifestations of life.*

'*This vision transformed the man's life. He talked about The Dream, a kind of smoke, which prevents us from seeing what we really are – pure love and pure light. He looked around and saw himself in everything and everyone. However, he found it difficult to convey this revelation to other people; they didn't understand because they were all dreaming – the Dream of Humans. He realised we dream all the time; we have a dream of society, of our planet, of family, religion, laws and beliefs. In the dream of the planet it is normal for humans to suffer, to live in fear. Fear controls the dream – it is a dream of hell.*

'*People who go before us such as parents, teach us to dream the way society dreams and to dream what is acceptable; they teach us by repetition, giving us a code, a Book of Law. We learn a system of punishment and reward, which we carry throughout our lives. We develop a way of hooking attention in order to get a reward and we pretend to be what we are not to please others and to get what we want.*

'*We didn't choose to learn our native tongue or to learn the values and beliefs of our society, they were already there – we didn't even choose our own names. However, we agreed with the information passed to us from the dream of the planet, as it is only by agreement that we can store information. We have faith in those who have gone before us and our faith is strong.*

'As a very young child, a toddler, we rebel for a while to defend our freedom, but we soon learn to comply and then we self-discipline with the Book of Law, which is now firmly fixed in our minds.

'If we are exposed to new concepts or we doubt the Book of Law and rebel, we feel guilt and shame; these beliefs still control our lives, determining what we accept and reject and we punish ourselves over and over for making one mistake. We are Judge to ourselves, even if these judgements go against our own inner nature; we judge everyone and everything. Part of us is also a Victim, carrying self-destructive blame and guilt.

'Our minds are a fog – the Toltec called it mitote while in India they call it Maya – illusion. We cannot see who we are; we cannot see we are not free. Being ourselves, being alive, is the biggest fear humans have; it is easier to be the creation of others.

'We have to have the courage to break the thousands of fear-based agreements we have made with parents, teachers, priests, God; agreements, which rob us of our energy. We should make new agreements, which come from love.'

I thought about my relationship with Nathaniel, which I had once considered to be pretty near perfect, yet he had taken actions I didn't understand, leaving me confused, angry and upset. I had been smug in the belief that we were exceptionally close, that we could almost read each other's minds, but in reality we had played out our relationship in a 'mitote'. I didn't really know him at all; it had been a dream, my dream. It struck me for the first time that if I were given a second chance, I would have to get to know the real Nathaniel, not an artist's, or rather my, impression.

Then I thought about Sara and the confusion I frequently felt in her presence; she threatened my Book of Law; she didn't sit easily within its pages. I had put myself in the role of victim, both in relation to Sara and to Nathaniel. In fact, if I really faced the truth, I had wallowed in this role at many points in my life – a victim of my past, a victim of circumstance, a victim of fate.

'The big mitote in the human mind creates a lot of chaos, which causes us to misinterpret everything and misunderstand everything. We destroy relationships in order to defend our position.

'Stop lying about what you really want. Say no when you want to say no and yes when you want to say yes. Be impeccable with your words. One word can create the most beautiful dream or destroy everything around you, like good and bad spells; they can be seeds of fear or of love.

'Don't take anything personally or you will allow yourself to be poisoned – nothing people do is about us but about them, they are in their own dream. Don't even take the voices in our own head personally, they are part of the mitote, like a huge market place where everyone talks at once and rarely agrees. Don't make assumptions, they lead to misunderstanding and create emotional poison. Just do your best in each situation.

'The first step to freedom is awareness. Be aware you are not free to be free. If you are not aware that your mind is full of wounds and poison then you cannot heal it. You are addicted to pain, that is why it is too painful to be touched by other people, it is like touching an open sore. Forgiveness is the only way to heal yourself; when you are healed you will enjoy being touched by others.

'Don't feed the parasite called fear in your mind. 'When the fear is too great the reasoning mind begins to fail and this is what we call mental illness.' Death can teach you to be truly alive, live each day as if it is the last, tell people that you love them – love without obligation or conditions or judgement. Resurrection is to be like a child again – wild and free but with the benefit of wisdom. Only then will you find happiness.'

I was troubled by the current state of the world – planetary disasters, terrorism and a growing rage that seemed an uncomfortable feature of modern life. I had escaped the terror in London only to run back into its arms in Delhi and I was desperately trying to find meaning in this.

I wondered whether people of my age had always worried excessively about the state of things – in so-called peacetime – whether they felt the weight of the world groaning on their shoulders, as I did now. If I hadn't lost the faith of my childhood I might have been tempted to believe in an imminent Armageddon.

But where did the Christian faith fit into all of this? While I knew the Bible stories – donkeys and mangers, the crucifixion and resurrection, and something about love and turning the other cheek – I had very little understanding of the true philosophy at the heart of the faith. Catholicism had been a comfortable and unchallenging part of my life for the first fourteen years; I still felt a warm glow when I saw a crib scene or heard carol singers, but surely there must be more to it than that.

I shivered and looked up to see the sun falling behind a building opposite. I had been reading for longer than I realised and hurried back to the hotel, buying water on the way. The room smelled of sickness and of something else, something bitter, which I couldn't place. Sara was still asleep. I watched her for a few seconds, struck by the vulnerability of the sleeper stripped of all defence, a lamb placing itself willingly at the mercy of wolves. Seeing Sara asleep made me realise, with a shock, just how ill she had become, just how much the illness had daubed its shadow across her face. Then, as if she could sense the scrutiny of my eyes, she struggled into wakefulness and her defences shifted haltingly back into place.

"How are you feeling?"

"Not too bad. I had some weird dreams though." She winced as she pushed herself to a sitting position.

"About what?"

"I was being cremated down by the ghats, but I was still alive."

"Oh my God, that sounds horrendous."

"That's the weird thing; it wasn't. I felt really warm, the flames kind of stroked my body. I felt quite horny, actually. I wanted to tell everyone that there's nothing to worry about but they couldn't hear me as they were wailing so loudly."

"I think our heads are a bit screwed up," I said.

"I guess so." Sara took a long draught of water. "Do you believe in God?"

I was shocked. Firstly because this wasn't the sort of question that came out of Sara's mouth, not without irony anyway; secondly because it was the same question that had been hovering on my lips for her.

"I don't know," I stuttered. "I think I probably do in some form or other…it's hard to imagine there not being a God, but then maybe that's just my programming…how about you?"

"I'm not sure either. I had some pretty amazing conversations with Raj, you know." She looked embarrassed.

"I thought you probably did."

"How?"

"You seemed different when I saw you again, kind of softer."

"So did you. I really love you, you know Marianne. You're the best friend I've ever had."

"I love you too." I kissed her on her burning cheek.

"Good, now piss off. I need more sleep."

Chapter 11

'Still as he fled, his eye was backward cast, As if his fear still followed him behind.' Edmund Spencer, *The Faerie Queen*[10]

That night we were woken by noises in the hotel. We had heard them several times before, but on this particular night they were more persistent.

"Oh God! What's going on?" Sara asked weakly.

"I'm not sure. I've been awake for ages; it's getting louder."

I climbed out of bed and switched on the light. I walked around the room to try to locate where the sound was loudest.

"It seems to be coming from here." I placed my ear next to a hefty pipe that ran along the walls.

"I'm going to look." With great effort, Sara pushed herself up. "I'm sick of this."

"You should stay in bed," I said. "You're not well; it's only four-thirty."

I was concerned about Sara's health and I was also reluctant to get involved in one of her clandestine adventures.

"I need to know what's going on night after night." She was already pulling clothes over her nightwear and with resignation I did the same. The previous day I had asked Mr Sultan about the noise; he had been dismissive, saying there was building work next door. I didn't believe him and I was sure the noise was coming from within the hotel.

We walked into the corridor and since we were at the top of the hotel there was no choice but to go down. However, we wanted to avoid the reception desk for fear of raising suspicion. There was a door opposite our room and at the other end of the corridor from the main staircase. We had already investigated and discovered a narrow staircase, probably a service route, not used by guests. We knew it was hidden from the reception area and so we took it.

The staircase was of mean proportions, with roughly plastered walls; it smelled like an old castle – of damp and stale urine. There were no electric lights and we made the descent with torches. On each floor, there was a door leading off the stairs, presumably onto each successive corridor.

We pushed the door on the second floor and discovered it was locked, as was the door on the first floor. We didn't dare try the ground floor, for fear of attracting attention, so we passed it and descended into the basement, where the volume of noise increased.

"Shit, I'm scared," I said, waving my torch wildly so as not to miss any lurking demons.

"Me too!" replied Sara. "Let's go for it." She pushed the door at the bottom of the staircase; it offered no resistance. We were instantly assaulted by bright lights, a pungent smell and loud clanging noises. We could make out what looked to be copper and stainless steel pots and tanks of various sizes spread around the room, and they had pipes running out of them into other tanks. I noticed that the equipment at one end was pushed against the wall and it had, no doubt, been responsible for sending eerie noises up to our room. Since the pipes in our room were exposed, unlike elsewhere in the hotel, I guess we heard the noise more clearly than other guests.

I recognised the mashing pots and grain mills from an educational trip I had been on with my school in Shropshire, as well as the smell of hops and yeast.

"It's a brewery!" I hovered in the shadows behind Sara.

"An illegal sodding brewery!" Sara laughed.

A voice shouted something in Hindi and Mr Sultan appeared from behind a tank – a large kukri glinted in his hand. He was lit from a lamp on the floor, which cast eerie shadows onto his heavy-jowled face.

"What are you doing here?" He growled.

"Run!" I shouted, already turning and stumbling up the staircase. I could hear Sara gasping for breath behind me and the shouts of Mr Sultan behind her.

"Come back you bitches!"

I pushed the doorway on the ground floor, praying it would open and, thank God, it did. We ran through the reception into the night. Mr Sultan stopped in the doorway of the hotel, breathing curses.

"I will find you and I will kill you," he called after us.

We ran until we could run no more. We eventually dropped on the steps of the Vishwanath Temple, hiding in the shadows of its golden spire, desperately sucking in air.

"What the fuck is going on?" Sara looked more fearful than I had ever seen her; she was still breathing heavily and her face was haggard. "I feel like I've been playing a part in some trashy B-movie these last two weeks."

"We have to leave!" I said emphatically. "I can't take any more of this place."

"It's ridiculous." Sara was regaining some of her composure; anger replaced fear. "I don't give a fuck about that prick illegally brewing alcohol; it's not like we were going to call the police or anything."

"I guess it's a pretty serious offence here," I said. "Apart from anything else, he's a Muslim and Varanasi is a holy city; he could probably be locked up...or worse. He certainly wouldn't want us reporting him."

"Yeah, his rat-infested hotel is obviously just a front for a more lucrative business."

"I bet he'd go a long way to find us...to shut us up." Reality was beginning to bite; I could feel the first clawing talons of hysteria. We hadn't exactly got off to a good start with the lovely Mr Sultan.

"I don't think he'll waste much time on us." Sara spoke with reassuring confidence, but I wasn't convinced.

"What are we going to do about our bags? Our passports and everything are back there. There's no way I'm going back to that place."

Sara lifted her top to reveal her money belt, wrapped tightly around her slim waist.

"I've started sleeping with it on," she grinned. "I've got my passport and some money, not much though."

"Well *you're* ok then," I said sarcastically.

"At least we can get a hotel room and some food." Sara was in control again. "We can go to the police station later."

"You must be joking!" I gasped. We still weren't sure if it had been a *bona fide* police officer that had chased us at the ghats before, but I really didn't want to find out.

"I don't think we have much choice; we have to get our things."

"No! I'm going to the railway station to get the first train out of here." I was shivering hard, partly from the cool dawn air, mostly from fear. Then I threw up on the steps of the temple.

"Look Marianne." Sara rubbed my back and held my hair from my face. "I know it's tempting to run, but we can't do anything without your passport. I think it's best if we book into a hotel-"

"Sara, we can't!" I wailed

"We *can* Marianne, at least for a few hours. We can get some rest, gather our thoughts, decide what to do. Then we can go to the police, try to get our stuff back. We could leave tonight on a sleeper train."

I was impressed by Sara's clarity of thought. Her argument was logical but my intuition told me to leave Varanasi as soon as possible, to go to the British Embassy in Delhi and sort things out from there.

"What if he finds us? I bet all the hotel owners know each other here."

"Marianne, there are hundreds of hotels in Varanasi. We'll leave Godaulia, go to a different area. He'll take weeks to find us, that's if he's even looking. Anyway, I still don't feel great; I think I need to rest for a while."

She did look terrible and I felt guilty for not considering her needs.

"Ok, just one more day, but then we're definitely leaving."

It was still only 5.30am, but hotels in India are used to people arriving at ungodly hours and the festival was over so we hoped to have more luck than when we'd first arrived. Sara suggested we make our way down to the Ganges and trace it north. We eventually stopped at Ghai Ghat, where we found a clean hotel with a light, airy room en suite. Fortunately, the owner was happy to accept just one passport.

It felt like heaven and there was even warm water. We showered and then climbed into our beds; the sheets were cool and smelled of soap. I didn't expect to sleep but I did. I guess it was the after-effect of adrenalin pumping through my body as well as sheer fatigue. When I woke up it was eleven in the morning and Sara's bed was empty.

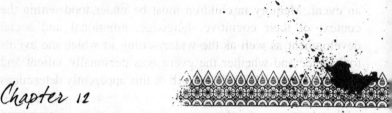

Chapter 12

On seeing that Sara was gone, my immediate reaction was annoyance but for the first time I began to wonder why this feeling of hostility instinctively occurred.

Memory is a fascinating subject as I found out when I did some research on it in my second year of university. The research was specifically related to the reliability of a child's memory in court hearings.

Nathaniel provided some useful information about child development and explained that the ability to remember changes at various stages in a child's life. If trauma occurs at a particular age then it's as if a hole is made in the child's life at that point, like a burn in a movie reel. It is hardly noticeable when played at speed but if slowed down the hole becomes very obvious; if it's not repaired then we have to replay that part of our life over and over in order to make sense of it. We have to fill in the gaps with something.

Very young children have the ability to store encoded information but children under five aren't able to store the information very effectively – like a badly-organised library. They might not understand that something is important or 'wrong', such as sexual abuse, as they do not have the language or cognitive ability to rationalise this. Retrieval of memories in younger children often depends on the ability of either an adult or the child's older self to ask the right questions, in the right way.

Concerns have been raised about the malleability of a child's memory when relying on their testimony in court. However, research suggests that children as young as three – if questioned sensitively – show very accurate recall, even several years after an event. Memory in children must be understood within the context of their cognitive, language, emotional and social development as well as the wider setting in which the events took place and whether the event was personally salient and experienced or only observed. All of this apparently determines how a child remembers an event

Certain types of information, however, such as time and distance are not encoded in the memory of younger children as these concepts have not yet been learned. Since children don't have any idea, at the time, that they should commit certain events to memory (unless specifically asked to do so) then they might not be able to later recall the information, unless prompted. A child must first encode the information, then store it and then be able to retrieve it. A child's understanding of an event to which they are exposed will have a profound effect on what they encode and what is stored in their memory.

An explanation for poorer recall of details in traumatic memories may be that the details are encoded in such a way that they are more difficult to access, or that their retrieval is hampered by continuous attempts to repress them or push them from consciousness.

Over time a child develops more sophisticated language and intellect; understanding of an event might then be altered by this newfound knowledge.

The memory of my mother leaving when I was three-years-old remained undisturbed, floating in the recesses of my mind for many years. I couldn't make sense of it because I didn't know the right questions to ask.

I do remember, on the night she left, waking up and knowing that everything was different. I remember feeling a shocking alertness and an unfamiliar fear. I did what was natural for any three-year-old to do: I called for my mum. When she didn't come I climbed out of bed and headed for my parent's bedroom – that strangely scented haven where sleep and whispered talk and other mysteries took place.

Before I reached the door, I heard unfamiliar sounds from within. I found my Dad alone, sobbing, my mum's nightdress clutched to his face. The sight terrified me. My mum's side of the bed was empty and this, for some reason, was the most powerful image of that strange night. It was the image of something missing – an empty space, one hand clapping.

I'm not sure how much of this was true memory and how much was supplied later, by my much older self, but what stayed with me was that sense of terrible emptiness: the emptiness of the house, the emptiness of my dad's face and the hollowness of his voice as he tried to explain.

I couldn't have known, at the time, the significance of what was happening; I couldn't have understood that my mother would never come back. Perhaps the nightmare of the weeks that followed were all rolled back into that one night for me: my father's tears, curtains left drawn, the smells of neglect and the fading away of smells which I only then realised I loved – my mum's perfume, cakes baking, fresh flowers, furniture polish – and the reliable monotony of meals on the table. It was all about absence.

When Nathaniel and I spent nights together in one or the other of our flats, he would sometimes jump up to make coffee before I awoke. When I did wake and saw his side of the bed empty I would find myself inexplicably irritated with him.

I felt a similar irritation when I saw Sara's empty bed on that fateful day. But, for the first time, I made the connection to my childhood; an empty bed equalled abandonment. I knew in that moment that I had to ask my father some very difficult questions.

PART 2
Chapter 13

'No passion so effectually robs the mind of all its powers of acting and reasoning as fear.' Edmund Burke, *On the Sublime and Beautiful*[11]

It was a hot day in November, a day broken in two. I remember every detail of it now and probably always will. I guess some memories are etched more deeply into the brain – the very good and the very bad. The sun was already burning low into the room when I woke up and I was sweating beneath the thin cotton sheet. I pushed the sheet away from my body and stretched out; only then did I turn to see Sara's empty bed. I had a flashback to Agra. Why did she have to do this? We needed to stick together.

I dressed and went down to reception, wary of what I might find. I was convinced I would meet Mr Sultan and a gang of heavies dragging Sara away, but it was empty except for the manager, a petite woman in a bright-yellow sari who greeted me with a warm smile.

"Good morning, can I help you?" She moved her head touchingly from side-to-side.

"Good morning." I held the panic at bay. "Have you seen my friend? She's not in the room."

"Yes, your friend is on the rooftop, waiting for you. Breakfast is being served." They were wonderful words. It was like waking from a nightmare, running out of a tangled jungle into

93

civilisation.

"Thank you!" I said, a little too enthusiastically, and climbed the stairs to the rooftop.

There was a fantastic view of the Ganges and Ghai Ghat from up there; the clear blue of the sky seemed to stretch out forever. Sara sat alone at a table, drinking chai and staring away from me into the hazy distance.

"Good morning!" I said, surprising myself with my cheerfulness. Sara turned very slowly. My heart lurched, punch drunk. She had aged overnight; her skin was sallow and her eyes, the only indication of her former beauty, stared huge and glazed as if surprised to find themselves in the wrong face. The pupils had retreated into black pinpricks. She didn't seem to know who I was. But then recognition came, she smiled and some of her luminosity returned.

"Sara! What's wrong?" I sat beside her, wanting to cry with horror.

"Nothing, I'm absolutely fine." Her words were elongated as if spoken in slow motion.

"God, you haven't taken an 'E' have you?" I was desperately trying to figure out what was going on. We had taken ecstasy once, at a Full Moon Party in Thailand; we danced on the beach all night with hundreds of other travellers. I thought perhaps Sara had smuggled one into India but I knew really that she wouldn't be so stupid; besides, she didn't look like someone loved up on MDMA. "Your eyes are so weird."

"I went to the pharmacy earlier to get something to clear up this bug. It must have been strong stuff."

I wasn't sure I believed her but it was the only explanation that made sense.

"Well, you shouldn't have gone out without me, you nutter. I thought you'd been snatched by Mr Sultan."

"Sorry Mari," she said. "I didn't want to worry you. I was just feeling crap."

"Ok, shall we order breakfast, I'm starving."

"I've had some; I'll just get another tea."

When the waiter came he took my order of vegetable omelette; he then turned to Sara.

"What can I get for you, madam?" His pen and pad were poised.

"Just chai please."

"Nothing to eat, madam?"

"No, just chai," she said firmly.

"You haven't eaten, have you?" I asked when he left.

"I'm not hungry."

"But why did you lie?"

"You worry too much Marianne. I thought it was easier."

I felt confused. Sara didn't usually cover up. I put it down to the illness, the stress of the past few days.

I decided not to pursue the point; there was too much else to worry about.

"So what's our plan?" I asked, relying on Sara to show the clarity of mind she had possessed in the early hours of that morning.

"Erm, I'm not sure; what do you think?"

I was taken aback for a moment.

"I thought we said we'd go to the police, ask them to get our bags and then take a train out of here."

"That sounds like a good plan," she said. "Why don't we do that?" She rolled a cigarette, like we had no pressing engagements.

"I think we should do it sooner rather than later." I was feeling increasingly worried by Sara's behaviour; she didn't seem to care about or even remember much of what had happened only a few hours earlier.

"Ok," she said, rising with some determination, "just give me a bit of time; I'll go back to bed for an hour, then I'll be fine."

I could see that Sara couldn't be persuaded otherwise so, reluctantly, I agreed.

It was noon and I desperately wanted to ring my dad, hear the unconditional tenderness of a parent's voice. However, even stronger was my desire not to worry him or put him in a position of helplessness. Instead, I asked for paper and a pen at reception and wrote him a letter telling him how much I loved him and how grateful I was for all he had done for me. At ten-past-one I wrote his name and address on the folded sheet and asked the woman at reception to post it.

"You girls are very busy with your letter writing," she said. "You must be missing your families."

"You girls…?" I was confused. "No, it was just me."

"No, the girl with the eyes; she was also wanting paper and pen."

My legs turned to water; I grabbed onto the reception desk.

"It's hot," I said. "I'm going to lie down."

The room was empty; a piece of paper lay in careless abandonment on Sara's bed. I sat down and lowered my head between my knees until the dizziness subsided. Then I read the letter:

Marianne,
I'm going to the police station alone. I've caused you enough trouble as it is. I will then go to find out times of trains to Delhi. Don't leave the hotel and try to relax. I may be some time!
Love and kisses
Sara x

To my shame, my first reaction was one of relief. I had been dreading the journey to the police station; I thought Sara would be less conspicuous on her own. The light tone of her letter reassured me that she was feeling better and able to handle things. It was only after a few minutes that I felt the first seeds of apprehension. I knew in reality Sara was still weak; I couldn't forget her face that morning. If she did get into danger she might not have the strength to run away and I wouldn't have a clue what had happened to her. However, I knew it would be ridiculous to follow her; I didn't know how long she'd been gone and we would probably end up crossing paths. All I could do was wait but waiting seemed the worst possible option. I curled up on my bed, wishing I could sleep until Sara returned, wishing that everything would be magically sorted out.

When I was ten-years-old, my aunt loaned me her pearl brooch to wear for my Catholic confirmation. Afterwards, I decided to take the brooch to school before giving it back to my aunt, so that I could show it off to my friends. Amanda Davies, an older girl and a known bully, snatched it from me and threw it down the toilet. The school caretaker managed to retrieve it but two of the pearls were missing. I never knew if they'd been flushed down the toilet or if Amanda had prised them out to keep for herself.

I was too scared to tell my aunt or my dad about the incident; instead I traipsed around jeweller's shops asking if they could fix the brooch. When I learned how expensive it would be to replace the pearls, or even match them with good fakes, I resorted to fervent praying, asking various saints to perform a miracle. Nothing happened and I eventually had to confess my sin. However, it didn't stop me from turning to prayer again at that moment.

Perhaps all religion grows out of our earliest need to be rescued. The profound helplessness of the human infant – a helplessness we share with no other animal – means that we must have the hope, the expectation, that the milky breast will magically appear in response to our cry, that the great parental arms will lift us from our cradle and remove our discomfort. Any delay in their response brings on near hysteria. We never forget that terror; we never quite relinquish the belief that we will somehow be rescued and we regress to this belief in the hour of our greatest need.

At two-fifteen, I returned to the now deserted rooftop and sat watching the endless flow of the Ganges. Many people were milling about on the banks of the river. I guessed there was yet another festival taking place; Indian people seem to possess endless energy for celebrating life and death.

I wondered about emailing Nathaniel – something I had resisted so many times over the past months – to tell him how much I missed him, to say how sorry I was that our relationship had ended. I played with the words but everything sound trite and impotent. Besides, I couldn't leave the rooftop; I was rooted there by an invisible force, like a saint or sadhu compelled to sit in silent meditation.

At three, I saw some heightened activity by the river. A crowd was bunched together at one end of the ghat like a dense and colourful knot at the centre of a tapestry. I guessed some ritual was taking place but couldn't make out the detail. I thought I saw figures in the water with white, plumy splashes around them – perhaps more plaster gods being ritualistically washed by the sacred waters. I thought how sad it is that we have lost so much of our ritual in the West – the festivals and carnivals that used to take place in every town and village, in churches, streets and on village greens.

At four-thirty, despair was creeping into my blood. I knew I should order food but I was amputated from my senses; there was no room for anything but fear and I felt powerless to dispel it. Sara had been gone for at least three-and-a-half hours and the light was dying from the sky, leaving an exquisite red and purple shroud above the earth.

At five, I heard a noise behind me and turned to see the Hindu lady from reception with two police officers. Well, I thought, at least the waiting is over.

"We have some very bad news for you," one of the police officers said. I noticed he had very prominent front teeth, which forced his mouth into a permanent smile when he spoke. I thought this was unfortunate considering the amount of bad news he must have had to deliver.

I searched all three sets of eyes for clues. The Hindu woman was wringing her hands in a peculiar, old-fashioned way. Then came the last words I expected to hear, words reserved for movies, or for other people, not for me.

"A body has been dragged from the Ganges. We think it is your friend."

Chapter 14

One of the best experiences of my life was standing in the sanctuary at Anapurna Base Camp, in Nepal, surrounded by eight-thousand-metre peaks. It was the highest I had ever stood on the planet and the air was so pure that it seemed to slice through my lungs, cutting away years of pollution and debris. I was looking at the earth with the filter removed, the sky a vivid dark-blue and the mountains caught in sharp focus. My mind was as clear as the air and everything made sense. It really didn't have to be any more complicated than this.

Sara and I laughed and hugged each other, exhilarated by the beauty of the scenery and the achievement of the climb. We had taken four days to reach base camp. On the way we stayed in a variety of lodges. The higher we climbed, the more basic they became. Lower down we had warm showers, then cold showers, then warm buckets of water and then cold buckets. Needless to say we didn't bother with the latter; the air was freezing and we slept in our clothes, not bothering to wash.

We met some interesting people en route, from the indigenous Nepalese people, who lived in high altitude villages, the guides and porters who trudged up the mountain in flip-flops (carrying impossibly huge loads on their heads), to the other travellers with whom we spent our evenings eating in kerosene-fumed canteens and playing card games to pass the time.

The climb was hard and at times the pain of the exertion stopped all conversation, locking us into our own thoughts. All concentration went into the present step, nothing else, just the present step. I experienced some of the purest happiness I have ever known, feeling the exquisite joy and pain of each moment – each one connected to the next like pearls on a necklace, each pearl possessing a self-contained beauty and purpose.

When I saw Sara's body in the mortuary I thought of those moments. I remembered her bounding up rocks and through streams, her sun-glazed legs strong and supple, hair flying about her like a horse's tail, proud and defiant. She was so young – we were both so young – her earthly body seemed hardly able to contain the life that flowed through it. Yet, was death waiting for her, even then?

Sara's body was laid out on a slab of stone in a grey room. I could tell it was her because of the ring she always wore on her little finger – a present from her father – which had recently been joined by the karra from Raj and the silver necklace I had bought her in the Pink City. I also recognised the beautiful hair, which trailed like ivy down the sides of the slab, reminding me of a picture of Sleeping Beauty from an illustrated book of fairytales I had owned as a child.

However, her face was barely recognisable. It was bloated and the muscles appeared to have lost their tone so that her strikingly high cheekbones sagged.

"Dragged from the Ganges…" I couldn't free my mind from those brutal words.

On a table next to her was her money belt, with the sodden contents laid out beside it: her passport, a few rupees, the receipt from our hotel – with still discernible numbers scribbled onto it – a pen, lip salve, an empty pill packet and a small key. Even now when I shut my eyes, with a little concentration, I can see all of those items clearly. The key was particularly enticing, holding a promise of something wonderful or something awful. Like all the other objects laid out next to Sara's body, it seemed to hold a greater significance than the sum of its parts.

I realised that tears were pouring from my eyes, down my cheeks and spilling onto the floor without any effort on my part;

I had never experienced such an involuntary flood. I was like *Alice in Wonderland*, except I was in Hades.

*****

A week after my first meeting with Sara and the day after the London bombings, she asked me to go to a party in Notting Hill. Nathaniel was on a training course that weekend – something to do with Freud – so I went on my own. It was my first introduction to Sara's world.

Most of my friends lived in north London and had completed degrees in subjects like art and philosophy, English literature and politics; we went to gigs, partied in dilapidated flats, ate in cheap cafés and took an interest in politics and social issues. Sara's friends were in law and finance or had slipped easily into Daddy's advertising company; they went to concerts and cocktail parties, dined at The Ivy and shopped in Chelsea.

I didn't fit in. I wore the wrong clothes, made the wrong conversations. However, Sara wasn't quite one of them either; she had her own style – a quirkiness that set her apart. I had the feeling she was taking the piss out of the world she found herself part of – whether by accident or choice – but played the game anyway. She was accepted because she was beautiful and confident and, at the end of the day, she knew the rules. I learned the rules as well, it wasn't that difficult, and the next time I met Sara's friends I had made subtle changes. I learned the gestures and jokes, what was ok to talk about and what was passé or taboo. I didn't change my politics or values; I just didn't mention them.

For a short time I lived a double life, swapping costumes between acts, saying the lines for each of my characters. I was a hypocrite, but then aren't we all? In the 1970s, my parents called themselves 'Catholic Socialists'. They adhered to the beliefs and rituals of the Catholic Church as well as handing out political tracts in the streets and protesting about Vietnam: They hated capitalism, war and homeownership. Yet, they bought their council house in 1981. Two years later, when Dad was more successful – aided by Margaret Thatcher's small business initiative – and just before my mother left us, they moved to a large semi with a garden in Shrewsbury. They were not alone; most of their 'socialist' friends did the same.

Nathaniel disliked the change in me and only came to one of the many parties that took place that summer. He thought Sara's friends were shallow, obsessed by property prices and the stock market. He didn't like their excessive use of cocaine, their 'hedonism' and the way he said I behaved when I was with them.

I thought he was being possessive, inflexible and petty. Nathaniel was always so true and honest; he didn't – couldn't – play games, or pretend to be what he wasn't. His integrity had challenged me at many times during our relationship; it was a sword, skilfully picking off my armour until I felt exposed. While I admired this quality in him, it could also make me feel uncomfortable. What was wrong with a bit of make-believe? Why did he have to be so damned straight? For the first time we had vehement rows that left us wrung out and weary.

At the end of August, Nathaniel ended our relationship, calmly and soberly. He didn't give any reason other than he thought we'd grown apart. No matter how many times I asked him, begged him for reasons, begged him to reconsider, he was like a stone wall. Then he refused to see me at all.

I turned to my old friends, people I knew and felt I could trust, even though I had neglected them over the past weeks. Sara's world seemed to vanish like a mirage, as if it had never existed; the party had ended. But Sara was still there, as real as ever.

She told me she was going travelling in September; she was sick of parties, sick of London. She asked me to go with her, said it would help me get over Nathaniel. I was a little surprised that Sara was prepared to take a year out when she was just about to move into her first job at a prestigious law firm. I was more surprised, however, that she had asked me to go travelling with her rather than one of her other friends, but then I couldn't really see Tara or Sophie 'slumming it' in India.

I really didn't know Sara very well; we had spent little time together away from noisy bars or parties. However, autumn was approaching, my favourite time of year, and I couldn't bear the thought of not spending it with Nathaniel. I remembered the exquisite rawness of my first autumn in London when I had fallen in love with the glorious seediness of its streets and the grandeur of its open spaces – where Nathaniel and I conspired together in mists and mellow fruitfulness. The secrets of the city seemed to unfold for us alone, like an enchanted thread, and gently weaved us into its cloth.

I agreed to go. My Dad tried to dissuade me with loving and cautious words.

"Marianne, sweetheart, you shouldn't run away. Don't you think it would be better to get some work experience…so that you can get on the journalism course next year?"

My friends were pissed off that I chose to go travelling with Sara rather than with them; it was a second betrayal. My own commonsense told me it was a crazy thing to do and my heart wanted to stay in the hope that Nathaniel would come back to me. I had asked him on many occasions to take a year out to go travelling but he always said he wanted to establish himself in his career first. Perhaps if I stayed, he would change his mind.

I'm not really sure what part of me made the decision to go but it felt like a strong and bold part, a part that I rarely allowed to flourish. The decision felt good; it felt magnificent.

*****

"Do you know why your friend was taking diamorphine?" A lilting voice broke into my thoughts.

"Diamorphine! What do you mean? What is it?" Sara lay dead, my mind was screaming, my guts were retching, my heart was breaking, yet I could still talk, I could still ask sensible questions. I had always wondered how people could behave so rationally after receiving bad news, why they didn't disintegrate into a mess of pain.

"It is a kind of medical heroin, madam, which in turn is derived from morphine." His accent sounded as if it had been acquired at Oxford in the 1950s, clear, correct but a little dated. "Very, very strong, according to our pharmacist; only used for severe pain."

"But Sara wasn't in pain; she couldn't have been taking it." What did Sara know about pain?

"The empty packet in her money belt once contained diamorphine, madam, and very high doses."

"I'm sorry, I don't know anything about it." I couldn't make sense of the situation. There was a viscous substance moving through my brain, slowing down my thoughts.

Dragged from the Ganges…

"How did she…die?" My voice was at first calm. I didn't want to be asking this question; I didn't want any of this to be happening. "Who killed her?" My voice grew loud, unstable, as my mind began to compute the possibilities. Then a shrill, hysterical note tore from my throat. "It was Mr Sultan, wasn't it?"

"Mr Sultan…? We do not know how your friend died madam; we don't even know that she was murdered. We must first carry out a post-mortem. In the meantime, I need to ask you a few questions. Would you like some chai?"

The lilting voice belonged to the chief of police who introduced himself as Mr Bakshi; he looked to be in his late-fifties with still thick but greying hair. He had a paunch, which only the comfortably-off can acquire in India. His voice had a strangely calming effect. He guided me out of the mortuary and into his office. My legs fell one in front of the other and somehow carried my weight. The outline of Sara's body was still imprinted on my mind – the sun's image on the retina. We were accompanied by an awkward young police officer in an ill-fitting uniform, who danced by Mr Bakshi's side like a faithful puppy.

Despite my shock, I was lucid enough to be selective in my statement. For example, I told Mr Bakshi about our trip to the burning ghats but not about the incident there; I told him about our meeting with Bert and Sam but didn't mention drugs. I did, however, tell him about the Avaneesh Hotel and the illegal brewery in the basement; I was convinced Mr Sultan had murdered Sara. Mr Bakshi and the young police officer exchanged looks, which I couldn't interpret, but they made no comment.

"My friend...Sara...she said she was coming here to tell you about Mr Sultan...and our bags. Do you have any record of it? It must have been some time after twelve."

"I will check our records, madam. In the meantime I will send someone to the Avaneesh Hotel to recover your bags."

"But you need to question Mr Sultan." I was desperate to convey my suspicion. "He threatened us, chased us with a kukri."

"Don't worry, madam, we will do our job." There was a tiny hint of irritation in Mr Bakshi's voice. "You must contact the young lady's parents in England," he said firmly. "They need to make plans."

"I don't know any of her family." I was shocked by my own words. "I don't even know where they live."

"She is your good friend, but you do not know her family? This could not happen in India." He spoke in firm, paternal tones.

"What about the key?" I asked, its image once again popping into my mind. "What is it for?"

"I do not know, madam; we must be patient. Now I have some other business to attend to."

Mr Bakshi asked me to remain in the office and wait. He then turned from me and uttered a few words in Hindi to the officer, who left the room and returned with a scrawny, dark-skinned man, who wore only a dhoti. He approached the desk with his head bent. He looked distraught and muttered unintelligible words. Mr Bakshi spoke in firm but kind tones, and then dismissed him.

Two other officers then brought in a large, hirsute man in handcuffs. This time Mr Bakshi had no hint of melody in his voice. He spoke in short, guttural barks and each bark seemed to hammer-tap the man's head until he was lying almost prostrate on the floor. He was then roughly ushered out.

This drama continued for some time – men, women and young boys were paraded before me like dogs at Crufts. I was appalled that I was permitted to be voyeur to these proceedings, embarrassed that I was a privileged member of an elite audience. I averted my eyes as the humiliating scenes were played out but, as at the burning ghat, I was compelled to watch rather than excuse myself as I know I should have.

"Would you like anything else, madam?" Mr Bakshi asked when he had completed his onerous task, his voice once again soft and melodious.

"No, I'm fine. What's happening?"

"We are waiting for my man to return from the Avaneesh Hotel."

At that point the young police officer burst into the room and, ignoring me, conversed in Hindi with Mr Bakshi.

"Excuse me, madam, I shan't be long." Mr Bakshi ushered the officer out of the room. They were gone for nearly half-an-hour.

A kind of numbness was setting in, crawling through my body like a slow poison. I wished Nathaniel could be with me; he would know what to do.

The office was a clutter of paper that seemed to be without order or meaning; I imagined there were countless statements of victims lost in these piles, never to be followed up, justice never done. I thought that Sara's file would end up here, working its way to the bottom until it disintegrated into dust and floated out of the window into the Ganges, where everything came to rest, and I had no power to prevent it.

"Madam, we have retrieved your belongings from the

Avaneesh Hotel." Mr Bakshi marched back into the office, causing me to jump from my thoughts.

"There are suspicious substances in your friend's bag, which we will have to send to our laboratory for analysis." Mr Bakshi looked displeased; any respect he might have had for me seemed to evaporate with his latest discovery.

Shit! Sara must have had some cannabis in her bag. I imagined my father's disappointment. Fear dried in my throat.

"We also found a locked diary," Mr Bakshi continued. "It appears we have solved the mystery of the key."

"A diary!" This information shocked me as much as the illegal substances. Not only because I had never seen Sara keep a diary, but it didn't seem a Sara thing to do. She had been amused by my daily scribblings and I had imagined she thought it to be a slightly old-fashioned or childish pastime.

"Can I have it?" I was deeply curious to see the diary. I felt it could offer clues to many things, not just Sara's death.

"I'm sorry, madam, we must detain it. It might contain important evidence. However, we have found several telephone numbers in the front of the diary, one belonging to the mother of the deceased – you must contact her immediately."

Mr Bakshi handed me a folded piece of paper. "We must also confiscate your passport, Miss Taylor, while we investigate your friend's death and carry out the post-mortem. You must report back here tomorrow morning at nine o'clock." Mr Bakshi turned, dismissing me with his back.

Chapter 15

It was ten in the evening when I arrived back at the hotel. I felt a hundred years older. I fell onto my bed, clutching the piece of paper. Scribbled on it in black ink was a UK phone number. At eleven, I ventured down to the reception to make the call. The telephone had an old-fashioned metal dial; my hands shook violently and I misdialled twice before finally getting it right.

"Yes?" It was a terse voice, impatient, cool.

"Mrs Fitzgerald?"

"Yes."

"This is Marianne…"

"Who? Speak up, I can hardly hear you." She sounded nothing like Sara.

"I'm calling from India." I increased my volume. "I'm a friend of Sara's."

"Oh yes, how can I help you?" It sounded like a command, not an offer.

How did people do this, what did they say?

"I have some bad news." There was silence at the other end of the phone. "Mrs Fitzgerald?"

"Yes, I'm still here, go on." The voice was more subdued.

"Sara's dead, I'm…sorry." I felt like I was apologising for getting her daughter into trouble at school or losing a letter she'd given me to post.

"Sara!" she gasped and then I heard a sob. She recovered herself quickly; in this ability she and Sara were alike.

I told her all I knew. She said she'd organise affairs back

home and contact me the following day. I didn't know what to make of the phone call but reasoned that everyone reacts differently to bad news.

I then called my dad; I broke into sobs the instant I heard the warm and familiar tones of his voice. He told me he would come to India as soon as he could. I begged him not to, saying there was no point; I told him that Sara's mother would be flying out soon. He hadn't been well recently and I really didn't want to worry him unnecessarily. I promised I would ring each day to update him and that I would return home as soon as I could. Eventually he agreed. I heard resignation in his voice. I imagined he regretted not being a stronger man.

I didn't sleep well. The night stretched out like the Ganges, littered with charred limbs and ghostly forms. At three in the morning, my mood was as flat and seamless as a sheet of cold steel. I feared that I would never leave Varanasi; I would end my days in a stinking prison cell, the smell of burning flesh in my nostrils and the sound of chaos in my ears. This seemed a worse fate than being bumped off by Sara's killer, who was still out there somewhere and no doubt intent on getting rid of me.

When the morning came, it brought uncertainty and fear that things could still get worse. There was a message from Mrs Fitzgerald waiting for me at reception. *'Arriving Thursday, will meet you at your hotel, 6pm.'*

It was only Tuesday morning; how could she take so long? What on earth would I do for three whole days? I had been asked to report to the police station each day but, apart from that, the rest of my time was free and time was not a luxury I craved at that point.

I couldn't face breakfast but went straight to the police station, jumping at every noise on the way. I waited for an hour and was then questioned by Mr Bakshi and his junior for a further two hours, covering the same ground as on the previous evening. I told them I was afraid that Sara's killer was still at large and that I was in danger; they were polite but dismissive, saying once again that they weren't even sure it was murder. I asked them if they'd arrested Mr Sultan and they avoided the question. I was increasingly suspicious that they were protecting him. They did say, however, that they had a record of Sara visiting the police station the previous day at approximately twelve forty-five. The officer who took her brief statement said she was confused and inarticulate; it seemed they didn't take her report too seriously.

I left the station light-headed with hunger and tiredness. I was shaken by the report of Sara's visit to the police station; it showed what a bad state she had been in, hardly fit to be roaming the streets of Varanasi alone. It left me feeling guilty and upset.

I bought some vegetable pakoras from a little street stall and returned to the hotel to eat them. I dreaded the time stretching out before me. I had no desire to meet new people or to see the sights but I knew I couldn't stay confined in my room day and night. I also had it in my mind that Bert and Sam might still be in Varanasi, although I had no idea where and I thought, perhaps irrationally, that if I found them they might provide clues to Sara's death, or at the very least offer me some company. I didn't, at that point, suspect them of Sara's murder; I was still obsessed by the belief that Mr Sultan was the guilty party, and if not him then the bogus policeman and his sidekick.

I made a decision to disguise myself as heavily as possible and venture out. I don't think I did this out of bravery, but rather out of fear that I might go insane if I remained alone in my room. I covered my hair with a large, brightly coloured scarf and twisted it into a knot on top of my head; I put on a mismatch of clothes, which I would never dream of wearing normally; I rescued my make-up, which was melting at the bottom of my backpack and, for the first time in months, applied it thickly to every part of my face. I even added a black beauty spot to my chin. Finally, I put on a pair of sunglasses. I looked like an eccentric hippy, or a mad woman, and I was pleased with the result.

At first I walked the streets aimlessly, unable to concentrate on any particular direction. I looked behind me constantly to see if I was being followed; I also hoped to catch sight of Bert and Sam.

I needed distraction more than anything and found it in the frenetic life of the bazaar. I ran my hand over silk embroidered throws and caressed brass candlesticks; I stared at mounds of exotic spices on silver platters and watched women in bright saris haggling with stall owners. I did it all with a strange sense of detachment.

Somehow the time passed and another night came. I did sleep, but fitfully. My dreams fell around me like splintered glass, cutting my nerves with their jaggedness. I dreamed of my mother for the first time in years; she had drowned in the Ganges instead of Sara. I saw her sliding into the water easily, as if taking an afternoon dip, blowing kisses to me as she sank beneath the ash-grey flow. I felt glad she was dead – it was better that she drown than abandon me. It was better that she was gone as a result of a cruel accident, than because there was nothing – no one – to keep her where she was.

I awoke with a feeling of dread and the sense that there was endless heavy time to sift through my fingers. I hoped there might be some progress in the investigations, but when I arrived at the police station there was a fracas going on in the reception. A group of sari-clad women were shouting at a police officer, while another officer was attempting to hold them back. I waited until the situation calmed down and then asked for Mr Bakshi. I was told he was dealing with a serious incident elsewhere.

"Can I speak to someone else then?" I asked, keen to get away from the grey confines of the station.

"That is not possible I'm afraid, madam." The officer seemed distracted by the wails of the women.

"Why not? I just want to know if there is any more news on my friend's death." I still gagged on these words.

"Oh, your friend…you mean Miss Fitzgerald?" He looked

more closely. "I did not recognise you, madam." I remembered my disguise and was glad it was so effective.

"I'm sorry, I cannot help you," he continued. "Mr Bakshi specifically asked that he deal with you himself."

"Well, what do you want me to do? I-"

At that point another officer interrupted us; he spoke in urgent Hindi.

"Just one minute, madam," said the young officer and left the room. The minute turned into fifteen, then thirty and eventually forty-five, by which time I felt exasperated.

I paced up and down, not caring that I must look like a crazy woman to the other people who waited with much more patience and decorum. Eventually, I asked a young man in an orange turban if he knew what was going on.

"There has been a case of sati outside the city," he replied.

"What happened?" I asked, distracted for a moment by the horror of the image forming in my mind.

"A young widow climbed onto her husband's funeral pyre while reciting prayers; she burned to death. There has been a riot among the women of the village."

"Oh my God!" I said. "Are they protesting against the practice of sati?"

"No, they want to make the site into a shrine in her honour. They believe the site of a sati can make barren women fertile or cure cancer. But sati is illegal; officials are trying to disperse the crowds, prevent it from becoming a pilgrimage site."

At that point the young officer returned. I jumped up to get his attention, prepared to block his exit if necessary.

"Look, don't leave again, just tell me how long Mr Bakshi will be."

"Oh, no need to wait, madam. Mr Bakshi asked me this morning to tell you to come back at three." He smiled ingenuously. I stared at him with unforgiving harshness. Without speaking, I strode out of reception and slammed the door.

I wandered the city, seething inside. I was angry about so

many things that I didn't know what to be most angry about. This time I went in a different direction and ended up at Vishwanath Temple where Sara and I had found solace a lifetime earlier. It was a very beautiful building, also known as the Golden Temple because of the striking gold plating on the spires.

I noticed a little plaque to one side. It informed me that: *'the temple was built by Ahalya Bai in 1776'*, and that it is the most sacred Hindu temple in Varanasi, dedicated to Vishveswara – Shiva as lord of the universe. The plaque also informed me that the temple is closed to non-Hindus.

"Madam, come here," a shrill voice called from across the road, causing me to literally jump with fear.

I saw a wizened woman waving her arms with great enthusiasm.

"Please madam, you can see the Golden Temple from my shop, come inside."

"Thank you, but it's ok." I waved back and started to move away. I wasn't in the mood for haggling. She came closer and looked deep into my eyes; her teeth were slightly bucked and red from the Betal nut she probably chewed in paan on a regular basis.

"You know, life is very short; it is like the flowers in the field – tomorrow they will be gone. Don't waste time saying no to everything. It is easier to say yes."

I was startled by her words. I had assumed she was just another poor shopkeeper trying to take advantage of a naive Westerner. But she seemed somehow wise.

"Ok," I said decisively. "I'll come and look."

The diminutive figure disappeared into the shop and up a narrow staircase. I followed. We climbed several flights past dozens of rolls of bright silk, which stood upright on every stair. We entered a dark and dusty room at the front of the shop, piled high with silk weave of every colour. There was a strong smell of incense, which caught in the back of my throat. The low, wood rafters of the ceiling made me feel claustrophobic and I was regretting my decision to follow her. Then, suddenly, she scurried towards me and pushed me with surprising strength towards the open window. The next minute, I was staring into the magnificent open heart of the temple.

For a religion that appears so chaotic and which defies any attempt to be defined, its place of worship is a picture of remarkable symmetry and order – a map of the universe.

I had read that for Hindus, the square is the perfect shape. Complex rules govern the location, design and building of each temple based on numerology, astrology, astronomy and religious law. Temples even store their own set of calculations, like religious texts.

In the centre, bathed in sunlight, I could see a simple, unadorned space – the inner shrine. I had read that this area is symbolic of the womb-cave from which the universe emerged. This is where the deity, to whom the temple is dedicated, resides. Above the shrine is a large structure, which symbolises a cosmic mountain. The womb and the mountain are linked by an axis.

Walking in a clock-wise direction around the shrine was a number of devotees dressed in white. Even from my elevated position, I could hear the tinkling sound of brass bells, rung by the devotees as they entered the temple.

"See how marvellous it is!"

I reluctantly turned from the light, back into the dark interior of the shop, to be met by the shrivelled walnut-face of the owner. She nodded with great enthusiasm.

"Yes, it is; thank you so much." I glowed inside, surprised that joy could visit even in a time of pain.

"You might have fallen dead and never seen it."

I took her small hands between mine and squeezed them.

"Thank you – you have lifted my spirits." I headed for the door and she followed me down the stairs. As I was about to leave she placed her hand on my shoulder. I turned to her again and looked into her unfathomable raison-eyes, waiting for the final words of wisdom to come from the blood-red mouth.

Perhaps she had a message for me about Sara or even about Nathaniel, something to help me in my moment of need. Her lips parted and she spoke.

"Do you want to buy any silk, madam? Very good price."

*****

I stopped for lunch at a small canteen where I had a simple plate of dhal and roti. I then wandered into the more modern part of the city, which still looked remarkably ancient, and I found a book exchange tucked down an alleyway. After looking around for some time, I swapped *The Four Agreements* for a Bible and self-consciously slipped it into my bag like porn from the top shelf. I thought of the words of Rajpal's father, "They come here clutching every single holy book to their chests except for the Bible, as if they're ashamed of it."

It was then time to return to the police station where Mr Bakshi escorted me into his office.

"Any news?" I asked.

"No," he replied soberly. "Although, we do have the results back from the laboratory. The substance in your friend's backpack was morphine, in powder form. The trace of powder in her money belt was heroin. I will have to ask you some very serious questions about your time in India, madam."

"I don't know anything about these substances." Fear rose in my throat like bile. "It must have been planted there by someone…perhaps Mr Sultan?"

Mr Bakshi's eyes didn't leave my face and for some reason I felt guilty. I was convinced that Mr Bakshi knew I had taken illegal substances. I thought back to the incident at the burning ghat – everything was becoming confused. My fear and grief were blending into a dangerous brew of paranoia and my mind was frantically linking unconnected episodes and creating meaning where there was none.

"You do know it is a very serious offence to have possession of such drugs in India?" His eyes bored into mine.

"Yes I do, but I have never used heroin or opium and never would – they're dangerous drugs – and I'm sure Sara felt the same."

"Well, you seem to know very little about your friend, Miss Taylor. There is certainly more to this than meets the eye." Mr Bakshi tapped his nose like some B-movie sleuth. In different circumstances I might have been amused by this gesture, now it just irritated me. I suspected he was enjoying the intrigue of such a high-profile case; it must have made an exciting change from petty criminals and demanding tourists.

"Look! I want to know what you are doing to find Sara's murderer. Have you questioned anybody? Are the public aware of her death?"

It was Mr Bakshi's turn to be amused.

"Miss Taylor, people die or go missing in Varanasi every day, and especially during festivals when there is too much chaos for anyone to notice or even care. Some people take advantage of the chaos to disappear, to escape from their lives, while other people use the opportunity to dispose of loved ones, who they have grown to hate…or perhaps of whom they are jealous." He looked at me pointedly and I suddenly realised I was a suspect. I stared back open-mouthed. I had the strange sensation – not for the first time in India – that he could see into my soul, or at least into my mind.

"Bollocks!" was the first word that came into my head.

"Pardon me, madam?"

"You are on the totally wrong track if you think I murdered Sara. Ask the hotel manager – she knows I was in the hotel all day."

"Does she?" he asked. "I was not accusing you of murder, Miss Taylor, but perhaps you feel guilty?"

"Of course not!"

"Miss Taylor, it is my job to deal with vandals, rogues and rascals, to solve mishaps and murders. We will solve your friend's death if you give us time, but you might not be happy with the conclusion."

Journey

"Just find her murderer!" I demanded and then, for the second time that day, I stormed out and slammed the door.

Chapter 16

I had to see for myself where Sara had died. I had been avoiding the Ganges, as if it were a cobra poised to strike. I was not even able to look out of the hotel towards it though I knew I had to face it now.

I left the police station on Kabir Chaura Road and followed the river, cutting down narrow lanes to Ghai Ghat, one of the most north-easterly of the ghats. The light was fading by the time I arrived and there were few people about – a group of small boys bathing at one end and a solitary woman washing clothes.

I walked to the opposite end of the ghat, where I had seen the commotion on the day of Sara's death, and I climbed onto a small mound that sloped into the Ganges. I looked back towards the city and could make out the top of my hotel, from where I had almost certainly witnessed Sara's death.

I walked over the mound, away from the ghat, and realised I was hidden from view – an ideal place for a murder, I thought. However, I still couldn't understand what Sara would be doing in this isolated spot, unless of course she had been taken there against her will. It was difficult to imagine how this could have gone unnoticed. Sara wouldn't be dragged anywhere without putting up a fight and the only way to reach this spot would be through the festival crowds or by boat. I just couldn't make sense of it. I searched the ground for any evidence of Sara's presence but found nothing, except for one or two handmade sweets that had been crushed into the dirt.

I stared into the Ganges for a while, trying to imagine Sara's last moments, her final thoughts. I felt myself drawn towards the dark welcome of the current, mesmerised by the oblivion it offered.

Then I saw a shape moving, just beneath the surface – black, human-like. My heart froze into a tight fist. I let out an involuntary scream and stepped back from the water's edge, looking around to see if anyone else had witnessed this strange sight, but the ghat was now eerily deserted.

I continued to back away from the Ganges, still keeping my eyes fixed on it, in case a ghostly hand – like that of Catherine Earnshaw – reached out to drag me down.

Then I saw the figure again, rising from the water, eyes glaring, lips blood-red, breasts perfect black mounds, arms…too many arms…flailing in the air.

The back of my legs hit one of the ghat steps and I fell hard on my backside, waiting for the final moment to arrive, my mind trying to compute what I was seeing.

Then I laughed hysterically, as involuntarily as I had screamed.

"You bitch!" I roared. For the figure was clearly the goddess Kali – she who devours time – in all her four-armed menace. She had probably been abandoned to the Ganges during a recent festival. An eddy had momentarily lifted her – Venus rising – from the water.

I walked back up the steps, still shaking and a little embarrassed by my loss of control. My head was now aching and my throat sore; I was worried that I had caught Sara's bug. It was the last thing I needed at that moment.

At the top there was a sculpture and I went closer to inspect it. It was the figure of a brightly painted cow, about five-foot high and carved from stone. I stood for a while, contemplating the significance of the sculpture and the place of the cow in Hindu culture, when a man's voice brought a new thrill of terror to my heart.

"Marianne?"

I instinctively grabbed onto the cow and looked up to see Bert and Sam standing on the steps above me.

"Oh God! What are you doing here? You scared me."

"Our hotel is just there." Bert pointed to a building close to the ghat.

"Marianne, are you ok? We hardly recognised you in that weird outfit."

"Oh, but you did recognise me?" I felt dismayed.

"Yeah, sure, I never forget a face," said Sam. They exchanged baffled looks.

I put my hand to my face and realised that I had pushed the shades to the top of my head.

"Hey, you're as fucked up as your friend," Bert laughed. "Where is she by the way?"

"What do you mean fucked up?" I asked. How had they gained that impression of Sara after only one meeting?

"Didn't she tell you?" replied Sam. "We saw her two days ago; she came to our hotel."

"She was frigging weird," said Bert, scratching his head. "We were just leaving to go to an Ashram in Kushinagar for a couple of days – get in touch with the spiritual side, if you know what I mean."

"Yeah, it's where Buddha said his last words." Sam threw his head back in a dramatic pose. "'Decay is inherent in all component things.' Cool hey?" He smiled like a manic clown.

"Sara's dead." I said. His grin disappeared, but only slowly.

"Oh shit." They spoke simultaneously.

"She was probably murdered, pushed into the Ganges, on the day you saw her." I'm not sure why I was so harsh with them. I felt instantly sorry. They were basically nice guys.

"You're frigging joking," said Sam, his face twitching with emotion.

"Wow, who did it?" asked Bert.

"We don't know. The police are supposedly investigating and a post-mortem is taking place. Why did she come to your hotel?"

"Erm…well…" They looked at each other as if deciding how much to say.

"I have to know," I said. "They need all the clues they can get."

"Well, she just turned up out of the blue; we had our backpacks on to leave."

"How did she know where you were staying?"

"That night we met you at the restaurant…" Bert looked uncomfortable. "She asked for the name of our hotel. I was flattered; I really fancied her. I didn't know she just wanted drugs."

"Drugs! What do you mean?"

"That's why she came to the hotel; she wanted drugs, not just Marijuana but class 'A' frigging drugs."

"Heroin!"

"Yep. Or opium."

"Did you give her any?"

"No!" said Bert firmly. "We're not into that shit."

"She practically begged us to get her some," said Sam. He suddenly looked young and scared. "She looked so different – kinda haggard."

"What time did she come to you?"

"God…about twelve-thirty. Our bus was leaving for Kushinagar at one o'clock; we were in a hurry."

"Did she say anything else to you at all…anything?"

"She said she'd give us a blow job if we got her some…" replied Sam sheepishly.

"Fuck man, you didn't need to tell her that." Bert thumped Sam hard on his arm.

I didn't know how to take in this information. It just didn't seem to be a Sara thing to do.

"Did you agree?" I pushed on.

"No man!" Sam looked at me in disgust while rubbing his arm protectively. "She looked a mess, nothing like the beautiful girl we saw a few days earlier. "

"So what happened next?"

"Er….we told her to go and get help," said Bert, "and then we left to get our bus."

"That's all?"

"Yeah, that's all." Sam shifted uneasily on his feet.

I wasn't convinced. I sensed they were holding something back. Of course it also crossed my mind that they had killed Sara, although it was hard to imagine they were capable of murder.

"When are you leaving Varanasi?" I asked

"Saturday," said Bert. "We're going to Kathmandu."

"The police might need to question you."

"Sure," replied Sam.

We exchanged mobile phone numbers and talked vaguely about meeting for drinks one evening. I then left them standing on the ghat, their faces a perfect mime artist's impression of bewilderment.

Chapter 17

'I will show you fear in a handful of dust.' T.S. Eliot, *The Waste Land*[12]

As I left the ghat I was hurled into darkness by another power-cut; fortunately my hotel was close by and there were enough oil lamps in the streets to light the way. I went straight to my room and lay on the bed, feeling unnaturally hot and my head throbbed painfully.

My conversation with Bert and Sam had thrown a whole new light onto Sara's death – and on her life. Somehow, I had to assimilate this information into what I already knew about her.

It dawned on me that Sara had known exactly what she was doing in taking us so close to Bert and Sam's hotel on Ghai Ghat. She wanted drugs and had been able to think on her feet, despite the terror of our departure from the Avaneesh Hotel. But I still couldn't believe she would use heroin.

My first impressions of Sara had been formed in extreme circumstances, but even then she came across as very astute, in control. At parties, I had seen her consume large quantities of cocaine and alcohol, yet at the end of the night she always appeared more intact than anyone else. I sometimes wondered if even this was an illusion, that she tricked us all. I imagined lines of coke and half-sipped glasses of wine abandoned in parties all over London. Being in control had seemed more important to Sara than anything.

In recent weeks, however, I had noticed a change in her: she drank heavily and practically chain-smoked dope, often seeming out of it. This had bothered me, but I resisted the urge to challenge her, reasoning that it was just her way of coping with the string of traumas we had experienced.

I went up to the rooftop for dinner and found myself sitting at the same table where Sara and I had sat for breakfast two days earlier. The power was still out and there were patches of impenetrable darkness, contrasted with pools of candlelight. I felt intense loneliness; there was no one I could talk to, share my pain with. I could hear the easy laughter and conversation of other travellers, while I was a dark shadow in their midst. I no longer felt part of them or of their journey; I was stuck in my own solitary, motionless, journey. I experienced an acute sense of solipsism – as I had on a couple of occasions in adolescence. It was as if I existed alone as a sentient being, while the rest of the world was an illusion. I no longer inhabited my life.

I stared into the chasm, where I knew the Ganges would be, crouching, waiting in the darkness. Perhaps that was my lowest point: sitting in a strange continent, feeling that there was not one human being I could connect with. Even the thought of London brought little solace – it was a place without Nathaniel, without Sara.

Leaving most of my meal on the plate, I returned to my room, shaken and tearful. I lit several candles, which I placed around the room trying to dispel shadows from every corner but only succeeding in creating more. I then poured a generous measure of Mahua – a clear spirit I had purchased from a dodgy market stall the day before to help me sleep. It tasted awful. I took great gulps of the stuff, which slipped thickly down my throat until I felt it kick in. I lay on my bed, the room alive with flickering shadows. My limbs were hot and restless as if they had a life of their own. I knew that sleep was a long way off.

Perhaps it was the effect of the candlelight coupled with the ancient sounds playing in the street below, or perhaps it was just that I had spent too much time alone with only grief and paranoia for company, but I imagined myself as some tragic heroine, one of those stoic Dickensian women or a tormented creation of a Bronte sister. My mind seemed extraordinarily alert and was racing with the multitude of words, ideas, philosophies I had heard and read in recent months. I realised how little time I normally gave to the act of simply thinking.

I envied previous generations their apparent certainty and I craved the earnest simplicity that the past seemed to offer. I perceived it to be a place where people grappled with important issues, sweated over questions of faith as if it really meant something. I often felt that I had to excavate the past in order to find something to speak to me in the present, to find a time when ignorance was bliss, when terror didn't reign.

I thought back to Sara's words about us belonging to a "lost generation, an atomised culture", and I kind of understood. Our generation is unshackled but also uncomforted by religion, the product of fractured families and absent parents who leave a void that we try to fill with so many things. We are unable to grow up or to settle down; we're a generation of terrified Peter Pans. We have more choice, more freedom, more money than any other generation, yet we live in fear: the fear of being seen by CCTV cameras, the fear of not being seen, the fear of dying through the pleasure of sex, the fear of not having sex, the fear of being alone, the fear of commitment.

I became acutely aware of my body and had a sense of myself as somehow separate from it. I tried to imagine where 'I' actually was in my physical body. Not in my limbs – if they were amputated, *I* would still exist. Perhaps my heart, the place poets and lovers locate as the seat of emotion, yet I could relate to my heart as something separate to myself, picture it as if *I* am not there.

I must be in my mind then, the modern seat of reason and control; the human computer, that's where *I* must exist. If my brain dies then *I* must die. But still I could think about my brain, picture it, discuss it as if it's not me but separate to me. I came to the conclusion that *I* was in fact a separate entity to my body; *I* was that thing called *spirit* or *soul*. I felt a sense of wonder, as if I had discovered something amazing.

I felt that a strange transformation was taking place within me; I can only describe it as a sense that I was becoming myself – so much myself in fact that I was going mad with it. I was awake and it hurt. I took another large gulp of Mahua to stop the frenetic motion of my mind; it was then that I remembered the Bible I had stuffed into my bag earlier that day – it actually turned out only to be the New Testament. With little else to do I pulled it out.

Despite being a Catholic for fourteen years, I had never looked at the words of this book for myself; it had been the job of the priest to interpret for the masses. I wasn't even sure where to start and so I placed the black Moroccan-leather book onto my knee and allowed it to fall open at random.

It opened on the first page of *The Gospel According to John*. I pulled the sheet around me – I was now shivering with cold. I could barely focus on the words:

'In the beginning was the Word and the Word was with God and the Word was God. He was in the beginning with God, all things were made through him, and without him was not anything made that was made. In him was life and the life was the light of men. The light shines in the darkness and the darkness has not overcome it. The true light that enlightens every man was coming into the world…yet the world knew him not…And the Word became flesh and dwelt amongst us full of grace and truth…the light has come into the world, and men loved darkness rather than light…but he who does what is true comes to the light…'

I was expecting wise men and shepherds, shalts and shalt nots. I was surprised by the poetic mysticism of what I was reading and remembered again the puzzlement felt by Rajpal's father that Christians appeared to be ashamed of their own holy book. I closed it and allowed it to fall open again.

'I am writing to you a new commandment…because the

darkness is passing away and the true light is already shining...The commandments are summed up in the sentence, 'You shall love your neighbour as yourself'...A new commandment I give to you that you love one another; even as I have loved you...Love bears all things, believes all things, hopes all things, endures all things. He who loves is born of God and knows God...for God is love...there is no fear in love, but perfect love casts out fear.'

'Perfect love casts out fear'. It couldn't be that simple. Where was 'an eye for an eye, a tooth for a tooth?' Where was God's revenge?

I quickly, almost frantically, closed and reopened the pages. A picture started to emerge of a man who seemed unafraid to live, unafraid to challenge the illusions of his day. Why was it all so strange to me? It was like reading a foreign language. I felt a mix of wonder and anger. I felt tricked.

'Forgive your enemies and love those who hate you...be kind to one another, tender hearted...'

Surely, if we dared to adopt such a radical philosophy there could be no wars or terrorism, injustice or poverty. It would be impossible for them to co-exist. Yet two-thousand years after his death, the simple message of Christ was hard to recognise. Why had the church enslaved itself to ritual and law? Why had there been inquisition, persecution, holy war?

I saw this man, Jesus – a sadhu, a political and social activist – speaking out for the poor and the dispossessed, yet the church had dressed him in elaborate robes, forced a jewelled mitre into his hand, built grand churches around him, surrounded him with synods and saints, gods and idols, popes and priests – *'Holding the form of religion but denying the power of it'.* Surely they were obscuring the simple truth. Stripped back, deconstructed, reduced to its essence there was a simple, terrifying message – love. Perhaps it was too radical – unbearably simple. Is it easier to talk about hate?

I remembered the words of Nelson Mandela scribbled on the blackboard by a half-hearted teacher nearing retirement who had been given the tiresome job of teaching that new fangled 'Citizenship' to a class of apathetic students. However, something had stuck and I could still quote the words he wrote that had profoundly moved me at the time.

'No one is born hating another person because of the colour of his skin, or his background, or his religion. People must learn to hate, and if they can learn to hate, they can be taught to love, for love comes more naturally to the human heart than its opposite.'

I had believed this fervently at fifteen and I still wanted to believe it now but sadly evidence from life was telling me otherwise.

'He who sows sparingly will also reap sparingly, and he who sows bountifully will also reap bountifully...'

The words swam on the page, floated and pulsed with energy. I was convinced I was being directed to certain passages, that I was being given a message. *'He who sows sparingly will also reap sparingly...'*

What had I sown in my life? Everything I did was for myself. I lived a small life. I remembered Miguel's quote from Marianne Williamson, *'Playing small doesn't serve the world... As we are liberated from our own fear, our presence automatically liberates others.'*

My father had become a small man, like a caterpillar rolled into a ball. He thought small thoughts, took small steps, held small hopes – his reward was a small life. I saw myself in him and I shivered as I pictured myself retreating into smallness, forever living in the shadow of maternal abandonment.

I pictured the house I had grown up in – a museum of abandonment. There were still hauntingly empty spaces on the walls where my mother had hung pictures, and bright throws bought during their trip to India in the 70s. It was as if, when she left, she took everything that was alive and colourful with her, leaving behind beige and magnolia and earthenware bowls of pot pourri that littered the house like abandoned urns, the contents as dry and scentless as ash.

'All flesh is like grass and all its glory like the flower of the grass, the grass withers, and the flower falls, but the word of the lord abides forever…for we brought nothing into the world, and we cannot take anything out of the world…Creation itself will be set free from its bondage to decay and obtain the glorious liberty of the children of God…Though our outer nature is wasting away, our inner nature is being renewed every day…You will know the truth and the truth will make you free.'

I pictured Sara's body floating in the Ganges, lying on that grey slab in the morgue. She had been so substantial, more alive than most. Yet, had death been on her mind?

'Awake, O sleeper, and arise from the dead and Christ shall give you light…you he made alive, when you were dead…Unless a grain of wheat falls into the earth and dies, it remains alone; but if it dies, it bears much fruit…do not labour for the food, which perishes, but the food which endures to eternal life…For we look not to the things that are seen but to the things that are unseen; for the things that are seen are transient, but the things that are unseen are eternal…God is spirit and those who worship him must worship in spirit and truth…'

Miguel said that truth is like the moon and the mind like a lake. When the surface of the lake isn't being blown around by thoughts and emotions it becomes still, only then can we clearly see the reflection of the moon.

'For now we see in a mirror dimly, but then face-to-face. Now I know in part; then I shall understand fully. Let each of you look not only to your own interests, but also to the interests of others. He who believes in me…out of his heart shall flow rivers of living water. Whoever drinks of the water that I shall give him will never thirst…'

I felt thirsty, really thirsty, but I didn't know what could quench my thirst. It felt bottomless. The candles danced and swayed and split into myriad flames, moving about the room like tiny spirits. I was getting closer to the answer, my mind was singing with energy, sharp and clear, ready to receive. I knew I was near to the truth.

'Unless you turn and become like little children, you will never enter the kingdom of heaven...'

These were the last words I remember reading in the early hours of that demented morning.

Chapter 18

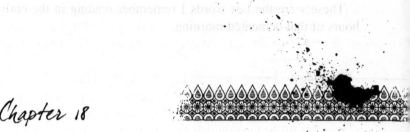

I woke up, my head thick as molasses, the bottle of Mahua half-empty at the bedside. The Bible lay awkwardly on the floor, its pages bent like the wings of a wounded bird. It had taken flight in the fluttering madness of the previous night, but now it looked crushed and impotent. Even so, I felt that its words had quietly slipped into my consciousness to confront the unwieldy flock of ideas, philosophies, hypotheses, already dipping and soaring there.

A battle was taking place and there, soaring higher than the rest, wings flapping relentlessly so that I couldn't ignore them, were the words – *'Perfect love casts out fear'*. These few words seemed to contain the essence of everything I had heard and read in previous months – from Buddha to Jesus to the Toltec of ancient Mexico; they provided a sense of connectedness in my otherwise fragmented world. If only, if only, we could take these words to heart.

I went up to the rooftop. My temperature had gone down and I felt a quiet and guilty joy. I devoured breakfast, after eating little the day before, and then donned my disguise (I was still too nervous to go without). I felt happier than I had for what seemed a long time, a small happiness but with the potential for growth. Mrs Fitzgerald would be arriving that evening, which meant I wouldn't have to spend another night alone.

But, I had only been out for half-an-hour when I saw Nathaniel, or at least I thought I saw him. I believed I knew every curve, every slant of his body, the angle of his back as it sloped into his firm round butt, the precise movement of his legs and the easy swing of his arms as he walked beside me. I saw the back of his neck, unprotected, exposed, smooth, feminine, the place I loved to kiss, moving round from the back of the neck to the side, to feel the warmth, the closeness of arteries, lifelines.

The sight turned me to liquid, nearly crumpled me to the ground. It was only in that moment that I knew how much energy I had expended in holding myself together – an incredible effort, every day, every night, to keep my heart beating, my lungs inflating, my flesh and atoms bound together, prevent them from scattering to the four winds.

Nathaniel possessed a classic beauty – Homer's Paris. I saw his hair stuck at odd angles from his head; it never obeyed the brush. It was him, or at least all the parts that I saw were his; if it wasn't him, it made a mockery of what we base love on – the parts, the pieces, the sound of the voice, the movement, the turn of the head. I called to him but he didn't look back, as if he wasn't mine.

I had dreamt several times in the months before of a glass maze. I entered it without Nathaniel, to explore on my own. It didn't matter – every time I turned I could still see him through the glass; I could still hear his voice calling me to come back.

"Just a bit further," I would say, "just let me explore a bit further."

But then I grew tired of exploring and wanted to be with Nathaniel again. I tried to get out of the maze but I found myself even deeper inside. When I looked again, Nathaniel's image was blurred by the thickness of the glass and his voice was faint. Eventually all I could see was my own distorted reflection and all I could hear was my own voice echoing from the glass. I banged on the walls until my hands were raw, screamed for him to find me until my voice failed. But he had stopped calling. He had given up.

The figure disappeared and, despite searching for hours, I

couldn't find him. I cried, unashamedly, and eventually stopped at a café. I found a dark corner and ordered chai. I made myself think logically. It couldn't possibly be Nathaniel; there was no reason he would be in Varanasi, other than to see me. He wasn't the impulsive type and would surely have made contact first. There is no way he would be wandering the streets, looking so at home in this chaotic city.

*****

Nathaniel and I fell in love very deeply, very quickly after our first meeting at University. At times I felt pissed off that I had met him so early in my life. I didn't want to become one of those annoying couples, joined at the hip. However, if I didn't see Nathaniel, even for a day, I missed him and I was always battling against my desire to spend every waking minute with him.

It ruined my plans to have a wild few years. Most of the time I felt grateful, ecstatic that I'd found my soul-mate so easily, found a love that most people only dreamt of. Looking back I guess I was pretty smug. I'd thought I had it all sewn up.

At the time I thought of relationships as having three parts: the physical, intellectual and spiritual. I believed that some relationships operate very much on the physical level, the first attraction. The physical is about how well two people function in terms of negotiating their leisure and work activities, food, sex, finance and living arrangements.

The intellectual level is about how they think – their values, morals, ideals, and how deeply they want to explore ideas. I don't mean just the day-to-day conversations that take place in order to communicate about practical actions such as food or finance – these come under the physical because they are only used in order to obtain something to meet the physical needs of the body. I am talking about the sort of conversations that go beyond this, necessary discussions about the way things work – the world, politics, science and the sharing of views about such things.

The spiritual realm is about the *why* of things, the questions, which some might say are unnecessary to our survival, questions about meaning and purpose.

Although a relationship can work for a while by finding common ground in one area, it has a better chance of success if it is strong in two – which is how I guess most relationships function. It is rare, however, to find relationships that flourish in all three areas, i.e. couples who find satisfying physical, intellectual and spiritual union, which I thought Nathaniel and I had.

I also used to believe there are three types of sex. The first is an animalistic passion; it can occur with or without love. It is solely about physical attraction and the satisfaction of sexual urges. Some people, even in long-term relationships, only ever experience this type of sex. While it can be enjoyable and exciting for a while, in time it can feel empty and unsatisfying – one step away from self-pleasure.

In the summer break after my A-levels, I met a guy at a party. He was gorgeous and very popular. We eventually slept together but it felt like play-acting. We went through the motions of sex, perhaps expertly, perhaps beautifully, making the right noises, finding physical satisfaction, but all the time I felt I had made no real connection with him.

The second type of sex is where a mutual tenderness and love exist between two people. They each want to give pleasure and to make a real connection with the other. This can be beautiful and satisfying; it feels warm and safe. Perhaps this is the most we can ever hope for.

The third type of sex is rare; it is the stuff of dreams, of novels. It is a spiritual lovemaking, an epiphany of two souls. It is that expression of ancient need found in Plato's *Symposium* – the yearning for the other half of our being, for lost regions of ourselves, cut from us by Zeus in primordial times as punishment for our pride. If we discover this other part of ourselves we are lost in an amazement of wonder and bliss; we sense a pre-existing fit, an inner rightness and we long for merger with the other.

The act of lovemaking is about surrender of mind, body and spirit; it is about entrusting all parts of ourselves to the beloved, desiring to love the beloved as a separate entity as well as the desire to become one with the beloved.

It is the chilling awareness of our own insignificance in the universe that causes us to seek this merger, but with merger comes exposure to fracture and madness. There is a demonic quality at the source of love, which may turn to destruction. In return for bliss, we can pay a large price; we can never again exult fully in our own separateness.

I believed I had found a superior love with Nathaniel and after finding it I was changed forever. It became an antidote to my existential anxieties, my soul's isolation from other souls, my mind from other minds, my complete sense of internal isolation and abandonment. But the price to pay was the possibility of an even greater abandonment, the abandonment by someone with whom I had entrusted my soul.

This is what I had once believed, but nothing seemed straightforward anymore.

*****

I shook myself out of this reverie to return to the hotel. I felt seriously concerned about my state of mind. Unlike the joy and clarity I had felt in the garden with Miguel – a lifetime ago – I felt disturbed by my fractured thoughts. I imagined I was experiencing the first dark trickle of madness.

Chapter 19

Mrs Fitzgerald breezed into the hotel like a lady of the Raj. She was the epitome of Englishness – fine hair the right side of mousy, pale skin, a pretty face, though a little pinched, blue eyes on the watery side, clothes a picture of simple elegance. I guessed Sara had inherited her father's looks; the dark hair and creamy skin that belonged to a certain section of the Irish population, combined with a playful sparkle in the deep blue of her eyes – a quality often lacking in cool, English beauty.

She made the hotel look shabby; she seemed too big for its confines and much too elegant. Her expensive perfume infiltrated every crack and I became painfully aware of my scruffy appearance. (I had abandoned my disguise before Mrs Fitzgerald's arrival, replacing it with my usual hippy garb.)

Mrs Fitzgerald managed to have this impact on me while smiling broadly and holding out a curiously white-gloved hand. It was only her eyes that wandered over me in cold judgement.

"Marianne! Good to meet you." There was little tenderness in her handshake; it was brief, perfunctory.

"Hello, Mrs Fitzgerald, I'm so sorry about S-"

"Call me Melissa, please; Mrs Fitzgerald sounds so old."

I knew I would find it almost impossible to call her Melissa; it is such a sensuous name, with those seductive 's' sounds followed by the gasping sigh of the final 'a'. I think it comes from the Greek work for honey-bee, totally inappropriate for the sharp woman who stood before me (perhaps she had been soft and sweet once?). I wished she'd had a name like Liz or

Jane, succinct and economical. I avoided using her name as much as possible and in my mind thought of her as Mrs F.

A man followed Mrs F into the lobby; he looked too hot, dressed inappropriately in a shirt and cord jacket with heavy trousers. I got the impression that he had been plucked from an English winter at short notice.

"This is Dave Holland." Mrs F waved an arm in his general direction as if it wasn't really important to locate him precisely. I was surprised that a woman like Mrs F would hook up with a man like Dave. He was attractive – thick dark hair, in need of a brush, a day's worth of stubble, an unreadable gleam in his eye. It gave me hope that Mrs F was more than I had first imagined.

"He's my private detective," she said dismissively. Her use of the word 'my' in this statement irritated me. It was typical of a certain class to want ownership of everything, especially people.

"Hi," I said, relieved that we would be a threesome; I hadn't enjoyed the prospect of facing the dark chasm that I was sure would gape between Mrs F and me. I was also more than happy to have a private detective in our midst who would hopefully solve the mystery of Sara's death more efficiently than I felt the local police were.

"I didn't realise you would be coming." My relief must have shown in my smile.

"Neither did I until two days ago." He had a reassuring East-end accent while also raising his eyebrows behind Mrs F's back and winking. I like men who wink. I know some people think it's old fashioned or corny but I guess that's why I like it. It's comforting that people can still do something so 'uncool'. It's a bit like whistling in public. I immediately liked Dave and, more importantly, felt that I could trust him.

"Anyway, no time to waste," said Mrs F, as if addressing everyone in the lobby. I expected her to clap twice, sharply. "We have to get you out of this awful place." Her eyes pierced every dark corner. I stood motionless, not sure what was expected of me.

"Come on!" she said in even firmer tones. "Our driver is waiting. Pack your things and we'll get going."

It didn't take me long to stuff everything into my bag and get back down to the lobby. A white Ambassador car was sitting outside the hotel with a local driver, erect and smart, behind the wheel. He jumped out to open the boot and help me load my uncouth bag next to two large cases with Gucci logos on the side. There was also an ancient battered leather case pushed into the back of the boot, which looked as if it was about to burst open.

We drove away from the river on the busy Kabir Chaura Road, competing with rickshaws and overloaded buses with a messy straggle of people clinging to the roofs. We crossed the railway line onto the Raja Bazaar Road and continued until we reached the Cantonment Area, where all the top-class hotels are located.

Ours was one of the best of the top-class hotels. It was only three or four kilometres from my former hotel but it belonged to a completely different world. As well as a swimming pool, tennis courts and jogging track, it had a sprawling garden filled with native trees, orchards and well-manicured lawns. It also had several good restaurants and cafés. A huge, domed ceiling with Moroccan-style arches graced the reception area.

"I have reserved three rooms." Mrs F took charge of the receptionist. "We'll be down for dinner in an hour." Dave and I stood behind Mrs F grinning like naughty schoolchildren. I was anxious about the cost of the rooms but Mrs F was insistent that she pay for everything. We were handed our keys with respectful nods and a porter came to take our bags.

"I suggest we go to our rooms to shower and change." said Mrs F. "We'll meet back here at eight-thirty. We can talk over dinner."

My room was more than I could have hoped for – elegant and airy with a view across the garden. I removed all of my clothes and caught my reflection in the first full-length mirror I had seen in months. I was brown and lean. I could see tight mounds of muscles in my arms and legs. I looked really good, if a little tired and grubby.

I went into the en suite and ran a bath; I then stared mesmerised by the wonderful steam made by really hot water. There were miniature rose-scented products arranged in a basket. I opened a bubble-bath and inhaled the scent deeply before emptying its contents into the torrents of water. Masses of bubbles magically grew into a white meringue. I sank into the bath and sighed loudly; I was surprised again that it is possible to find happiness in such simple pleasure.

I was loath to leave the bath, even though time was short – it was a womb, a haven, protecting me from Mrs F and what I imagined I might be about to learn. I suddenly realised that she hadn't once used her daughter's name.

I climbed out of the bath at ten-past-eight and wrapped myself in a soft, white towel. I couldn't pull the plug; it seemed so wasteful. I then emptied the whole contents of my backpack onto the floor and selected a skirt and linen shirt that had lain untouched at the bottom of the bag; they had never quite seemed the right things to wear in India. I pulled them over clean underwear, brushed my hair and put on some minimal make-up.

I arrived in the lobby, creased and awkward at exactly eight-thirty. Mrs F was already there looking fresh and neat.

"That's better," she said, looking me up and down. The slight disapproval in her eyes didn't match her words.

"You don't come across many irons in India." I attempted to explain. "Well, not in the sort of hotels I-"

"Never mind!" she interrupted. "Perhaps we can do some shopping while we're here." I felt shocked by her remark. Surely we had more important business to attend to.

Dave arrived at eight-forty looking exactly as he had before. I imagined he had slept for an hour, grateful to be alone, or perhaps he had stared out of his window, blowing smoke rings into the night. I wondered why Mrs F had chosen him to solve the mystery of her daughter's death. Her choice seemed incongruous.

"All present and correct," said Mrs F. "Shall we go and eat?"

We followed her into the main restaurant where we were seated next to a large French window with wonderful views across a moon-lit lily pond. The lilies were huge and looked like they could hold the weight of a small child.

Everything was immaculate, including the service. Even so, Mrs F extracted a white handkerchief from her bag and wiped the rim of her wine glass in swift, efficient movements. She then unwrapped gleaming silver cutlery from another napkin and placed it carefully on the tablecloth, pushing the existing cutlery to one side. She showed no embarrassment about her actions but I cringed inwardly and looked around to see if anyone else had noticed.

The food was exquisite; wonderful spices, which I had tasted all over India, but with top quality ingredients – the sweetest, firmest okra and the freshest, most succulent fish I had ever tasted. I was still a little overawed by my surroundings. It is funny that the culture shock of returning closer to what you're used to can sometimes be stronger than that of entering a completely new environment. Perhaps the mind is better prepared for the latter.

Most of the guests at the hotel were white Europeans, dressed in casual elegance – light-coloured linen and silks, with a small amount of tasteful jewellery. Mrs F fitted in perfectly.

"At some point, I want to know everything about my daughter's death," said Mrs F after the first course. Why couldn't she say her name?

"I can't tell you how devastated I have been about all of this; we really need to sort it out." Mrs F reached over for her wineglass and raised it to her lips, lowering her head in the process. I thought I saw the glimmer of a tear in her eye. I felt sorry for her and retracted my earlier judgements; she was obviously trying desperately to control her emotions.

"I know; it's been a nightmare." I said. "I still can't believe what's happened." My eyes filled up; it was a relief to talk about Sara to someone who knew her.

Mrs F looked at me, really looked at me for the first time, as if seeing me as a person in my own right, rather than as just a slightly strange friend of her daughter's.

"Yes, yes, this must have been bloody awful for you – and in such a dirty, chaotic country too. Never mind, things should start coming together now."

Dave, who had been totally engrossed in the act of eating up until that point, paused for a minute.

"I'd like us to talk tomorrow morning, Marianne, if that's ok. I want to start piecing together the events of the past few days."

"That's fine," I said. "I have a lot to tell you."

Following the meal we had a slightly awkward drink at the bar. Now that the subject of Sara's death had been broached it was difficult to return to trivial topics such as the length of flights or the English weather. After a stilted conversation, Mrs F and Dave, who were both obviously exhausted after their journey, retired to bed.

I took the opportunity to call my father and tell him about the change of hotel and Mrs F's arrival. I then wandered into the garden; it was fragrant with jasmine and magnolia. The evening air was sweet and refreshingly cool and the only sound was the comforting drone of insects and the popping of catkins. Silence *could* be found in India but only at a price.

I found a little stone bench under a eucalyptus tree and sat for a while, drinking in everything through my senses. I thought about my imagined sighting of Nathaniel earlier that day and I felt a deep, deep longing for him. I could easily picture him in this garden. It was warm and fragrant with a calculated wildness; it both calmed and excited me, soothed and stirred up my senses like the presence of a new lover.

A strange thought came into my mind – I am ready for Nathaniel now. I wasn't before but I am now. At that moment I felt a startling certainty that I would be with him again soon. This feeling wasn't coming from my rational mind but from a deeper, more instinctive place. With this thought I went to my room and sank into the impossible comfort of the bed.

Chapter 20

'To fear love is to fear life, and those who fear life are already three parts dead.' Bertrand Russell, *Marriage and Morals*[13]

I had a wonderful night of almost dreamless sleep but I woke early and lay for a while staring at a strip of sunlight on the ceiling. How stupid to imagine that Nathaniel would come back to me just because I wanted it, just because it fitted my plans. Travelling, even for a short time, had taught me that the world is a much harsher place than I'd ever imagined, that shit happens. What was the point of magical thinking, or in making wishes like a child? Life moved on like the eternal flow of the Ganges.

I went to the bathroom; the bath was still full from the night before and it looked completely unappealing. The bubbles had disappeared and the water was surprisingly dirty. I pulled the plug and took a shower.

Only Dave appeared at breakfast; he told me he'd had a brief conversation with Mrs F – they were situated on the same floor while I was on the floor above. She was apparently tired and had a headache, and would spend a few hours in her room and meet us for lunch in the conservatory.

Dave and I had an easy breakfast together. I asked him questions about life back home and realised how out of touch I was with current affairs in Britain. I noticed again that Dave was very attractive, although in a totally different way to Nathaniel. He was much older than me and not particularly tall.

142

He had the rough appearance of a man who had lived more life than his years, but there was an energy in his movements and a softness in his eyes that made him unexpected and intriguing.

After breakfast we agreed to meet in the garden. Dave asked me to bring film from my camera so that he could get a recent picture of Sara to distribute on posters around Varanasi. He arrived with a notebook and pencil in one hand and a coffee, most of which had spilled into a saucer, in the other. He sat next to me on the bench – where I had foolishly dreamed the night before – placed his notebook down and poured the coffee from the saucer into his cup. He then disposed of the saucer on the floor and took a slurp of coffee.

I handed Dave the film, which he stuffed into the top pocket of his jacket.

"Now, I know this is difficult for you, Marianne, but I really need as much detail as possible about the events of the past few weeks – people you have met, places you have been, anything unusual that has happened etc, etc."

I laughed. "Dave, there is nothing *usual* in India, *everything* is unusual." Then I cried. I don't know where it came from, but Dave's modicum of sympathy seemed to open a tap to grief. I cried for Sara and for myself. Dave put his arm around me and spoke in soothing tones.

"It's alright love; it'll be over soon."

"It doesn't feel like it will *ever* be over." I said with dramatic emphasis.

"Hey, come on." He squeezed me tightly. "You'll be back in damp old London before you know it, fighting for a seat on the bleeding tube, working every damn hour of the day and wishing you were back here." I half-laughed, half-cried but felt better. I wiped my eyes.

"Ok, sorry about that; I'm ready to go."

"Ok," he said, turning over his spiral pad to find a doodle-free page – which wasn't easy. At the top he wrote the date. I realised with a shock that Sara and I had been due to leave India for Australia the following day.

"Ok!" he said. "From the beginning!"

"I'm not sure where the beginning is."

"Just tell me everything."

Then it all came tumbling out – the first time I met Sara, the freckled man, Nathaniel, the plan to go travelling. I told him about Rajpal, Miguel, Bert and Sam, and about our frightening experiences at the burning ghat. I told him about the brewery and shared my suspicions about Mr Sultan. In fact I told him everything I thought he would need to know, drugs and all. I had suppressed my feelings so deeply over the past few days, not daring to break down in front of the local police, and I realised I was bursting with the burden of it all. The only thing I omitted was my sighting of Nathaniel, real or imagined, the previous day, as I felt this reflected poorly on my state-of-mind.

"Shit!" he said when I'd finished. "You certainly have been having an adventure!"

"You sound like Enid Blyton," I laughed. "I guess you cram more experience into a day when you're travelling than most people do in a month."

"Sounds like it." Dave grinned. "Anyway, I'll start making enquiries. We should be able to eliminate the bogus policeman and his sidekick pretty quickly. Did you give the police a good description?"

"I didn't tell them about that; I was scared they weren't bogus."

"I don't think in the scheme of things the police are going to be arsed if you had a bleeding camera or not. Trust me." I was happy to trust Dave, let him carry the whole burden.

Over two hours had passed. Dave had made several pages of notes; some words were heavily underlined two or three times. It was a good feeling to know that he was taking the chaos from my mind and putting it into some kind of order on paper.

"You two are working hard." Mrs F emerged into the light wearing a white dress and a large straw hat tilted at an elegant angle; she seemed to shimmer in the sun.

"Hi," I said," are you feeling better?"

"Much! Thank you. But I'm positively starving; shall we go for lunch?"

We sat in the bright conservatory, which was decked with exotic plants and beautifully carved furniture. Mrs F ordered a bottle of Chardonnay and poured Dave and me a glass without asking and, after performing the wiping ritual, poured a generous measure for herself. I knew the combination of wine and heat would knock me out but I sipped it anyway so as not to offend Mrs F. I refused a second glass, however, as did Dave; Mrs F polished off the rest.

"I want you to take me to the place where she died." She drained her glass and placed it firmly on the table.

"Oh...are you sure?" I asked. I don't know if I was concerned for Mrs F or for myself.

"Of course I'm sure." She held me with her omniscient blue eyes.

"Ok." I decided it wasn't worth arguing. "I have to report to the police station at three; we could all go together and then visit the ghat later, when it's cooler."

"Oh! Do I have to go to a dreadful police station?" she looked to Dave.

"I think we should *all* go," said Dave. "We need the co-operation of the local Bill. We can help them; they can help us."

We left the hotel at two-thirty in the gleaming car and arrived early at the police station. We waited for Mr Bakshi in reception, which, unlike the hotel, was devoid of air-conditioning. It was crowded with locals, sitting two to a chair or cross-legged on the floor. Some of the women were even preparing food, pulling a selection of savouries from cloth bundles for a huddle of bird-like children. Mrs F looked extremely uncomfortable, perched on the edge of her chair, arms wrapped protectively around her body as if she could somehow prevent contamination by making herself smaller.

When Mr Bakshi finally emerged from his office I noticed a

change in his usual demeanour. I think it was partly to do with Mrs F, who seemed to command instant respect from everyone, but probably also due to the presence of a male in our group. Whatever the reason, I felt he treated our situation with a little more gravitas.

"Please, please, come through to my office." He waved us in. "Samir, some tea for these good people!" Mrs F picked her way through the chaos of the office and sat on the newest-looking chair. There were not enough seats and I sat on a dusty tea crate.

I introduced Dave and Mrs F to Mr Bakshi and then Dave went on to explain his purpose in Varanasi. Mr Bakshi's forehead creased into a frown when he heard the words 'private detective'.

"We are making good progress with the enquiries." Mr Bakshi spoke with a purposefulness I had never heard from him before. "But we have some real puzzles in this case." He looked pointedly at me and I knew he was referring to the drugs. I noticed a questioning look glance across Mrs F's face; she didn't yet know the full story surrounding Sara's death and certainly not about her daughter's penchant for drugs. Dave had told me he would "fill her in later". I could already anticipate her disapproval.

"I am aware of *all* the details." Dave spoke with an authority that filled me with confidence. "Miss Taylor has brought me up-to-date. I'm sure there's nothing that can't be sorted out." A tray of tea arrived and Mr Bakshi waved to the boy carrying it to indicate that it should be passed around.

"Of course, of course." I detected irritation in Mr Bakshi's voice and sensed a verbal battle for dominance between the two men.

"Any news on Mr Sultan?" I asked, hoping to break the tension.

"He appears to have a good alibi, madam, but we are following it up." Mr Bakshi forced a smile. "You and your friend had a very…eventful… few weeks in India. It is difficult to untangle the knot."

"Perhaps you'd better tell Mr Bakshi about the incident at the burning ghat, Marianne." Dave lifted his eyebrows.

"Oh yes," I stammered and tentatively recounted the story to Mr Bakshi.

"Why didn't you tell me this on Monday, madam?" His eyes bored disapprovingly into mine. "It is no use trying to bamboozle me you know; I will always find out."

I noticed a boyish smirk playing on Dave's face. I wasn't sure if it was about Mr Bakshi's quaint use of the English language or the fact that my face must have been glowing deep red.

"I wasn't…I-I don't know. I thought perhaps he was a real police officer."

"You Westerners think the police behave like this in India?"

"No! I just…"

"Well, I could have told you that your description fits that of two men arrested last Sunday for physically assaulting a tourist near Manikarnika Ghat. We have had many complaints about them." Mr Bakshi walked over to a grey filing cabinet. He pulled hard on the second drawer and extracted a file, which he brought over to his desk. He took out a photograph, clearly showing the faces of our two pursuers.

"That's them!" I said, feeling like a child in the head teacher's office. I could feel Mrs F's eyes judging me.

"I know it's them, Miss Taylor."

"Anyway," Dave came to my rescue, "I will be making my own enquiries." He drew a small white card from his jacket – despite the heat he was rarely without one – and handed it to Mr Bakshi. "I would very much like us to work together to solve this case, Mr Bakshi, but I know you are very busy and don't have the same amount of time at your disposal as I have. All of my details are on there, including my mobile phone and the hotel number. Feel free to contact me at any time."

Mr Bakshi rubbed his thumb over the glossy black lettering on the card; he lifted a pair of reading glasses to his eyes, hanging from a gold chain around his neck.

"Yes, Mr Holland, and the same applies to you. Now Mrs Fitzgerald, would you like to see your daughter's body?"

I had never seen blood drain from a face so quickly. Mrs F reached out for Dave's leg and clung to it like a life raft.

"I certainly do not!" It was odd to see her so thrown off-guard; her eyes darted between Dave and the officer like a frightened rabbit.

"I'm sorry if I have upset you, madam; in India we are not afraid of death or of the rituals around death. Perhaps it is different in your country?" I had a feeling that Mr Bakshi was well aware that it was different in our country.

"No…yes!" Mrs F stumbled. "It's just…well, it's just… she's been dead for over four days."

"Yes, it is unfortunate, madam; we usually deal with corpses much more quickly here. However, we are lucky in Benares to have freezers in our mortuary." Mr Bakshi strode purposefully to the door and held it open for us; he smiled ingenuously. "We should have the post-mortem results soon and then perhaps you should make arrangements for the disposal of your daughter's body."

It was difficult to know if Mr Bakshi was being purposefully cruel or whether the language barrier was responsible for his uncompromising choice of words. Mrs F looked distraught; her eyes were awash with tears.

I trailed behind while Dave supported Mrs F out of the police station and into the merciless heat.

"Ridiculous little man." Mrs F extracted her arm from Dave's and brushed herself down, like a bird unruffling its feathers. "I need a drink!"

We decided to return to the cool of the hotel, where Mrs F sipped a large, icy G & T.

"I know it's difficult." Dave stepped carefully, his eyes soft; I was impressed by his compassion for this virtual stranger. "But you will have to think about what to do with Sara's body. If you want to repatriate her then you should be making arrangements now."

"But I don't know what's best...I really don't know what she would have wanted." Mrs F looked lost, out-of-control. I felt quite sorry for her. "I have no idea really what I believe," she continued. "I was brought up Church of England, you see. We went to church as a kind of social outing, somewhere to be seen. I suppose it was a soggy kind of faith." She laughed apologetically.

She then made a sparrow hawk turn of the head and her eyes focused on me. "Marianne, do you know what she would have wanted?"

I felt instantly guilty, as if I should know.

"No, not really." I stammered. "We did have one conversation about death recently. She said she liked the idea of being cremated, like Hindus, at the ghats."

"Oh God!" This idea seemed more abhorrent to Mrs F than it did to me. "Why...why would she want that?"

"When we watched the ceremony at the burning ghat she looked really peaceful...it didn't scare her like it did me. She even had a dream about being cremated."

"Think about it Melissa. You don't have to make the decision right now." It was the first time I'd heard Dave use her name; there was tenderness in his voice, which I found very attractive. I also felt something a bit like jealousy.

Chapter 21

At six in the evening we ventured out again, this time to Ghai Ghat. Mrs F had consumed several G & Ts and appeared calm. She said very little as we stepped down to the Ganges. Dave and I left her for a few minutes to stand alone in the dusk, staring into the purple swell of the waters. I strongly wished I knew what was in her mind. I suspected it might help me to understand Sara better.

I walked with Dave up to the sculpture of the cow and pointed out the hotel where Bert and Sam were staying. After a few minutes Mrs F joined us.

"I want her wishes to be carried out."

"What do you mean?" I asked.

"I want her to be cremated, her ashes scattered here. It is a peaceful place."

"Melissa, are you sure?" Dave seemed concerned. "Remember you will have nothing of her back in England, no grave to visit, no ashes-"

"I have never been more certain about anything," Mrs F interrupted. "It is the least I can do. Anyway, I don't need a place to visit her; I have my memories here." She tapped her head in a way which seemed hard, self-punishing and I wondered what her memories were made of.

"Now, can we go back to the hotel?"

"The car will take you and Marianne. I need to make some enquiries here." Dave nodded towards Bert and Sam's hotel. "I'll join you later."

Back at our hotel I showered and changed and then went down to Mrs F's room, as she had requested, so that we could go to dinner together. I knocked several times but received no answer. I could hear the sound of running water and guessed she must be showering.

I pushed the door, it opened and I went in. From where I stood I could see into the en suite, which was over the other side of the room. The door was open and I could see Mrs F standing at the sink; water was running hard from the taps and clouds of steam plumed around her, softening her appearance in the mirror.

She twisted her hands beneath the water and rubbed them together savagely so that every part of them was cleansed, time and time again – between her fingers, under the nails, up to her elbows. She frequently pumped soap from a plastic bottle and repeated the ritual over and over. As she did so I heard her muttering to herself, although the torrent of water masked the words. I found the sight distressing – a human being so compelled to perform a ritual, to purge herself repeatedly. This controlled, controlling woman, so out-of-control, so at the mercy of a compulsion.

I don't know how long she had been doing it before I arrived, but I watched for several minutes. I was about to leave when she looked up and saw me in the misted bathroom mirror. I expected her to freak out, to order me to leave, but she didn't; she twisted off the taps, grabbed a white towel and turned slowly towards me.

"Insane, isn't it? I know that." She was patting dry her hands. "I see dirt everywhere, especially here." She glanced around her. "Sometimes I think everyone else is insane for not seeing it, for being so bloody disgusting in their habits. I've lived with it for twenty years; in a peculiar way, it's part of me now."

"Have you ever-"

"Sought help, seen a shrink? I did once, a long time ago, but I think I'd left it too late. Too entrenched, you see. It costs me a fortune in soap and moisturiser, but there you go." Mrs F smiled, almost a warm smile and I felt that, at last, I was seeing something real about her. She applied a generous amount of moisturiser to her hands. "Now, shall we go to dinner?"

We didn't mention the hand-washing ritual again. In fact, over dinner, we had a pleasant conversation about literature. We found common ground – safe ground – in our reading interests; I enjoyed the normality of our conversation.

Dave still hadn't returned so we moved to the bar where we drank G & Ts. Mrs F had two to every one of mine and I suspected she had a problem with alcohol as well as with dirt. By eleven she was decidedly drunk. I guessed the day had been very stressful for her – the chaos and dirt, death and decay.

"I need to tell you something." Her words were slurred. "I've never told anyone this."

"Perhaps you should wait." My stomach bunched into a knot and I wished Dave would return. At that moment I didn't want to have to deal with whatever she had to say.

"No, no, Marianne, this is very important." She moved closer, so that I could smell her gin-soaked breath as well as the subtle layers of her expensive perfume. These smells seemed somehow to tell her whole story.

"Sara's father died when she was four-years-old." Her daughter's name dropped from her mouth like a heavy stone. "A brain tumour, but you probably knew that, didn't you?" I nodded. "He was playing with her in the garden, as he often did, twirling her around. He just dropped dead, fell to the ground with Sara on top of him, no warning at all."

"Oh God! I didn't know that."

"I loved him...James. I'm not a woman with a lot of love inside me, Marianne. My mother and father didn't have much love to spare, and I don't have much to give. But I loved him, as much as I could love anyone – perhaps I used it all up on him. I couldn't bear it when he died; it felt like a punishment." She drained her glass and indicated to the barman that she wanted another. I declined one for myself.

"James was the opposite of me; I never knew anyone with so

much love inside him. He had plenty for me and for Sara. He adored her; I was sometimes jealous of how much." Mrs F fixed her eyes on me as if to gauge my reaction. I tried to keep a look of fixed sympathy. I had a sudden and unexpected image of a younger Mrs F, blooming with love, free from her peculiarities, and I saw the cracks that can open up in a person.

"I'm very weak, Marianne. I'm one of those women who can't be alone, especially with a four-year-old child. I had no support. The obsessive-compulsive behaviour was triggered by James's death; it was getting worse by the week and I was finding it increasingly difficult to care for Sara. I hated her playing in the garden, bringing mud into the house, so I put a padlock on the back door so she couldn't get out. When I met Charles, it was convenient, fortuitous. I married him."

Sara had never mentioned Charles. My feeling of uneasiness was growing.

"You look surprised."

"Sara never mentioned him."

"She hated him."

I wondered how you could hate someone so much as to erase them from your life story altogether.

"He moved in when she was five. She resented his presence from the start. No one could take her daddy's place. I realised my mistake after a year. He was a demanding man, in every way, and I was finding it more and more difficult to meet his needs. Another drink please!"

Mrs F waved to the barman. Her words were slurred, her eyes bloodshot and her hair, which had been piled into a sophisticated knot, was now falling all over her face. Perhaps I should have insisted she stop, give her a way out, but I was now hooked by her story, despite my concern. I felt it might be crucial to the bigger picture.

"I couldn't bear him to come near me. He wasn't a clean man, not like James. Charles was a drinker – I hardly touched the stuff until I met him, after which I hardly refused it. At first I drank just so I could let him touch me, then even that didn't work. I moved into the spare room and locked the door each night." Mrs F stared into her drink and tapped the side of the glass with the tips of her sharply-manicured nails.

"Marianne, it's very hard to describe what it's like to have an OCD; it's a curse. The fear of contamination is with you every second of every day. Your whole purpose is to avoid it, to survive. It's like you're operating on a deeply primitive level." Mrs F began to cry, in a peculiar way, like a cat's meow, as if she wasn't used to it; her eyes didn't seem familiar with the action of pushing out tears and her face was screwed up with the effort. I was frozen and couldn't reach out to her as I would normally reach out to someone in distress – touch their arm or pat their leg. It was as if I was watching a play, sitting on the front row in an intimate theatre so that I could almost touch the actors but would never dream of doing so.

I clutched my empty glass; I couldn't tear my eyes from the stiff, red gash of her lips. With absolute dread I think I already knew what was coming. I did wonder why she was telling me this sorry story, but I guessed she had held it inside the cold shell of her life for a very long time; perhaps her daughter's death had widened the crack so that she could contain it no longer.

"I noticed a change in Sara when she was about seven," she continued. "She had always been a happy child, more like her father than me; she had some of his Irish optimism, his playfulness." A small smile flickered and then died. "Suddenly she became secretive and withdrawn. I blamed my OCD; by this stage I could hardly bear to touch her – my own child – without having to wash afterwards. I guess I didn't give her much physical affection; she had to do everything for herself – brush her own hair, tend to her own childish wounds.

"Charles was drinking more than ever and often came home late from whatever seedy bar or club he frequented. He seemed to have accepted a sexless marriage and his demands stopped. I was so relieved, I didn't ask why. Once or twice I heard Sara cry. I never went to her because I knew I couldn't give her comfort…Have another drink; you must want another drink, for God's sake!"

"Yes, I will." I placed my glass down hard on the bar. I could hardly bear the feelings that were welling inside me, the image that was forming in my mind.

"I think I knew." Mrs F's hands suddenly shook so that the ice clattered violently in her drink. She quickly placed the glass on the bar and clasped her hands together.

"Why?" I asked. It was a small, croaky "why". I was watching her hands twist, listening to the dry sound of their contact, one on the other. She didn't answer.

"Why?" I asked more forcefully, looking uncompromisingly into her face. Her tears were black with mascara, her nose and eyes angry red. I wasn't going to let her off the hook. She was silent for a long time.

"I need to know why." I emphasised every word as if slapping her in the face with each syllable. I was surprised by the hatred I was feeling towards this woman. Other customers looked our way as the volume of my voice increased.

"I don't know," she answered in a stage whisper. "I was never certain, not really."

"But you said you *knew*!" I could feel my facial muscles clench as I attempted to control my anger.

"Subconsciously, maybe, but I wouldn't allow myself to believe it."

"You mean it suited you not to believe it. While he was abusing her, he wasn't touching you. How could you, how could a mother-"

"Stop, Marianne, please stop! There is nothing you can say to me that I haven't said to myself in the empty hours of every long night." Her distress looked real. She was breathing in short, sharp gasps and tears were now flowing freely. Her shoulders were shaking violently. This time I did reach out to her, but I could only manage a quick, perfunctory pat on her arm.

"When did it stop?"

"He disappeared when she was twelve. He just walked out of our lives; I haven't seen or heard of him since. Sara and I had never been close, but I lost her completely after that. Her eyes were dead when she looked at me. I couldn't bear it." Mrs F tried to focus on my face but her eyelids struggled to stay open and continually slid down like heavy shells over watery molluscs. She looked pathetic and I didn't know which was stronger, my sympathy or my disgust. It seemed that the more loathing I felt for Mrs F, the more love I felt for her daughter – the victim of this woman's weakness and selfishness. Many things about Sara suddenly made sense and I wished I'd been a better friend to her. However, there would be time later for regret.

"Now I've lost you as well." Mrs F reached out her hand and laid it on mine. It was as cool and dry as grass in an English summer garden. I knew it must have been almost unbearable for her to place her gloveless hands on human skin. Close up I could see the damage caused by obsessive washing; the skin was thin, exposing a network of veins. Her nails were, of course, perfect and she wore a selection of expensive rings – the sort wealthy women of a certain age often wear, too big for their bony hands. While her face still looked young and smooth, her hands were rough and aged as if all her sins were written there; her picture in the attic.

I resisted the almost overwhelming urge to pull my hand away, but this seemed too cruel. I didn't understand her comment; how could she think she had ever had me to lose?

"I can see how you feel about me, Marianne, and I don't blame you. I hoped somehow that you could understand; that we could be friends. We had such a nice chat over dinner."

I was horrified by her bizarre assumption that a 'nice chat over dinner' could mean anything more than that.

"Mrs Fitzgerald, I'm finding it really, really difficult to take in what you have told me. But, surely you can't think you can make things right by turning me into a kind of surrogate daughter?" She must have seen the hatred in my eyes and I saw the fear in hers. Our looks froze together for several uncomfortable seconds; perhaps we both saw betrayal.

"Hello ladies." Dave appeared like an unexpected but welcome breeze. Mrs F and I jumped away from each other, like cats caught in mischief.

"You were deep in conversation," he said, looking from one to the other of us. His brow was drawn into the centre with puzzlement. "Hope you weren't talking about me." Neither of us spoke and we must have looked a strange sight, open-mouthed, guilty.

Chapter 22

Neither Mrs F nor Dave appeared at breakfast the following morning though I was relieved. After a troubled night, splintered by more disturbing dreams about my mother, I needed to be alone. I finished breakfast quickly and escaped to the garden with a coffee. I sat on my bench with a book open as a decoy but my thoughts were far from the words on its pages. I was trying not to think about Sara's experiences at the hands of her stepfather; it was too horrendous. I couldn't equate the Sara I knew with the helpless child.

I had been wondering all through the restless night what I should do with the information that I felt had been forced upon me and, secondly, how I could ever face Mrs F again. A crime had been committed and the perpetrator was probably still at large, ruining the lives of other children. But it had all happened so long ago.

It struck me for the first time that Sara might have taken her own life. Perhaps she could no longer live with what had happened to her. This thought caused such a powerful reaction in me that I jumped from the bench and paced around the garden, pulling at my own hair.

Why didn't she talk to me? Didn't she consider me to be a good enough friend? Perhaps I had been too caught up in my own selfish world to be really available to her. I understood what it meant to be tormented by your own thoughts; they clattered around my head like a multitude of bells.

I had to tell Dave; he would know what to do. Where the hell was he? It was nearly eleven o'clock. I marched back into the hotel, up to the first floor and banged on Dave's door but there was no answer. I called his name though still no reply and the door was locked. I then went to Mrs F's room; I really didn't want to see her but panic was taking over. I was met by the same, cruel silence.

I marched down to the lobby.

"I am looking for my friends, room twenty-six and twenty-seven. I haven't seen them since last night."

"Yes, madam. Mrs Fi-t-serald..." The receptionist had difficulty pronouncing the name and giggled at his own attempts. "Mrs Fish-ger..."

"Mrs Fitzgerald," I snapped. "Where is she?"

"I am apologising, madam; she checked out early this morning and the gentleman, Mr Holland, left with her."

"No!" The world fell away, miles beneath my feet. My paranoia wasn't far below the surface and it came crashing back up. Perhaps Dave was protecting Mrs F...he wasn't interested in Sara at all, or in finding her murderer...perhaps he and Mrs F were romantically involved and they had just been hiding it from me. I remembered Dave's unexpected softness towards her. I felt angry, betrayed.

"No...no, it's not possible. Dave wouldn't do this to me..."

"Madam!" Seeing my obvious distress, the receptionist reached quickly into an antiquated wooden pigeonhole on which my room number was inscribed in gold paint. "I have a message for you. We are very sorry...we didn't see you at breakfast. Mr Holland asked me to give you this note."

I took the note without speaking and fell into a chair to read it.

Marianne,
I'll be back soon. I have taken Melissa to the airport. Will explain everything later.
Dave.

The world re-formed and the panic subsided a little. Things still didn't make sense but at least I wasn't alone in the chaos. I guessed Mrs F had insisted she return to England after realising, in the cold light of day, the significance of what she had told me. I was glad I didn't have to deal with her again. Dave and I didn't need her anymore, although she had provided an important piece of the puzzle.

Dave returned to the hotel, hot and flustered, at three and immediately came to my room, where I was trying to lose myself in sleep.

"I need a stiff drink. Now!" he said. "I don't think I could spend another minute with that neurotic woman…Don't worry," he added, "she's still paying my fees."

I think he mistook my sleepy expression for disapproval and he checked himself.

"Sorry, I didn't mean to be disrespectful, it's just-"

"You don't need to explain Dave; let's go to the bar."

"She was knocking on my frigging door at five in the morning." Dave's eyes were ringed with dark shadows. He banged a brandy down hard on the table. "I was having a bleeding great dream as well – which I'd better not tell you about." He smiled, a mischievous smile. "She was in a real state; she demanded I take her to the airport. I could have bleeding killed her. I've wasted a whole day of enquiries trying to sort out a flight for her. I knew I shouldn't have agreed to come to India with her in the first place. I think I was about her fifth choice anyway, the only mug who could come at such short notice…" Dave pulled an unlit cigarette in and out of his mouth between each sentence; in his other hand a disposable lighter was poised, ready for use.

"Did she say why she was leaving?" I was eager to find out what Dave knew.

"She said she couldn't stand the dirt anymore – it was driving her insane; she needed to be in her own place, with her own things. I mean it doesn't come much cleaner than this place, does it?" He moved his hands around to demonstrate the cleanliness of the hotel. "You could eat off the frigging floor. Now if she came to my flat, she'd soon know about dirt-"

"Is that all she said?" Dave must have picked up the strain in my voice. His brow furrowed.

"Should there be another reason?" He finally bent his head towards the lighter, lit the cigarette and inhaled, blinking his eyes in the smoke.

I explained the events of the previous evening – my observation of Mrs F's compulsion and her account of Sara's abuse.

"Fucking hell, excuse the French," he said. "It gets more complicated by the minute. What a bastard!"

I could see Dave trying to grapple with what I had told him; his face was a picture of mixed emotion. He scratched his head. "That girl certainly had a lot to deal with."

"She didn't tell me anything about it."

"Are you thinking she might have topped herself?" Dave scrutinised my face.

"Maybe, but it still seems out of character. I feel so fucking angry, Dave. I want that man to suffer…and Mrs F." Tears pushed at the back of my eyes. Sympathy softened Dave's expression.

"I don't think Mrs F does much else but suffer." He laid his hand on my arm. "Look, I'll call my mate Phil in London, ask him to make some enquiries about that bastard, see what he can find, hey?" I nodded. Dave hesitantly stroked my cheek. He then visibly shrank back into character and lit another cigarette. He inhaled deeply, as if to calm himself and then blew the smoke away from me.

"At least I didn't totally waste my time at the airport. I managed to ask Mrs F a few questions about her daughter. She knew surprisingly little, which makes sense in light of what you've just told me. She didn't have a clue why Sara was taking prescription diamorphine and certainly not illegal drugs; she seemed quite shaken by the news."

"Guilty more like." Venom coated my words. "She probably realised Sara was taking drugs to deal with her awful experiences, which that woman could have prevented from happening."

"As I said, I think she has suffered for her crimes," said Dave. I felt he was trying to divert me from the subject. He reached into his jacket and pulled out a bright yellow folder. "I also managed to get the photos developed at one of those 'One Hour' places." He extracted the prints and laid them out like a deck of cards. Sara was on nearly every one. The sight of her face staring out of the glossy paper, beautiful, vibrant, was like a stab to my heart.

"Very pretty girl." Dave traced her face with his index finger and once again I felt the uncomfortable crawl of jealousy.

"Yes, she was," I said. The thought popped into my head that if Sara was here, Dave wouldn't look twice at me. I shook the thought away.

"I'll take a couple to the police station tomorrow so that posters can be circulated. Mrs F has also put up a substantial reward for information leading to an arrest. She wanted to put up a lot more but I told her it was inappropriate here."

"Guilt money."

"Probably."

"Can I keep the rest of the pictures?" I was drawn into the world of the photographs; they told a story of a time past, an unreachable time.

"Of course." Dave selected three close-up shots of Sara, which he returned to his jacket pocket; he placed the rest in the folder for me.

"I'll tell you what I found out last night." He was back in detective mode. "Then I'll start to chase some new leads."

"Go on," I said, unsure of how much more I could bear.

"I went to see your friends, Bert and Sam; nice guys but living on another planet."

I smiled at his accurate description.

"I checked out their alibi and it holds up, but I felt they were being a bit cagey; they kept contradicting themselves. Eventually they admitted that while they didn't give Sara any drugs on the afternoon of her death, they did give her the name of a guy who could get her some."

"Oh God!" I said. "The bastards! Who?"

"A German guy, Kratz; he's been living in Varanasi for years, a well-known dealer. Every addict gets to hear about him sooner or later. Apparently he's a nasty piece of work, few scruples. He can get hold of anything."

"He killed Sara, didn't he?" I could feel the sobs rise to my throat.

"Hold on Marianne, don't jump to conclusions-"

"But he must have met her by the river that afternoon to do a deal...on the other side of that mound thing; he must have pushed her in."

"Hey! Has anyone told you you'd make a good journalist? Don't let your imagination run away with you, girl." Dave gave me a friendly thump on the arm.

"But it's a possibility, isn't it?"

"Of course it is, but after meeting him I'm not convinced."

"You've already met him!"

"Last night, that's why I was back so late."

"God, Dave, you shouldn't have gone on your own, that's dangerous."

"Look, babe, I'm not as sweet and innocent as I look."

I giggled. The phrases 'street-wise' and 'weather-worn' could have been invented to describe Dave's face.

"So, where was he?"

"I found him in this bleeding opium den on Chaitganj Road. I'd always wanted to go into one of those places. Everyone was too mashed to really notice me, except a guy at the door who 'kept watch' in the loosest sense of the words. It was just like I'd imagined, a big circle of people shrouded in blue smoke, passing a chillum around – Indians, Europeans, Africans; others were chasing the dragon, or injecting." Dave drained his glass. "Kratz was sitting in one corner. He looked rough but was surprisingly open with me. It was like he saw himself as some kind of model citizen, a pillar of the community – like no one could touch him. I asked him about Sara. He remembered her well. He said she came to see him about two on the day of her death; he sold her some heroin and then, he said, she left."

"But he would say that, wouldn't he?"

"Of course, but what would be his motive for killing Sara? If he got his money he'd be happy. Other people in the joint told me that Kratz rarely leaves the place before nightfall, and nobody remembered any dodgy incidents between him and a Western woman."

"He might have followed her…raped her."

"And risk his lucrative business? I doubt it. Anyway, we'll have to wait for the forensic results before we know if there was a sexual assault."

"Did Kratz say how Sara came across?"

"He described her as "hot but way too cocky". He also recognised her as an addict."

"An addict…" I could feel my defences rise. "I would have known if she'd been an addict."

"Not necessarily, sometimes it takes one to know one, if you see what I mean. People hold down responsible jobs, have mortgages and still maintain a habit."

"But it's just so unlike her, Dave. There might have been stuff I didn't know, but I think I knew that much."

"Well, we're still trying to piece things together, aren't we? All might not be as it seems."

"What do you mean?"

Dave lit another cigarette from the old one. "We have a term in my business; it's called 'the secret compartment'." He paused to inhale. "In order to solve a crime it's sometimes necessary to discover that part of the victim which is hidden, even from the people closest to them."

"Well, Sara certainly seemed to have a few of those," I said. "But I still don't think being a smack-head was one of them."

"You're being a bit judgmental, Mari. People often have very good reasons for opting out and Sara seemed to have more than most. Like you said, she had shit to deal with."

"I know, but heroin! I mean it just makes me think of run down council estates and filthy squats; it's just not Sara. Why not carry on using coke or the occasional ecstasy tablet if she wanted to escape?"

"That's the thing, Mari, it's a different experience altogether. Some people just use heroin recreationally, to get a nice warm, woozy feeling, but for most compulsive users it isn't about opening doors into other worlds, like LSD. It closes doors; it stupefies and kills feeling. It's an antidote to a wretched existence. Heroin doesn't promise anything except neutrality."

"But Sara never seemed wretched; she was full of life, always looking for adventure. And, anyway, why did she use amphetamine if she wanted neutrality?"

"Probably as an anti-soporific – just to appear normal. Heroin is a narcotic analgesic. It belongs to the opiate family, which derives from the opium poppy. Morphine is up to ten times more potent weight-for-weight than opium. Medical heroin, which Sara had on prescription, is known as diamorphine..." Dave stopped in mid-flow and grinned. "Is this too much information for you?"

"No, I want to know everything, carry on."

"Well, heroin is a bit of a bastard child of mother opium and the laboratory. In its purest form it is up to three or four times more powerful than morphine. Having said that, most street heroin is heavily adulterated. The stuff Sara had in her money belt is known as 'Brown' and originates in Pakistan. It can be smoked but not injected unless first dissolved in an acid, like citric acid. It is usually mixed with cheap cuts, such as lactose, glucose or even chalk dust and battery acid, to maximise the dealer's profit."

"Shit! Could that have killed her?"

"Unlikely. The post-mortem results should tell us more. What we *do* know, at the moment, is that at some point in the last year, Sara started taking diamorphine on prescription from

London and when this ran out she moved on to some pretty pure morphine, in powder form. She finally resorted to 'Brown', supplied by Kratz. That's what was found in her money belt. Any idea where the morphine came from?"

"No."

"What about the times you and Sara went your separate ways?"

"She spent a few days with Rajpal, the Sikh guy I told you about in Agra."

"Were you aware of any friction between them?"

"I have no idea what went on during that time. They got pretty close though; they were even planning on seeing each other again. He seemed like a really nice guy, but it might be worth questioning him."

"I intend to, tomorrow."

"What! You're not going to leave me again...I'll come with you."

"You're better off staying here Mari; anyway, you have to report to the police station. There's a shuttle flight tomorrow morning that takes less than an hour – cost courtesy of Mrs F. I'll be back in time for aperitifs tomorrow evening."

"Oh well, I guess I can do without you for one day."

"It's nice to be so indispensable." Dave did something close to a blush and then seemed to shrug himself out of it. "Out of interest, can you pinpoint when the change in Sara occurred?"

"Well, she seemed a bit listless when we were in Agra, but she only got really ill the day after we were chased by that so-called policeman at the burning ghat – it was like flu with vomiting."

"Could be the side-effects of the morphine."

"There was also this weird smell in our room; I noticed it a couple of times."

"Probably the morphine as well; it's got a strong smell." Dave screwed up his face as if recalling it. I could have watched his face all day and never got bored. He blew out a strong and orderly stream of smoke. He then turned to me a little tentatively. "I've also decided to get my colleague back in London to follow up on the 'freckled man' as you call him."

"The freckled man! But why?"

"Not sure, just think he might be a significant lead, if he's still alive."

"Don't say that, Dave; I still feel guilty for not checking Sara's story out for myself."

"Well, don't beat yourself up; let's keep moving forward, hey?" Dave patted my arm and sort of grinned, revealing surprisingly white teeth for a man who smoked so much. Again I felt comforted by his presence and was grateful to have him there.

"You know a hell of a lot about drugs Dave."

"I know a hell of a lot about a lot of things, usually from personal experience."

"You mean you've used heroin yourself?"

"I was addicted between the ages of sixteen and twenty-two."

"Do you still use drugs?"

"Only the worst kind – alcohol, caffeine and cigarettes – but no one's going to arrest me for that, are they? Anyway, enough about me, how are you coping with this shit?"

I shrugged my shoulders. "You know. In the best way I can."

"Good kid. Sorry you've only got a ragged old sleuth for company."

"Dave, you don't know how happy I am to have you around."

"Not many women have ever said that." He looked at me intently. His eyes were cocoa-brown, a little sad; the lines radiating around them told a hundred stories. "In fact, they usually say *"piss off out of my life"*!"

I laughed and found myself holding his warm, rough hand. My desire to lean towards him, to meet his lips, was very strong. I wanted to lay my head on his chest and breathe in the comforting combination of Cussons Imperial Leather and fresh cigarette smoke – my first olfactory memories of my father. I thought I sensed the same desire coming from Dave; his eyes were soft and he didn't resist my touch. We had been thrust together into a small and intimate place, a place neither of us would have chosen to inhabit in normal circumstances, and, despite the pain and adversity surrounding us, the space had become our haven, our cave. The more adversity we faced, the smaller we made the space; we drew it around us like a protective cloak. With Mrs F gone it felt there was no place for us to go except towards each other, closing the space between us. I felt confused by my feelings and resisted the urge to give in to them. Instead I squeezed Dave's hand, lifted it to my mouth and kissed it.

"We've got that much in common then."

PART 3

Chapter 23

'Two roads diverged in a wood, and I – I took the one less travelled by, And that has made all the difference.' Robert Frost, *The Road Not Taken*[14]

Dave left for Agra at eight the following morning; Nathaniel arrived at eleven, just after I returned from my daily visit to the police station. He came to me as I could only have dreamed. I was in the garden reading, when a shadow crossed the pages of my book. I looked up to see the person I loved most in the world, the person who had hurt me the most. I didn't think a face could evoke such a strong reaction.

They say a newborn baby is fascinated by the human face more than anything else and by the mother's face more than any other. Even minutes after birth he or she will express great pleasure on seeing the mother, suggesting that there is a bond which pre-exists birth. I remembered my first meeting with Nathaniel, having the sense that I had always known him, as if there was a pre-existing fit that could not easily be explained.

I jumped up from my seat, I think the book fell to the ground, and I threw my arms around him. I wanted his lips but he was kissing me all over my face; we were in competition to find cherished skin. I kissed his neck and then chased his lips again, but he was lost in his own pleasure. He kissed the tears from my face, my eyelids, until eventually he remembered me and met my lips.

"Marianne, I have missed you so much."

"Not as much as I've missed you." I laughed and cried. Then the words stuck in our throats. They were too big, too weighty to flow out. He sat on the bench and pulled me onto his lap; we clung to each other as if our lives depended on it. I don't know how long we stayed like that.

"I'm desperate for a drink." Nathaniel said eventually, and I remembered that he must have had a long journey.

"Oh, I'm sorry." Strangeness, convention, now intruded. "I'll go and get you one. Wait here." I couldn't take my eyes off his face; I was so afraid he'd disappear.

"No way!" he said. His voice was a soothing balm to my ragged senses. "I'm not leaving your side." We walked into the conservatory like Hansel and Gretel, clasping hands, afraid to be torn apart by wolves.

Then we sat in a quiet corner, sipping iced water like strangers until the words came.

"When did you arrive?"

"I came straight from the airport to you."

"How did you know where I was?"

"Your dad told me."

"How come you spoke to my dad?"

"I couldn't stop thinking about you. I called him and he told me what had happened. I had to come to you."

"How long do I have you for?"

"Forever, if you want me."

"I mean, here…?"

"Stop asking questions and take me to your bed, you skinny, gorgeous creature."

We didn't leave my room until two o'clock, until we had found each other again. Then we went out, blinking in the harsh sunlight after the sweet darkness of my room. For two hours we walked the ancient streets of Varanasi; the city seemed to join up into a magical, coherent whole. Nightmares fled from tangled lanes, demons hid behind medieval walls and dived into the sludged depths of the Ganges. I floated besides Nathaniel, fascinated by the place that had held me captive for seven dark days.

"I thought I saw you here the other day," I said. I wished I hadn't mentioned it. It opened the door to reality and as T.S. Elliot once said, 'Human kind cannot bear very much reality'.

"What do you mean?" he asked. Did I hear defensiveness in his voice or was it just an innocent response?

"Oh nothing. I guess I was so desperate to see you, I imagined you everywhere."

"Poor baby!" He kissed my nose and pulled me closer to him. "You've had a really crap time, haven't you?" We walked in silence for a few minutes, taking in the scenes at the Bazaar, stopping to examine objects we had no intention of buying.

"You didn't tell me what time your plane landed." My voice was as flat as I could make it.

"Oh, about nine at Babatpur Airport; it was an hour-and-a-quarter flight from Delhi."

"What time did you arrive in Delhi?"

"I arrived last night and stayed in a hotel at the airport."

"So when did you leave London?

"What's going on Marianne? You're suddenly very interested in my flight details. You're not turning into an anorak, are you?" Nathaniel laughed, but nervously.

"Oh, sorry, just wanted to know. Anyway, we'd better get back to the hotel to meet Dave." I had of course told Nathaniel about Dave, but suddenly the thought of the two men meeting filled my insides with butterflies as well as a small flutter of guilt.

It was five-thirty when we arrived back at the hotel and Dave was sitting in the bar sipping King's Beer. He looked surprised when he saw me walking towards him with another man and again I thought of our close encounter the night before. I was glad nothing had happened between us.

"Dave, this is Nathaniel; he arrived unexpectedly this morning."

The two men shook hands; I thought I saw Dave's jaw tighten, very slightly.

"Pleased to meet you, Nathaniel; can I get you a drink?"

"A beer would be great, thanks."

Dave nodded at me but avoided eye contact.

"Same for me please."

"So what brings you here, mate?" Dave asked. He pulled a cigarette from a crumpled packet and offered one to Nathaniel. Nathaniel hated cigarettes and shook his hand at the packet, like he was being offered arsenic. I felt a little irritated by his prudish show of distaste.

"Marianne's dad told me she was in trouble."

"Right, yeah, she's certainly been through the mill." It sounded accusatory.

"That's why I'm here." Nathaniel seemed to glower.

I felt a little uncomfortable with the bloke-speak, so I intervened.

"How was your trip to Agra, Dave?"

"A bit of a waste of time, to be honest."

"Didn't you see Rajpal?"

"No, he'd gone away on business for a few days; his brother was holding the fort."

"Oh, shit! I really thought he might shed a bit of light on things. Didn't he know you were coming?"

"I like to surprise my suspects. Anyway, I left my details and asked him to call me when he returns; you never know. I did manage to ask a few questions though and it seems pretty clear that Rajpal was in Agra on the day of Sara's death."

"So what did you do with your time there?"

"Went to see the Taj Mahal. Bleeding hell, it's some frigging coffin."

"It's great, isn't it? You see the photographs, but you just don't have any idea until you go." I was aware that Nathaniel wasn't part of the conversation and tried to fill him in as we went along.

"And how was your visit to the cop shop this morning?" Dave asked, not making too much effort to include Nathaniel. "Any news from that quarter?"

"Nothing, although they did say they would put posters up at Ghai Ghat."

"At least that's something. I might take a wander there tomorrow, ask the locals a few more questions; it'll be a week to the day, you know."

"Yes, I can't believe it. I thought about taking some flowers to the river tomorrow afternoon."

"That'll be sweet; there's not much more you can do at the moment."

"When will they have the post-mortem results, Dave? It's taking so long. Surely we should be allowed to cremate her soon."

"They said about a week, perhaps tomorrow."

"Are you any closer to knowing who might have killed her?" Nathaniel asked. He had been listening intently until that point.

"Hasn't Marianne filled you in on the details?"

Nathaniel smiled and held my hand. "No, we sort of had other things on our mind."

I felt guilty; we had hardly spoken of Sara all day. In fact, we hadn't spoken about anything of importance. There had been a kind of mutual understanding that we needed time before tackling difficult issues. Now our omission seemed callous.

"My Dad told him quite a bit." I could hear the defensiveness in my own voice. "And I'll tell him the rest later."

"Well," said Dave, observing us with eagle-eyed astuteness, "we've already ruled out several suspects but I'm still waiting to hear from my colleague in London and hopefully from your friend, Rajpal. I'm also going to ask to see Sara's diary tomorrow; we might get a few names from that."

"She kept a diary?" There was a sharp edge to Nathaniel's question.

"Could be something or nothing, but the police have been

reluctant to hand it over."

"Well, I think we should have it," I said. The diary had been playing on my mind since I'd learned of its existence. The fact that Sara had kept it a secret seemed to imbue it with greater significance. I felt, irrationally, that it belonged to me; perhaps I harboured that narcissistic compulsion to know what others think of us. "Surely the diary is private; I don't want the whole Varanasi police force ogling it."

"I'm afraid," said Dave, "nothing is private once you're dead."

I turned to Nathaniel for support but he was washed of colour; he had a distant look in his eyes.

"Are you ok?" I asked.

"Yeah, yeah. Just feel really tired…jet lag I guess. I might go and lie down for an hour before dinner."

"Has your boyfriend got something to hide?" Dave asked after Nathaniel had left; a smirk played on his lips.

"Of course not," I said. "Nathaniel never has anything to hide."

"You know best."

"Piss off Dave." I rose from my chair. "You don't know everything."

"Marianne, I didn't mean…"

"I'll see you at dinner. Eight o'clock."

I didn't go back to the room immediately. I felt confused about Dave's words. I thought I should have told him about my sighting of Nathaniel – real or imagined – three days earlier, but I couldn't bring myself to do it. It seemed more a reflection of my poor state of mind, my precarious dance at the edge of madness, rather than anything of significance.

I was also troubled by my feelings towards Nathaniel. I had fantasised about a blissful reunion for so long that I had failed to take into account the passing of time. Nathaniel seemed incongruous with Varanasi and with the world I had inhabited for the past few months.

I suppose spiritual and emotional growth are the same as physical growth – we only notice it has happened when we measure it against something else. I remember my dad putting a giraffe height-chart on my bedroom wall when I was four or five-years-old; every few weeks I stood in front of it and he drew a neat pencil-line over my head. We were always amazed that I had grown some more in only a matter of weeks.

When I first saw Nathaniel again, I had the weird sense that he had shrunk physically. In my memory he had towered above me like some Greek god brandishing a mighty golden sword; now he appeared man-like, less impressive. After the initial exhilaration of our reunion, I must admit to feeling some disappointment and this disappointment was now turning into irritation mixed with anger. Perhaps anger that I had elevated him so highly in my mind and in consequence made myself appear smaller.

The constant shift in my feelings for Nathaniel between ecstasy and irritation confused me deeply and the niggling suspicion that he was lying to me didn't help. Lies from an honest person are so much more weighty than those from an habitual liar.

When I eventually returned to the room, Nathaniel was fast asleep. A single tear glistened on his cheek.

Chapter 24

Dinner was a surprisingly pleasant affair and I concluded that I'd probably imagined the tension between Nathaniel and Dave. They talked about sport and current affairs; Dave joked that it was a relief to have male company for a change.

Nathaniel and I had a reasonably early night and we made love again, with less passion but more tenderness than that morning. Nathaniel reaffirmed his love for me over and over again in words that soothed me. I shook off my earlier doubts.

Soon after breakfast the next morning Dave left to continue with his enquiries.

Nathaniel and I stayed in the shade of the hotel and I told him everything that had happened in Varanasi. He seemed shocked and visibly moved by my account and gripped my hand supportively.

After lunch we went to the police station. I thought I detected disapproval in Mr Bakshi's expression when I introduced Nathaniel to him – yet another man I was apparently so casually acquainted with. Mr Bakshi informed us that they would have the post-mortem results later that day and that they would soon be able to release Sara's body. This news brought relief as well as sharp anxiety; I was afraid of what else I might learn about Sara's death – or, for that matter, about her life.

From the police station we made our way to Ghai Ghat to mark the seven-day anniversary of Sara's death. I stopped at a market stall on the way to buy several marigold garlands.

The ghat was busy but, as usual, it was quieter by the mound.

There was a different light that afternoon, richer, softer; it stroked the river with tender fingers, sculpting the water into golden mounds.

We sat for a while, just looking into the Ganges and saying very little. I felt strangely isolated from Nathaniel. Although he sat close enough for me to feel the warmth of his body, I resisted its comfort.

I wondered what had happened in the space of time between Sara leaving the hotel and the point of her death. I thought I would probably never know.

Three o'clock came and I stood up. Nathaniel joined me. I could think of nothing to say that wasn't trite or sentimental, that didn't convey my fear, my thousand questions, so I just cast the marigold chains silently into the river, one by one, and watched them pirouette in the current. It struck me violently that it was into these greedy waters that Sara's body had been swallowed whole; that her hair, which had tangled about the limbs of many grateful men, had danced for a few seconds, like reeds twisting among the debris and decay, before following the rest of her into the sacred depths.

As I let go of each garland I tried to conjure up memories of Sara and I offered them to the Ganga, until my hands were empty and the last flower had disappeared from sight. A moment of silence fell.

I eventually turned to see Dave standing behind us.

"Well done," he said.

We all walked together up the steps of the ghat and stopped once again by the sculpture of the cow.

"I have been piecing things together." Dave ran his rough and deeply tanned hand over the cow's haunch. "Shall we get a drink and I'll tell you what I know?"

We found a café by the river. Dave pulled his increasingly battered notebook from his jacket pocket and laid it on the table. He turned the pages until he found a reasonably neat, bullet-pointed list. The heading said '*Sara's last movements*'.

"Ok. This is the story so far; some of it needs to be confirmed by the post-mortem. Tell me if anything doesn't scan:

● *On the day of her death it's likely that Sara used the last of the morphine in her money belt, before M...*that's you – I've used initials for speed...*joined her on the hotel rooftop. The rest of the morphine was in S's backpack, which had been abandoned at the Avaneesh Hotel. It is unlikely the amount taken was enough to feed S's habit; she knew she must find another supply.*

● *At approximately 12.10pm S leaves the hotel after placing a note on her bed for M. She goes straight to Bert and Sam's hotel, less than ten minutes walk away (we'll give her ten minutes because of her poor state of health), and asks for drugs. Bert and Sam are in a rush, but give her Kratz's details before leaving.*

● *S then goes to the police station on Kabir Chaura Road, (probably by auto-rickshaw) where she arrives at approximately 12.45; she reports the incident that had occurred at the Avaneesh Hotel in the early hours of that morning and mentions the abandoned bags. S appears confused and inarticulate and isn't taken seriously by police.*

● *At approximately 1.15pm S catches an auto-rickshaw to an ATM on Station Road.*

● *At 1.23pm S withdraws £500 worth of rupees from the ATM – the maximum amount she could withdraw. She then uses the remainder of her traveller's cheques inside the bank to withdraw a further £720. (Two separate receipts show the exact amounts and times of withdrawal.)*

"Why would she do that?" I asked

"I'm not sure yet," replied Dave, hardly raising his head from his notes. He continued:

● *She walks to Varanasi Junction railway station and gets the times of trains to Delhi, which she scribbles onto the back of the hotel receipt.*

● *At approximately 1.45pm S takes another auto-rickshaw to Chaitganj Road, where the opium den is situated. She gives a very generous tip to the driver – approximately 4,000 rupees. (It is possible she gave more, but the driver is reluctant to say.) He remembers S because of her troubled appearance, the dodgy destination and the large tip.*

● *S enters the opium den and spends approximately 30 minutes buying heroin (brown) from Kratz, giving him 5,000 rupees. She injects while in the den.*

"How do you know that?" Nathaniel asked

"Know what?"

"That she injected while in the den?"

"Only by Kratz's account; it's usual practice... I guess he's got no reason to lie. He also said she was in a pretty bad way and needed a quick fix-"

"Carry on!" I said, not wishing to hear more on that subject.

● *At 2.25pm S leaves the opium den with large quantities of H (according to Kratz). She probably takes another rickshaw to Ghai Ghat. We can't trace the rickshaw driver but it is possible Sara also gave him a large tip.*

● *S arrives at the ghat at approximately 2.40pm and probably goes to the south side of the mound, which is where her body is later recovered.*

● *At 3pm she is either pushed, falls or jumps into the river. When found, she has no money on her person, except for a few loose rupees and there are only traces of heroin in her money belt. It is possible she was mugged, put up a struggle and in consequence was murdered.*

"Pretty likely wouldn't you say?" Nathaniel sat forward in his chair.

"Except that she was in a generous mood that day; she might have given the money away before reaching the river."

"But why?" I asked. "It's one thing to give fifty quid or so to a few rickshaw drivers, but why would she give away her last penny? Surely she would have kept some for the rest of her travels."

"You'd think so, wouldn't you?" Dave nodded slowly. "Could be an argument for suicide, of course; although the fact she bothered to get the details of trains out of Varanasi and bought such a large quantity of heroin seems to discredit this. Or, it could be she was holding the money in her hand, along with the heroin, and it got carried away by the Ganges."

"Or, she might have been followed by one of the rickshaw drivers after they saw her flashing the money around," Nathaniel suggested.

"There are quite a few possibilities." Dave frowned and rubbed his chin.

"Anything else?" I asked

"Only that there was a Hindu festival at Ghai Ghat that day – Govardhana Puja – a festival in honour of the Sacred Cow. Apparently it is connected to the story of Lord Krishna – also known as Gopala, the cow herder – lifting this hill, Govardhana…something or other…to protect the inhabitants of Vrindavan from torrential rains. Devotees build a replica of the hill with sweets-"

"I found some sweets!"

"Where?"

"On the mound; I found them crushed into the ground."

"Yeah, well maybe that's what the mound was being used for, to represent the hill. It's not a widely-practised festival in Varanasi but there might have been a few devotees. Ghai Ghat is used because it's dedicated to the Holy Cow, hence the statue."

"But what's the significance for Sara?" Nathaniel asked.

"I'm not sure if there is any," relied Dave. "It's just part of the bigger picture."

"I did read in the *Lonely Planet*," (I heard Sara's mocking laughter) "that there's an increase in incidences of rape and assault during festival times."

"Well, there are a hell of a lot more people around," said Dave.

"And more outsiders," added Nathaniel, "who then disappear back into remote villages. Surely it's like finding a needle in a haystack."

I felt irritated by Nathaniel's pessimism. I didn't want to believe we would never know the truth.

"I've got some news on Mr Sultan as well; it might explain the police's reluctance to get involved."

I sat forward. At last, I thought.

"As well as owning a dodgy hotel and running an illegal brewery, he's an ex-police officer. He sits on committees and crap like that. Ironically, on the afternoon of Sara's death, he was sitting on a committee set-up to look at reducing crime against tourists in Varanasi. A cast-iron alibi. He might get done for the illegal brewery though, if that makes you feel any better."

"No!" I just felt disappointment that we couldn't indict Mr Sultan and was afraid that Sara's murderer might never be found.

"Anyway," Dave gathered his papers under his arm, "I think we should get back to the police station to take a look at this post-mortem report."

*****

The only death I had experienced in my life prior to Sara's had been that of my dog, Trilby. My maternal grandparents died in a car crash before I was born, and my dad's parents were still alive and having a ball. In fact they had been the main source of support for me and Dad after my mother abandoned us. I spent many happy hours after school in the old-fashioned cosiness of their home, relishing my gran's cooking and soaking in the warmth of their solid love until dad picked me up after his day at the office.

Trilby died in my second year at university, not of old age

but, true to character, he escaped through a hole in my dad's garden fence and traced a substantial walk through fields and woods where Nathaniel and I had often taken him. We guessed this because of the place where his body – which had once pulsed and twitched with too much life – was found mangled from the impact of a car's bumper.

I imagined him trotting and meandering along soft paths edged by ancient oaks and grassy banks riddled with rabbit holes and badger lairs, perhaps resentful that I wasn't there to take him on his favourite walk. I felt his resentment had caused his death and I was left with guilt and grief (the latter is so often fuelled by the former).

My grief was probably disproportionate to that permitted for an animal; it crippled me for a week and Dad and I sobbed in each other's arms for the first and only time.

Nathaniel, who was an observer to this and at that time enthusing about the psychoanalytical concept of transference, shared his view with me that both of us were transferring onto Trilby our unexpressed grief for my mother. I was dismissive of this, insisting, "That's rubbish. I'm indifferent to my mother; why would I grieve for her?"

It was only now that I was beginning to understand how deep a gash my mother's abandonment had carved through my life.

*****

"I'm afraid we don't have the technology here that is available to you in England," Mr Bakshi said, while holding a single, solitary, A4 sheet of paper. "I did spend several months observing your illustrious police force in London and I had the privilege of viewing your fabulous forensic laboratories."

"Is that all you have?" I asked, nodding towards the paper, which he guarded closely to his chest.

"I think it tells us most of what we need to know." Mr Bakshi laid the paper down on his desk. The report was written in beautiful Hindi flourishes, giving a kind of cryptic mystery to the occasion and making it impossible for me to take a sneaky look, despite my skill at reading upside down.

It also meant that Mr Bakshi was in a position of power. We waited for him to speak. I could hear my own irregular breathing and feel the urgent pounding of my heart. He slowly lifted his small, gold-rimmed glasses to his face and perched them on his nose. He looked up briefly, as if to make sure he had our full attention, then back down again, making a small adjustment to his glasses before reading.

"The body temperature, level of rigor mortis and putrefaction of soft tissues suggests the time of death was within three hours of the body being removed from the Ganges, i.e. at some point between one and four o'clock. High levels of opiates were present in the bloodstream, consistent with use within twenty-four hours of her death."

"Did this kill her?"

"It might be best if you wait for me to finish, Miss Taylor." Mr Bakshi looked at me, judge-like, over his glasses.

"She had bruises on her left inner arm consistent with injection by use of a syringe; the bruises were recently inflicted and there was no suggestion of long-term intravenous drug use."

"I knew it," I said. "I knew she wasn't a junkie."

Mr Bakshi ignored me and lifted the page, moving it backwards and forwards before his eyes, as if trying to find the optimum spot to decipher the script.

"There is no evidence of sexual assault; although evidence might have been lost after submergence in water."

"Thank God!" I said. I had been dreading news to the contrary.

"Neither are there any injuries consistent with struggle. However, there was an injury found to the occipital region of the skull-"

"The back of the head," Dave supplied.

"Yes, yes, consistent with a heavy blow from a hard object."

"Oh God!" I felt nauseous. "See, she *was* murdered, wasn't she?"

Mr Bakshi didn't reply but gave me another one of his looks. "The report concludes that the cause of death was drowning, following a blow to the head that rendered the deceased unconscious."

A heavy silence fell in the room for a few seconds as we digested this information. Dave broke it.

"Is that the full report?" he asked with a wry smile, which told me he was also disappointed by the lack of detail.

"It is a summary of the most important points, Mr Holland. It will be typed up and you may take a copy."

"What about the injury to her head? Is there any indication of what might have caused it – a blunt or sharp object; what pressure was used; from what angle was it applied; and what about the internal autopsy?"

"This was not deemed necessary when the cause of death was clearly external." Mr Bakshi tapped the inadequate piece of paper with a firm index finger.

"Well then, can I speak to your forensic team myself and see if they can shed any more light on these injuries? It would *appear* to be important to the case." I wasn't sure if Mr Bakshi picked up on the sarcasm.

"That is your choice, Mr Holland; they are located in Delhi."

"Well perhaps I can telephone."

"Of course, I will supply the number."

"Much appreciated. When will the body be released?"

"It may be released immediately. I suggest you make arrangements as soon as possible; there is now significant putrefaction."

"We are going to cremate her," I said, trying to ignore his last comment. "At Ghai Ghat."

"Oh." Mr Bakshi looked surprised. "I didn't realise." He removed his glasses and stared more intently at us all. "That is most unusual. Cremation is a Hindu custom and only certain ghats are commonly used."

"We are aware of that Mr Bakshi." I strained to keep calm. "But cremation is also used in Christian funerals and, anyway,

184

it was Sara's last wish."

"We'd really appreciate it if you can give us the name of someone who could help us to arrange it." Nathaniel's calmness counteracted my near-hysteria. I hadn't been prepared for the impact of the post-mortem report on my emotions.

"Anything is possible." Mr Bakshi tapped his nose in a sleuthish manner. "India usually gives you what you want but not always in the way you expect it. Anyway, I have a friend who would be happy to help. He also worked in England for a number of years." (I imagined he wanted to add, "and understands the peculiarities of the English".) There was a subtle shift in Mr Bakshi's tone and I wondered if he respected our decision to cremate Sara in Varanasi. He scribbled two numbers next to two names on a piece of paper and handed it to Dave.

We all stood up. There was an air of sadness in the room, as if the words of the post-mortem still hovered, ghost-like in our midst. We reached the door and were about to leave when Dave turned back.

"I nearly forgot! Miss Fitzgerald's diary, you said I could take it." I couldn't help but look at Nathaniel and noticed a slight clenching of his jaw.

"Of course, I will get it for you now." Mr Bakshi went to the filing cabinet and extracted a manila envelope from the bottom drawer.

"You will follow up on the matter I mentioned to you earlier." Mr Bakshi laid a firm hand on Dave's shoulder as he handed over the envelope. Dave nodded.

I had no idea what Mr Bakshi was talking about.

"And what about the investigation?" asked Dave.

"I still hope that we can nab the villain. I will let you know if anything turns up."

Chapter 25

Dave's face was fixed into an unusually serious expression. At first I thought he might be put out that we'd started dinner without him – in fact he joined us just as we were rising to leave.

"I'm sorry, we've finished," I said. "We can wait around if you like."

"No worries, I ordered room service…had stuff to do. I fancy a coffee though."

We sat down again.

"I rang forensics in Delhi," Dave continued. "They had nothing much to add to the post-mortem report, except to say that Sara was struck with some force by a curved implement."

"I still think it was Mr Sultan with the kukri," I said. "He's lying."

"No, the wound was too rounded for that and, as I said, he has a cast-iron alibi. I also managed to speak to Bakshi's mate; looks like the cremation is on for Wednesday evening."

"That's a relief," I said. "Thanks for arranging that Dave."

"No problem." Dave coughed as if about to make a speech and shifted uneasily in his chair.

"I read the diary too, not much there really."

I felt disappointed; I'd been hoping for answers.

"So, nothing of importance?" Nathaniel asked, clumsily wiping spilt coffee from the table.

"Sara does say a few odd things, which neither the police nor I can figure out."

"Like what?" I was eager to know everything.

"She writes stuff about being in a lot of pain, but it's not clear if she means physical or emotional pain; could even be the start of a psychotic episode. It also sounds, at times, as if she knew she was going to die, though it's all a bit cryptic.

"I want to see it Dave; I knew her more than you or the police…I might be able to help."

Dave didn't seem to hear me.

"She also mentions a 'Him' – capital 'H'," he continued, rubbing his chin between his finger and thumb and staring intently at the wall. "She said she saw 'Him' everywhere." Dave turned his focus back to me. "Did Sara ever mention being followed, or think she saw someone she knew from back home?"

"No never, and she always seemed calm and cool, even after we'd been chased by those guys at Ghai Ghat and by Mr Sultan with that knife. Who do you think it might be?"

"We're not sure. She did suggest it was only an illusion brought on by too much cannabis, but I just wondered."

"Please Dave, can I see the diary for myself?" I tried again, "I might understand…"

"I need to ask you a few questions first." He was looking at Nathaniel.

"Me?" Nathaniel faltered.

"Yes, shall we find somewhere quiet? It shouldn't take long."

Nathaniel followed Dave out of the dining room; he glanced backwards and I saw naked fear in his eyes. I headed for the garden in a state of confused limbo.

The only reason I could imagine Dave would need to question Nathaniel was because he considered him to be a suspect. In different circumstances I might have been amused by this, but recent events left me feeling uneasy. I thought there must be something in the diary to cast suspicion on Nathaniel. Perhaps Dave thought Nathaniel was the mysterious 'Him'? Maybe Sara wrote about seeing Nathaniel, as I thought I had, before his supposed arrival in Varanasi? It seemed horribly possible and the thought sent sickening waves through my body. But why hadn't she said anything about the sighting? None of it made sense. I knew Nathaniel had disliked Sara, but surely not enough to kill her?

Nathaniel had followed a fairly predictable course in his life. He did well at school and gained a good degree in psychology before embarking on his psychoanalytical training, in which he excelled. He was on a work placement at the time and told me he was having very good feedback from his supervisor. His future seemed mapped out, secure. I had often wished I could be more like him, more accepting of my path. Though suddenly I wasn't so sure. For the first time I saw traits in Nathaniel that reminded me of my father.

I once read that we choose our partners, consciously or unconsciously, because they share characteristics with one or both of our parents. This gives us the opportunity to resolve the issues we have from childhood. Even if the similarity isn't at first apparent – in fact we might even choose a partner because we think they are the exact opposite of a parent – in time we begin to see an uncanny resemblance.

I thought I had been attracted to Nathaniel because, unlike my father, he appeared strong, fearless, sure of his own mind. I guess it is easy to mistake inertia for equilibrium, stolidity for self-possession. I sometimes thought that I was a new soul while Nathaniel was an old one. I was seeing everything for the first time, a child in the sweet shop; Nathaniel had been here before, he knew how everything tasted, he knew the novelty would wear off.

A great deal had happened in the past few months. I was more confident, more self-assured. The question was whether I still needed Nathaniel. I wondered if one of my main reasons for being with him was because I'd been sure he would never abandon me, although that is exactly what he had done.

I think aspects of our personalities come to the forefront in different relationships. With some people we become the child while the other person takes the role of parent or adult. With others we are the parent, taking responsibility for nurture and care. With others still, we allow the adult in us to take a lead so that we become serious and responsible, sometimes punitive.

I think I had most often related to Nathaniel like a child to a parent – testing boundaries, exploring away from the secure base, knowing I could always return. Perhaps I even tested whether he would abandon me, being prepared to sabotage the relationship to push this to the limit.

With Sara, I had often found myself in an adult role, compensating for her carefree attitude, taking responsibility where she wouldn't. Once these roles are established it is difficult to change the pattern.

"Marianne, I need to talk to you." Nathaniel appeared from nowhere, his voice breaking like gentle waves into my consciousness. His face looked odd, slightly swollen; I realised he'd been crying. I saw his life, my life, our life, shadowed by what he was about to tell me, his heinous confession. It was like the people you pity in newspaper stories, their lives turned around in an instant – a moment of road rage resulting in the death of a child or an act of jealous passion in which the beloved's life is abruptly ended. In one dark moment the predictable course of happiness is severed forever, the mundane joys of life are confiscated, leaving the hollow sounds of 'Why?' and, 'If only'.

"No," I said childishly, "I don't want to hear." As if by not speaking it, it wouldn't be true, as if I could hold back reality with one word, "No."

"I have to tell you." Nathaniel's eyes pleaded with mine.

This wasn't just about me. He needed to confess, share the burden with me. I had to be strong. He pushed me along the bench, where I was rooted by fear, to find a space for himself. He then clutched my unresponsive hand.

"I love you, Marianne. I love you so much. I wanted to live my whole life with you."

I was too young to hold hands through prison bars, watching his skin grow sallow with lack of sunlight, my face growing immobile with lack of life, the absence of words echoing between us. Two people with no life to talk about.

I loved him but did I want this? "I love you too."

He started to cry again, in the strange way that men often do, tears forcing their way through taunts of 'sissy' and 'cry baby'.

I could never leave him, never. He was my life and this is the life we would live together.

"Don't worry, it will be ok."

He calmed a little and lifted his head to face me, his cheeks glistening.

"Marianne, I'm so sorry. I betrayed you."

It seemed an odd choice of words and my puzzlement must have shown. I suppose killing my friend was a betrayal of sorts.

"Wha-t do you mean…?"

"Marianne, I slept with Sara." He said it carefully, as if speaking to a young child, so that I couldn't mistake the meaning.

It took me a few seconds to digest what he'd said. Slept with, killed – at first they seemed to have nothing in common. The sentence was mixed up, nonsense, a line from *Alice in Wonderland*.

"What do you mean?"

"I had sex with Sara, only once."

"You mean you didn't kill her?"

"Kill her? You thought I killed Sara?" Nathaniel emitted a dry, half-laugh.

"What did you expect me to think; I saw you in Varanasi before you said you'd arrived, you've been behaving suspiciously, then Dave gets all serious and calls you for questioning."

"But why would I kill Sara?"

I jumped up from the bench, my muscles fuelled by adrenaline.

"Because you loved her but she didn't want you, did she?

You followed her here but when she still didn't want you, you killed her."

"Shit, Marianne, where did all this come from?"

"Tell me the truth!" I screamed, emphasising each word.

"He is telling you the truth." Dave's hand was suddenly around my arm and only then did I realise I was just about to bring the full force of my fist down on Nathaniel's head when Dave had arrived.

"Dave, why didn't you tell me…?"

"Marianne, I'm sorry, I didn't realise you were suspicious of Nathaniel; you didn't tell me you thought you'd seen him. Sara made reference to the fling in her diary; it made Nathaniel a suspect, but I'm satisfied he isn't guilty of murder."

'Fling', what a fitting word for Sara, a mix of flippancy and fun and fucking, but so inappropriate for Nathaniel.

"But how do you know he didn't kill her?"

"Mari, I'm a detective; it doesn't take long to check out a few details. You don't need to worry. It wasn't Nathaniel you saw in Varanasi; it could have been any Western traveller. The mind can play odd tricks when you're traumatised."

I think I felt disappointment. Murder somehow seemed a better option than infidelity.

"You've been under a lot of stress, Marianne…" Nathaniel reached out to take my hand.

"Get off me. Don't touch me."

He looked startled.

"I'll leave you two to talk." Dave raised his hands as if to say he wanted no part in this and walked back towards the hotel.

"Please let me explain, Marianne."

"Just get out of my life, Nathaniel. You were so perfect; you made me feel so imperfect. You always seemed to be looking at me with your wise old eyes, judging me as if I was a silly little girl."

"I know, I know." Nathaniel was gripping his head between his hands as if trying to stop it from bursting open. "I've been a hypocrite. I'm so sorry."

"Sorry isn't enough Nathaniel. You don't know the agony I've been through in the past months, trying to figure out why you ended our relationship and *so* coldly, blaming myself…"

"Marianne, I know, I'm a coward; I always have been…you're so much braver than me." His body looked hunched and defeated.

These words calmed me a little and roused my curiosity. Brave was the last thing I felt. I stood over Nathaniel, noticing how small he looked, like he wanted to disappear into the bench.

"I've no idea what you mean by that."

"I always take the safe option, the easy option; you push yourself, try new things. When you became friends with Sara I felt like I was losing you and I didn't know what to do about it. I didn't want you to shake up our happy little world. I couldn't handle it; I shut down from you."

"But you obviously didn't shut down from Sara, did you?" The anger returned in a bright flare that seared through my body. I felt loss, bereavement; a part of Nathaniel had died to me.

"It was more an act of anger."

"What the fuck do you mean? You couldn't have had sex with her if you didn't desire her." I couldn't allow my mind to wander over the scene, to see the embrace, the desire, his face next to hers.

"No one would deny that Sara is…was…a very attractive woman, but I wasn't attracted to her. She was too edgy, disturbed. Marianne, I know you will find it hard to believe…you might never be able to believe it, but I have had a long time to think about this. Maybe what happened that night wasn't about Sara; it was about you."

"How on earth…?"

"I felt you were moving away from me; I felt impotent. Perhaps it was transference…"

"For God's sake, Nathaniel, don't use all that psychobabble on me. Just be honest and say you wanted to fuck her."

"To fuck someone can have different meanings, Marianne; it really wasn't about sex."

With a different man I might have seen these words as a clever ploy, an excuse, but I knew deep down that unfaithfulness was not natural to Nathaniel, that what happened with Sara was about other things. But I didn't want to be reasonable. I had too much to punish Nathaniel for. I hardened myself towards him.

"Well, when I fucked a Spanish guy a few weeks ago it was definitely about sex, and bloody good sex too." I saw the pain glance across Nathaniel's face. It silenced him. I saw him trying to absorb my words, trying to figure out what they meant for him, for us, yet also knowing in his intrinsic reasonableness that he had no right to be angry. I regretted my words; I felt they were disrespectful both to Miguel and to Nathaniel.

"Anyway Nathaniel," I continued, not giving him a chance to react, "this isn't about my actions; it's about yours. Tell me how it happened; where it happened." I hadn't wanted to get into the logistics, not yet, but there seemed nowhere else to go.

"The party...Notting Hill."

"What?" This was a shock. "The party we were at together?"

"Yes." Shame painted Nathaniel's face with a strawberry blush. I had rarely seen him colour. The back of his neck was raw and, despite my anger, I felt tenderness towards him. I also felt power. I stood over him, turning the rack. There was something false about my outrage, but I felt compelled to act it out anyway. In truth, some part of me still trusted Nathaniel.

"Marianne, it lasted for two minutes."

"Where?"

"In the bedroom; where all the coats were left."

"What! Did you slip up there together after flirting all evening, giving each other seductive glances over my head?"

"No, nothing like that. I went up to get our coats...we'd decided to leave. Sara was in the bedroom already."

"That doesn't sound likely. What would Sara be doing up there alone?"

"I don't know, she seemed startled when I came in, and then angry."

"Angry?"

"Sort of. She asked what the fuck I was doing in there, as if I was an intruder. It got my back up. I asked her what the fuck she was doing in there. Then we got into this really childish banter. I could see all this anger in her eyes; I felt like she really hated me. Then she went weird and started coming on to me big style..."

"So, you're blaming Sara then?"

"No, Marianne, it was my fault. I really don't know what happened. It was like something clicked in me. Next minute we're lying in a bundle of coats."

"Sure." I laughed a vulgar laugh that I didn't know I had in me.

"Oh God, Marianne!" Nathaniel stood up and clasped his hands to his head again. He looked truly distressed. His eyes darted about as if searching for hope.

"When I say it out loud it sounds so implausible. I just know you will never believe me, or forgive me...that's why I ended our relationship, although it was the last thing I wanted to do." Tears were now pouring uncontrollably down his cheeks. I could picture the ten-year-old Nathaniel, golden hair tousled by sleep, a childish nightmare still haunting his mind.

"I'll pack my stuff, get the next flight home."

"No!" Whatever compassion I had in me twitched into life in the bones and muscles of my body. My arms opened to embrace him and I found myself moving towards him, taking him in my arms. I pulled him down onto the bench with me, placed his head to my breast and rocked him; I held him like a mother, kissing the waves of his hair, the back of his neck.

"We'll deal with this somehow Nathaniel but it will have to wait until after the funeral."

Chapter 16

'An idea is something you have; an ideology is something that has you.' Morris Berman[15]

"You have a message, Mr Holland." The receptionist handed Dave a slip of paper after breakfast.

"Interesting," he said coyly.

"What?"

"It's a message to call Phil, my colleague in London."

"You'd better call him now," I replied. "It might be about the freckled man."

Dave glanced at his watch.

"Too early, it's only four in the morning in the UK. Phil'd scream blue murder."

"God, I'm sick of waiting. I feel like I've been doing it for an eternity."

"How about a change of scene?" Nathaniel was tentative. We hadn't talked any more about his misdemeanour; we were like two strangers who happen to find themselves in the same railway carriage on a very long journey.

"What do you mean?"

"Perhaps get out of Varanasi for the day."

"I can't just leave," I said sharply. "There's a murder inquiry; I have to report to the police."

"I agree with Nathaniel," said Dave. "Sara's cremation is tomorrow; it would be good for you to have a change of scene. Just show your face at the police station. By the time you get

195

back, I'll have spoken to Phil."

"Why do I have the feeling you two are in collusion?"

"Because we are." Nathaniel's eyes pleaded. "Marianne, I don't want you to think about anything or worry about anything, just for a day."

I still had a strong urge to punish Nathaniel, but I also wanted to be convinced by him so I agreed to go. We made our routine visit to the police station – I had given up asking if they had any leads – then we went to the auto-rickshaw stand on the Kabir Chaura Road, the one Sara had used on her final day.

"How much to Sarnath please?" asked Nathaniel.

"A hundred rupees, good price."

"No, no," responded Nathaniel, "too much. I'll pay fifty." The rickshaw driver raised his hands in horror as if Nathaniel had offered to buy his whole vehicle for a pittance.

"That's not possible," he said, tilting his head from side to side.

"Ok, you name a fair price."

"Eighty rupees, very good price."

"I'll give you seventy."

"Yes, yes, seventy." The driver still looked deeply offended.

"I would have got it for sixty," I whispered as we climbed into the tiny vehicle.

"You drive a hard bargain," said Nathaniel with a wry smile.

Sarnath is about ten kilometres north-east of Varanasi and the journey only took twenty minutes but I felt my spirits rise in proportion to the distance we travelled away from the city; I knew it had been a good idea to get away.

Nathaniel and I were bound together in the sandalwood-drenched interior of the rickshaw like two wide-eyed children, travelling alone for the first time. We passed fields and shanty villages; the same rural scenes were acted out over and over again – children playing in the dust, women carrying baskets on their heads, men repairing ramshackle houses or smoking in shop doorways.

"So where are you taking me?"

Nathaniel pulled the *Lonely Planet* from his day-pack and flicked through the pages.

"The Holy Bible," I said.

"What?"

"That's what Sara called it; she used to take the piss whenever I looked at it."

"Yeah, well maybe both books have something in common."

"Oooh, profound," I teased. "I thought you were a confirmed atheist, Nathaniel. You haven't turned, have you?"

"No, of course not. I just mean they're both interesting guide books, an opinion of how things are, that's all…but I *have* been doing a bit of thinking in the past few months."

"Like what?"

"Sarnath." Nathaniel turned the page of the *Lonely Planet* and sliced through my question. "*'The Buddha came to this hamlet to preach his message of the middle way to Nirvana after he achieved enlightenment at Bodhgaya. It was known as the Deer Park, after the Buddha's first sermon, 'The Sermon in the Deer Park'. Later, the great Buddhist emperor, Ashoka, erected magnificent stupas and monasteries here.'*"

The first thing we saw as we stepped out of the rickshaw was the striking thirty-four-metre-high Dhamekh Stupa, which Nathaniel informed me is believed to be the site where Buddha preached his first sermon.

For the first couple of hours I felt an incredible sense of peace and acceptance, as if anything was possible, anything could be overcome. Nathaniel and I strolled through the ruins of monasteries and temples, breathed in the exotic scents of ancient gardens, all the while clasping hands. Nathaniel had once said that our hands fitted together perfectly, that he could never imagine holding another woman's hand. This thought had come to me many times over the past few months – the rightness of my fit with Nathaniel, despite my continual pulling away from him.

As the day went on, however, I found it difficult to fight off the image of Nathaniel and Sara in a passionate embrace. This thought was a cloud in my mind, shadowing the possibility of sunshine. Each time the cloud came, I wanted to pull my hand away, scream at him, run. It was as if he had scribbled over a beautiful painting, spoiled my perfect picture.

"I'm not sure if we can make it work Nathaniel." The words spilled from me and I saw the happiness flood out of him. He stopped walking, dropped my hand and turned to face me.

"Please don't say that, Mari. I can't bear the thought of not being with you."

I felt the power that we possess in love, the power of the lover over the beloved, the beloved over the lover.

"You've managed until now." My voice was cold. "Anyway, I can't stop thinking about it."

"I can't tell you how meaningless it was."

"You know better than to say that, Nathaniel."

He opened his mouth to speak his defence, but closed it again. I saw the despair come into his eyes. He was wise enough to know there was nothing he could say.

"It's not just what you did with Sara. I've changed in the past few months – so much has happened to me. It's like I'm a million miles from where I was when I left London." I knew this would hurt him.

"I haven't stood still either, you know." Now there was anger in his voice and it was my turn to feel insecure. It hadn't occurred to me that Nathaniel might have changed too.

"I've been doing a lot of self-analysis; I've discovered a few things about myself, some of which I don't particularly like."

"Like your prudish self-righteousness?"

"I guess you could put it like that. I made things into a moral issue rather than being honest with you about my insecurities. I didn't want to seem needy."

"You never seem needy, Nathaniel, that's part of the problem. You're so self-contained."

"It's fear, Marianne."

"Of what?"

Nathaniel led me to a piece of grass by a Bodhi tree and we sat down.

"Karl Jung talked of the struggle between the Ego and the Shadow. The Ego is the public aspect of our personality, the carefully constructed persona or mask we present to the world as the 'truth' about us. The Shadow is our unconscious, our 'dark side'. I've realised, the more I've analysed other people, that I'm really afraid of my dark side."

"What do you mean by your 'dark side'?" I felt slightly irritated by this talk.

"Well, my dangerous, unacknowledged, unacceptable feelings and reactions that I'd rather not look at and definitely don't want other people to see."

"I can't believe you have a dark side, Nathaniel; you're so, straightforward."

"Not really. I come from a family where emotions are never talked about, secrets never shared. On the surface we're a crisp, shiny family of do-gooders, upstanding citizens."

I had met Nathaniel's family on many occasions – his busy, humanistic parents, always involved in community activities, his bright younger sister Molly who got As in everything. They lived in a sunny, modern house where I imagined any secrets would be swept out with the dust each day.

"My parents are so proud of their humanistic beliefs, their freedom from the bondage of religion. They tried so hard to keep us away from any religious influence – 'keep your minds as clear as fresh slates', they'd say, but this carried its own kind of bondage. They were slaves to other things, like personal achievement and the rituals of family life."

"So what's wrong with that?" I said sharply. "At least you had a proper family; at least your family stayed together."

"Yes, at any cost."

"What do you mean?"

I saw a momentary struggle in Nathaniel's eyes.

"Well, don't get me wrong, I love my parents and they did a great job compared to most. But I always felt we were elevated in the community as this perfect family while under the surface there were serious flaws." Nathaniel cracked his fingers as he had a tendency to do under pressure. I waited.

"Molly has been anorexic since the age of thirteen." Nathaniel's voice was strangled. "Typical profile, I suppose: high achiever, unrealistic expectations from the parents."

I was shocked by this and by the fact Nathaniel had kept it from me. I had never detected so much as a scratch in the glossy surface of his family. In fact, I had been jealous of the hive of bright activity that typified his home and which contrasted with the often nullifying stillness of mine.

"But how…I mean I saw…"

"We closed in around her to protect her. She was educated at home for a few years. My parents told people she was too bright for school, a gifted child, and it was partly true. She was given every opportunity in life and the best private doctors for her eating disorder, but it was never fully acknowledged that she had an illness, a mental health problem. They used to call it 'Molly's appetite', as if it was another string to her bow, her lack of appetite, her fantastic stamina and determination. In reality, Molly lost touch with her own needs; they kind of got swallowed up in her efforts to please everyone else."

"What about now?" I asked.

"The anorexia is under control, though she will never be completely cured."

"I'm sorry to hear it." I suppressed my sadness and curiosity about Molly so as not to get side-tracked. "But that's not your dark side, Nathaniel; you were maybe then just a victim of other people's actions."

"Ok, you're right, but when I found out about Molly's illness I felt so much anger. I despised her for doing this to herself, for doing it to our family. I judged her harshly and blanked her for years. In fact, I've never really forgiven her, yet I speak about her in glowing terms to everyone else. I'm a hypocrite, Mari."

An almost unbearable emotion was evident in Nathaniel's face, moving under the surface like a storm cloud. He clasped my arm, a little too tightly, as if unaware of the physical world due to his mental turmoil. He spoke quickly, breathing in short, shallow, gasps; I had never seen him so disturbed.

A sudden gust of wind blew across the park, lifting jasmine and rose petals, which were strewn about the grass, rustling the leaves of the Bodhi tree and disturbing several picnic parties. A lady screamed with laughter, her voice made ragged by the wind; she jumped up to retrieve a paper plate that was hurtling across the lawn. She looked like an exotic bird, screeching and flapping in her bright yellow sari. For some reason it made me feel how alike we all are. I felt tenderness towards her and towards my fellow human beings in all their twittering turmoil.

"Marianne, I know I'm a relatively straightforward bloke." Nathaniel loosened his grip on my arm, his voice calmer. "I don't have loads of baggage, but I do have dark thoughts and repressed rage."

"That's no big deal," I replied, turning back to meet his troubled face, "everyone does." I couldn't yet soften towards him.

"I know, I know, but, without getting too Freudian about it, I elevated my mother and sister too highly and when they fell I took it personally. I felt they'd let me down. I did the same with you. When you changed, I couldn't handle it. I was so jealous of Sara's hold on you, but I couldn't talk to you about it – I had to be Mr Reasonable. It's the same in work. I sit and listen, nodding wisely as clients give me the mess of their lives. Secretly, I judge them all, call them losers in my mind. That's why I've packed in my training. I had to face my fear of being out-of-control-"

"Nathaniel, you didn't!" My ice-mask cracked; this was a drastic course of action for Nathaniel. "It's all you ever wanted to do…you're such a good listener."

"People who listen aren't necessarily wise," replied Nathaniel, his eyes soft with tears. "It's often a way of deflecting attention from themselves."

For a minute I was able to shift my focus from my own wounds to Nathaniel's. I glimpsed what he'd been through over the past few months and this began to dissolve some of the anger.

"I can't let you do this Nathaniel; we have to talk more."

"I don't see what else I can do; I'm not being real, Marianne."

"Look, Nathaniel, I'm so sorry that I pulled away from you." I took both of his hands in mine, as if I was calming a lost and panicky child. I felt the strangeness of the role-reversal. "I know I was distant, I know I withheld myself from you. It was like I was split into two people, each person wanting different things. I loved you so much and just wanted to be with you, but another side of me wanted to explore further. I felt I was… missing out on something."

"I know hon." Nathaniel extracted one hand and stroked my face. "I tried to keep you to myself. I always felt you needed more than me; I was just so scared of losing you."

"You're not the only one who is scared, Nathaniel. It sometimes seems that the world is a fragile place." I searched his eyes; I felt I was exposing my weakness to him. "I've been doing loads of thinking…about different philosophies and religions, trying to find some answers."

"To be honest, I think religions just create more fear." Nathaniel shifted his position and moved away from me slightly. "They are human constructions for human ends."

"But there must be something in them – so many people believe in some kind of god."

"So many people live in fear, Mari. Osofsky said that each culture has a different belief about fear and uses it to tame the human infant. Plato believed that children should be exposed to events that will help them conquer fear, desensitise them, while many Europeans held the opposite belief, seeing fright as physically and psychologically dangerous to a child, even leading to insanity; they tended to overprotect their children."

I observed Nathaniel visibly pull himself together as he moved onto familiar ground, comfortable ground. His voice was steady; he was in control again.

"Infancy is a period of maximum plasticity, the time when adults teach children skills and ideas, which they carry with them throughout life. The human infant is totally helpless, unlike other animals; that means they can be sculpted by the parents, by society and end up as the most complex of creatures.

"I suppose what I'm trying to say is that whatever culture we grow up in we try to find ways of dealing with fear in a culturally appropriate way; that usually means adopting the values and beliefs...the religion...of our parents. The longer we walk in a particular pathway, the harder it is to choose another pathway or to retrace our route."

"Our patterns."

"What...?"

"Oh, it was just a conversation I had with someone." The thought of Miguel made me blush and I lowered my head, feigning a sudden interest in a string of giant ants weaving past us in an orderly line. Nathaniel hadn't asked me about Miguel yet, but I knew I would have to tell him at some point if we were ever to be together again.

"But why do so many people believe in the same things, all over the world?" I asked to deflect my discomfort.

"I don't know if you've heard of 'memes'." Nathaniel continued. "They're a kind of pattern of behaviour which has evolved in such a way as to make groups of people want to copy them. Anyone who can't get their head around a new meme is at a disadvantage in that society. Memes are ideas, words, tunes, strategies, catch phrases, anything people can copy or appear to copy from one another; I suppose they're a kind of idea-virus. I really think that's how religions start. They are maintained because it suits the leaders of the day; it's a way of controlling their subjects; it also provides catharsis, a release from worry and guilt or an escape from the fear of death. We form clubs, alliances, interest groups and various memes to deal with fear, real or imagined."

Nathaniel was now in full academic flight, his hands illustrating his point with an obscure sign-language. A lot of what he was saying made sense and fitted with my own recent thinking, but in that moment I desperately wanted the softer, more vulnerable Nathaniel back. I wanted to be lost in the bliss of emotional honesty and physical intimacy of a few minutes earlier.

The sun was now low, burning through the trees, casting our shadows before us on the ground, long and distorted.

"You seem to have it all sussed Nathaniel." My voice was a little terse. "Don't you believe in anything?"

"Yes, I do." He looked up sharply. "I believe in self-actualisation; I believe in the beauty of things; I believe in meeting the need of humans in the here and now, not in some mythical future world. I believe in taking responsibilities for ourselves and for each other, not expecting some idea of God to act for us in the world. We've got to act ourselves to stop injustice, war and terror; I believe in human compassion…" Then his face softened and he saw me again. He leant over and kissed my forehead gently and looked into my eyes. "I also believe in us."

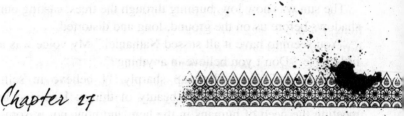

Chapter 27

When we returned to the hotel, Dave was sitting in the conservatory with a cigarette, as usual, perched between his lips. He was reading a book. For some reason this surprised me.

"Nice day?" He snapped the book shut and placed it self-consciously face down on a side table, but not before I saw the title, *The Meaning of Truth* by an unpronounceable author.

His look was questioning and he searched our faces, perhaps for signs of reconciliation.

"Yes," I said, "interesting place; any news from Phil?"

"Yeah, but first I need to eat. You're late; I'm bleeding starving." After a quick freshen up, Nathaniel and I met Dave in the hotel restaurant where we had eaten every evening since moving to the hotel. The bill was still being paid for by Mrs F, so we weren't inclined to spend our money elsewhere.

"So, what's the news? I can't wait any longer."

"Palak paneer, basmati rice, butter naan…oh yes, and throw in a couple of bhajias for good luck." Dave closed his menu with a satisfied snap and the waiter left with our orders.

"I guess you are hungry, mate." Nathaniel laughed. He looked more at ease than I'd seen him since his arrival in India. It sounds ridiculous but he also looked taller.

"Forget your stomach for once Dave and fill me in," I demanded.

"I can't fill you in, sweetheart, until I'm filled up. It's just the way it is." At that point the waiter brought a complimentary selection of starters, which Dave immediately tucked into. It was clear he wasn't interested in conversation.

I had noticed before that nothing else mattered to Dave when he was eating. It was as if all of his senses were locked into that one pleasure. He ate quickly, hunched over his food like a hungry wolf. I was fascinated by it – kind of repulsed and turned on at the same time. It made me wonder if he was the same when having sex, whether his whole mind, body and soul were involved in the act of lovemaking, to the exclusion of all else. I couldn't help feeling curious. Dave belonged to a different world, a *film noir* world, which I imagined to be exotically dangerous and edgy, a place I knew nothing about. He and Nathaniel were diametrically opposed. Nathaniel was thoughtful, analytical, reserved; he made careful judgements and valued honesty. In contrast, Dave acted on instinct and impulse. He used creative – not always honest – means to get the information he required. I guess these qualities were necessary to each in their chosen professions.

"That's better." Dave gave us his full attention again.

"I've got some very interesting news, but it will be upsetting. Are you sure you don't want to wait until after dinner?"

"No, I can't wait. Anyway, I'm hardened to bad news."

"Ok, here goes." He pushed some lime pickle into his mouth and continued to talk. "Phil managed to trace the 'Freckled Man', who turns out to be a Mr Gerald Harvey. Shit, that's hot!" Dave waved his hand in front of his open mouth.

"Thank God! He's not dead then?"

"Alive and kicking. He's a private medical consultant and his practice is situated on the top floor of a house in Islington, which is also where he lives with his wife and two kids. He told Phil that Sara first contacted him in May of last year; he saw her on five occasions after that, the last time being on the day you first met her."

"That's a completely different story to Sara's."

"There's a lot more to come. Sara confided in him about the abuse. She also told him she'd never had a smear test because she couldn't bear an invasive medical examination. Too much like the abuse, I guess.

"On her third visit she finally agreed to Harvey doing the test. The results showed she was in the early stages of cervical cancer."

"No!" The world shattered and the pieces hovered precariously in space before coming together again in a different form. "Sara? Cancer? It doesn't make sense." I put a half-eaten roti down; my appetite was dead.

"My God!" Nathaniel gasped.

"Certainly throws a different light on things, doesn't it?" said Dave. "And explains some of Sara's entries in her diary. Harvey said he tried to persuade Sara to accept treatment. There was a reasonable prognosis if it started immediately. She asked him a lot of questions but finally refused, saying she'd made the decision to go travelling for a year and die naturally. All she wanted from him were enough painkillers to make her journey as pain-free as possible."

"But she seemed fine," I stammered. "At the start of our travels anyway."

"Yes, but look at the mess she was turning into in the final week or so. Apparently cervical cancer can sit for a while and then suddenly turn really nasty and virulent. It fits with what you told me about Sara. The opiates and cannabis would all help with her symptoms. She might have been able to carry on for a few more months, even up to a year, except you both suffered some pretty nasty shocks – bombs in Delhi, being chased all over frigging Varanasi by angry men. It's not surprising she deteriorated quickly."

"Why didn't she tell me?"

Dave shrugged. "Perhaps she didn't want you to treat her differently. Harvey said she just wanted to be normal; she couldn't bear the thought of being a 'sick person'. He said he grew really fond of Sara over the weeks; he described her as sparklingly intelligent, with great potential as a lawyer – he didn't want to see her waste her young life. But when he refused to give her a prescription for large quantities of diamorphine and tried to persuade her again to have treatment, she became very angry. They had a heated row and he suffered one of his epileptic fits. When he came round Sara was gone. It was a few days before he discovered one of his prescription pads was missing. He called the police but it had already been used at several pharmacies where Sara had given false details. He was gutted to hear of her death."

"But she told me he'd tried to rape her; why would she say that? Could he be making up some elaborate-"

"No, Marianne, he's *bona fide*. Anyway, by chance, Rajpal also called today. He said Sara had told him she was dying of cancer. He's coming to the funeral tomorrow, to pay his last respects. He sounded devastated. His alibi holds as well; I think we can safely rule Rajpal out of the inquiry."

"I don't believe all this; it's too much to take in."

"It's crazy," said Nathaniel.

"Well, it seems Sara's drug use was about pain control," continued Dave. "You were right about her not being an addict, in the usual sense of the word."

"I wish she'd told me." That was all I could think about in that moment. "She told Rajpal, why not me; didn't she trust me?"

"Of course she did, hon," Nathaniel spoke softly. "Perhaps Sara chose you as someone she could be normal with."

Despite my distress and confusion, Nathaniel's words, "Sara chose you," seemed to switch a light on for me and I could see that I had, in some way, been chosen by Sara. Many of her actions and words suddenly made sense. But in that moment I didn't know whether to be angry or flattered by this thought. I didn't know if I had been grossly manipulated or gently led by Sara.

"Two other things," Dave ploughed on. "Phil managed to do some detective work on the stepfather. It seems he dropped dead ten years back from a heart attack. He was serving an eight-year sentence for molesting three other children. There is some justice, hey?"

"I guess so," I said flatly.

"What's the other thing?" asked Nathaniel.

"I've got something for you, Marianne." Dave laid his hand over mine. "It might help." He thrust his other hand into his pocket and pulled out a black book – Sara's diary. "I think it's time you read it."

Chapter 28

The diary was black and substantial, private and forbidding. I felt I shouldn't be reading it, even though jt had already been pored over by the eyes of Dave and at least a dozen police officers.

It was late and the air was sharp with the edge of a chill, inhibiting the usually intoxicating fragrances of the garden, where I had gone to be alone. I felt a strange tremulous wistfulness, which sometimes surprised me in England in the early autumn; the sense of another summer lying shrivelled and faded, a fallen rose petal, things past that can never be regained. Yet it was also a time for new beginnings, the start of a university term, a new job, a time to move on. Mixed with the wistfulness was a lurking anxiety. I had important decisions to make and yet there was still so much unfinished business in India.

Sara hadn't bothered to complete the front page of the diary – no name or address, G.P. or next-of-kin. However, several pages were set aside for other people's contact details and this is where her mother's number was listed, as well as mine and those of numerous friends – more male than female – many of whom I had never heard of. She had left blank the space for addresses and just inserted telephone numbers, mainly mobile. This created a temporary quality to the entries, as if each of them could easily be replaced.

When I first turned the pages I felt disappointed. I had hoped to find enlightenment in Sara's account of our travels, an answer to each of my many questions, but there were very few entries and most were just factual descriptions of the places we had visited.

There were a few amusing descriptions that made me laugh. I was envious of her ability to write – as she spoke – with a concise and sharp wit, to see the details that I often missed. She also documented the occasional flirtation or sexual encounter. (It was no wonder the police had held onto the diary for so long; it must have offered them a cheap thrill.)

10th September – Ozzie Greg was hassling me again today. He seems to turn up wherever we go, despite the fact he's travelling on one of those tour buses, with the herds, while me and Mari are travelling independently. He even popped up like an expectant wallaby in a temple in Chang Mai.

"G'day, fancy a beer?" he said.

I take the piss out of him constantly, but he never gives up; in fact, he seems to like it. I guess I shouldn't have shagged him in Koh Samui; he now thinks he has the right to drag me by the hair back to Tasmania, marry me and put me to work on the ranch.

There were a few glimpses into deeper regions of Sara's mind when she wrote in a voice new and strange to me – thoughtful, reflective – and I was grateful for these small insights.

20th September – Trouble in paradise. Marianne and I had a fall out, over nothing. I guess I can be pretty evasive at times. It's like I just want to be in the present; any talk of the past sends ripples through me. She worries too much, about the past, the future, what might happen, what might never happen. I want to say to her, for God's sake Mari, stop analysing everything; just enjoy your life, you have so much of it. Sometimes I want to tell her so badly, for her sake as much as mine, but then I worry that everything will come spilling out and she'll find out about me and Nathaniel. I'm too much of a coward to face the consequences of that.

I suspected that Sara was talking about her illness when she wrote, *'I want to tell her so badly'* whereas Dave had initially assumed she had meant her liaison with Nathaniel. This must have been the entry that had raised suspicion about Nathaniel and while it shed some light on things for me, Sara's brief, almost careless, reference to the event that had caused me so much devastation then seared through my heart for a second time, like a hot knife through butter. My feelings towards Sara were deeply confused; my love for her and my grief about her death were mixed with something bordering on hatred.

9th October – For every thousand metres we climb we seem to descend in equal measure. I know I'll pay for it tomorrow. I feel I'm doing really well, then some Nepalese guy in flip-flops, with a fucking fridge on his head, strolls past us and I feel like giving up. I've been feeling really good lately, and almost dare to imagine I'll be ok, but then I picture this evil thing crawling through my body, like ivy getting its grip.

I couldn't believe Sara had hidden her pain from me so effectively; it seemed incredible that she had managed to achieve so much when her body must have been screaming for her to stop. I could also see that this entry would have caused confusion to the police and might lead them to think that Sara was slightly unhinged.

13th October – Reached base camp and feel so grateful. It's as if Marianne's strength got me here, her blissful ignorance. I threw an invisible rope around her waist and allowed her to pull me up. Never felt so close to life and to death at the same time, like they are all part of the same thing.

I turned a few blank pages, battling with my emotions,

seeing my time with Sara in a completely different light.

4th November – Why has love come to me now? Is it a joke or a blessing? At least I won't have to face the end of love, or its fading into disappointment. After three days with Rajpal I can finally understand the love-poets and writers whose words were ridiculous to me before. I had to have these few days with him, although I know I hurt Mari in the process.

India has burrowed under my skin and nestled down. Nowhere else, no matter how beautiful, how welcoming, has had the same effect on me; I'm deliriously possessed by her and so glad that of all the places we've visited this is where it will end.

I'm smoking so much fucking dope that I'm sure I'm developing cannabis psychosis. I imagine I see things everywhere, especially Him, and it scares the shit out of me. I can't believe I didn't calculate enough diamorphine; I'm such a stupid bitch at times.

Being with Rajpal has helped. He held me for hours and I soaked in his strength; he made the pain more bearable. Then he took me to Fatehpur Sikri to see his brother, who happens to be a doctor – can you believe it! He got me some morphine and I feel sane again.

Pain kind of has a life of its own; it becomes a creature in its own right, an inconsiderate and nagging bully. I could control it at first, switch it off – probably a result of my early experience when I became an expert in visiting other worlds – but then it persists and persists until it wins.

So if the 'Him' wasn't Nathaniel, who was it? I wondered briefly if it was her stepfather but I couldn't find his name mentioned anywhere. Neither the police nor Dave had considered this worth pursuing after ruling Nathaniel out of the equation; they had assumed that these references were proof of some kind of drug-induced psychosis in Sara. But I wasn't satisfied.

This was Sara's last entry, followed by weeks of blank pages. I still turned them one by one in case there was anything else – a bit of scribble, a doodle etc. Her words had helped me to understand, but I still felt cheated. Sara owed me more than this.

Then I found the letter – several sheets of airmail paper. They lay hidden in the otherwise snowy white pages of December. I turned the sheets in my hands, feeling the paper – as thin and fine as silk. I brought them to my nose and breathed in the fragrance, a mix of incense and perhaps a whisper of Sara's perfume.

I carefully opened the letter and saw my name written at the top of the first page in Sara's bold flourishes. The handwriting was tiny, as if she'd meant to use as little paper as possible, probably so that the letter could be concealed. Yet, it seemed likely that it had already been discovered by Dave and/or by the police though I really hoped not. I hoped something of Sara remained un-desecrated by the touch of those for whom it was never intended.

It was after midnight and the air was growing cooler. I only had on a flimsy t-shirt and decided I would read the letter indoors. I was also in need of a stiff drink.

I folded the paper again and placed it back in the diary.

I was surprised to find Dave propping up the bar – Nathaniel had long gone to bed – sipping what looked to be a whisky.

"Hi Dave!" I said. He turned sharply, as if shaken out of deep thought. He looked a little rough and I felt sorry that I'd caught him off-guard.

"Hello darling." His voice was slurred. "Are you stopping for a drink?"

"I'll have a brandy." I sat awkwardly on the edge of a barstool. "By the way, thanks for the diary."

"I know there wasn't much in it, but I thought it might help."

"It did." Perhaps he hadn't read the letter after all. "Dave…" I hesitated. "Did you find anything else, besides the diary?"

"What do you mean?"

I pulled the letter out and held it in the air.

"Bloody hell. No!" he reached out to take it but I pulled it away.

"Look Dave, I haven't read it yet but it's addressed to me. I'd really like to keep it private. Is that possible?"

He smiled. "I'll do you a deal. If you promise to tell me if there are any clues, anything at all that could help with the investigation, then I won't tell the police you have it."

"I promise, but how do you know they haven't seen it already?"

"They showed me the list of all the evidence they'd gathered and it wasn't on there."

"But it seems weird that no one saw it but me."

"Just be glad that weird and wonderful things happen sometimes, darling. Of course shit happens more often, but…"

I couldn't stop myself; I flung my arms around Dave's neck and kissed him full on the lips.

"Thanks Dave!"

"Whoa girl. What was that about?" He reddened.

"Just so glad you've been around."

Dave took hold of my hand. There was a real tenderness in his eyes.

"Marianne, Varanasi has been a life-changing experience for me too, you know. It's like I've opened my eyes for the first time in bloody years."

I felt a mix of curiosity and concern. Perhaps he'd taken my kiss the wrong way; he was obviously drunk.

"How?" it came out as a whisper.

"My life's a mess back home. I've missed so many opportunities because I was afraid to take them; I've trashed relationships 'cos I couldn't commit." He kissed my hand. "I've grown really fond of you, Marianne."

"Dave…I-"

"You remind me of someone I was once involved with."

"What happened?" My curiosity took over.

"I let her go. She was intense like you, questioned everything; I couldn't cope. Her love was almost too rich for

215

me. She was also very beautiful."

I felt heat rise and throb beneath my skin.

"Being here has padded me out a bit, made me more real. Crazy bullshit, I know, but I suddenly can't understand why I didn't just enjoy it, relish it. It seems so fucking simple here in India."

"Is it too late?"

"Probably." He let go of my hand and turned back to the bar. He drained his glass and then looked at his watch, although I could see he could hardly focus on the hands.

"Big day tomorrow; I'm going to hit the sack."

I watched Dave walk across the room; his back looked lonely and wounded. The sight of him made me shiver. I thought of the decisions we make, which can so easily cast us into a place of despair.

Before Dave reached the door he turned, his eyes now sparkling like a child's on Christmas Eve.

"I might give it a try, though; but only if you promise to do the same with that lucky bastard boyfriend of yours." Dave winked.

Chapter 29

Marianne,

I haven't kept a diary since I was thirteen-years-old; it feels kind of adolescent. I ended up burning all the others. I remember it vividly. I went up to Hampstead Heath with James Knight, this cool sixth-former. It was midsummer night and still light at 10pm. His parents lived nearby and I made him steal two bottles of really good wine, I think it was Chateauneuf-du-Pape, from his parents' cellar – yes they had a wine cellar! We sat on Parliament Hill getting wasted.

This amazing moon was rising above St Paul's Cathedral, huge and eerie, like some kind of sci-fi, end-of-the-world thing. It suited my crazy mixed-up mood.

Then, we left the hill and headed for the woods where we could get privacy – except for the usual Peeping Toms and some gay blokes having a shag. I had matches, lighter fuel and some ceremonial stuff – I guess I still believed in magic back then.

First, we got a nice little fire going.

"You're fucking crazy," James said. I think he was a bit nervous; he kept looking over his shoulder, as if a policeman was gonna jump out from behind a tree. I guess it was his parent's neck of the woods and he didn't want to get busted. He liked to think he was a bit of a rebel in school but, underneath the surface, he was as conventional as the rest of them.

Anyway, next I laid out the artefacts – the pile of diaries I kept between the ages of eight and thirteen. They looked pathetic, lined up like little refugees; especially the early ones, spilling out their futile hopes and childish wishes.

Next to them was a rag doll that He gave me, one of His first bribes. Then my piece de resistance, a plasticine doll made in His likeness; it had His huge, ugly nose and gross, bulging belly. I made clothes for it out of a shirt He left behind. It still reeked of His filth. Best of all, a few strands of His greasy hair, left on my pillow; I stuck them into the plasticine head.

I got the fire really hot; James and I smoked a joint and drank more wine and then I started the ritual. I made James chant the same lines with me seven times, as I dropped each item into the fire, leaving the doll until last.

'With these flames the past is dead, no more nightmares, no more dread,

I'll live each day like it's the last, now is now, the past is past.'

Crap hey? Well I never claimed to be a poet.

Before I cremated the doll, I stabbed it with a pin and got a real thrill from it. I had to resist tearing it limb from limb. I wanted to see Him burn. Slowly.

"You look like you're possessed." James had a weird mix of fear and lust in his eyes.

"I am." I said. "I'm possessed by life."

Then we fucked.

So, here I am, twelve years later, scribbling in another diary. I haven't been very faithful in my recordings; it's a bit patchy to say the least. I won't go down in history as another Samuel Pepys, never mind Bridget frigging Jones. Anyway, I thought I'd write you a letter as well, to tell you things I couldn't when I was alive. (Wow that sounds weird).

First, that I was raped by my stepfather from the age of seven to twelve. I prefer to say raped than abused; it's an onomatopoeic word – Rape. It sounds like rip, scrape, rapacious; it's violent and grasping. That's how it felt. Abuse is soft in comparison. You can abuse your own body with alcohol or drugs; even self-pleasure is defined as self-abuse in the dictionary. I refer to Him with capitals because His name is still too powerful to utter; like Yahweh.

Secondly, I found out I had cancer on my 24th birthday. Not that I was planning to celebrate; I'm not a big birthday person, but another day might have been preferable. I'd never had a smear test, for obvious reasons, although I read somewhere that women who have sexual intercourse at a young age are more vulnerable to cervical cancer. I guess I didn't want to equate what had happened to me with the sexual act.

Anyway, it was only when I had some weird discharge that I decided to see Gerald, a private consultant in Islington – a long way from home. I liked him straight away. He was honest, non-patronising. He was the first person I ever told about the rape and it was a relief to share it. Especially with someone I could walk away from. The only true identifying detail I gave him was my first name.

When he gave me the diagnosis, I wasn't surprised. Back then I still felt the rape was my fault. The fact I hadn't told anyone seemed to implicate me in the crime, prove I was complicit, that I wanted it, although of course I didn't.

It's nearly impossible to explain why you don't tell anyone. Of course He used the usual threats – if you tell your mother she'll get really ill and die etc. etc. That worked for the first three years and then I stopped caring. My mother was a mess and didn't seem to care what was going on for me. I started to worry more about what people would think of me if they found out.

There is a survival mechanism that kicks in; it is a kind of splintering of the psyche, which enables you to compartmentalise what is happening to you, making it unreal. He raped me while I thought about schoolwork or about my favourite band.

But when I turned twelve, I started to get really bolshie. I mocked His manhood, spat in His face; He had to use brute force to hold me down. I think a combination of that and me starting my period put an end to the rape. He disappeared into the night. The ignorant bastard didn't even say goodbye.

I knew I didn't want treatment for the cancer, for the same reason I'd never had a smear test. The endless invasion of my body with needles and drugs, prods and prongs, would have just taken me back, while all I wanted was to move forward. Gerald said the cancer was unpredictable; it could take up to a year to kill me. It could be months before I even felt severe pain. I begged him for a supply of diamorphine, but he categorically refused. He didn't think it was ethical; besides, he wasn't convinced I wouldn't OD, even though there's no way I ever would. I wanted life more than anything.

I don't know why I told you that Gerald tried to rape me. I don't regret much but I regret that and you were right not to believe me. I was so angry that I had allowed him to examine me internally and then he refused to give me what I needed. It felt like rape. Crazy and irrational, I know, but it made sense at the time. Anyway, it seemed easier than telling you the truth.

Marianne, I think you were brought into my life, through that window. I bet you never thought you'd hear me use sentimental bullshit like that, did you? I still don't know what it means, or who or what brought you, but it makes some kind of sense.

You were different than any of my other friends. You struggled with things – injustice, right and wrong, truth, meaning – in a way that none of them did. I knew that I needed someone like you in my life, to be with me until the end. I guess I used you, but only because you were given to me, like a gift. I didn't need bullshit and pretence; I didn't have enough life left for all of that.

I suppose you also helped me to commit a crime. Gerald had an epileptic fit; I was terrified. I did check he was still breathing and put him into the recovery position (some school lessons did come in useful), but I couldn't move him. You helped so that I could run upstairs to his surgery and steal a prescription pad.

I'm sorry I couldn't tell you about any of this. I just wanted normality – well, as normal as you can get while dragging a backpack around the world. I didn't want concern or pity, questions and allowances.

I am not under any illusions about the sort of person I am, Marianne – selfish, unforgiving, judgmental, and there aren't any 'buts' to follow. I don't even know if I would have been much different if He had never come into our lives, if my mum and I had struggled on together after the death of my loving father. I don't blame my mum anymore. I knew her parents; I just pity her. I think we all get fucked up by life eventually; she and I just got there sooner than most. Anyway, I don't want to get all philosophical on you, Marianne; I just want you to understand that it wasn't that I didn't trust you – I was just doing what I needed to do for myself.

I've left the hardest thing until last. From the age of twelve, I used sex to get things. It nearly always worked. Most of the time I didn't even need to go through with it; just the promise of sex or the suggestion of it was enough for most blokes to slobber and fall at my feet. I learned that very early on.

I didn't do it with boys my own age; they were easy and, anyway, I wasn't interested in anything they had to offer. I was only interested in older men; men who could give me the things I wanted. I never saw myself as a slut – just a clever business-woman – and I never saw sex as making love; it was a tool of my trade.

A psychoanalyst would have a field day with my life – the sexually abused child who continues to be abused by men; the fatherless child who spends her life looking for a father. I guess Gerald became that for a while. But I don't see myself as a victim. I think we all use and abuse each other in various ways, get what we want and then move on. None of us like to admit it, we disguise our intentions in clever ways, but it all amounts to the same thing. We are all terrified of not getting what we need and so manipulate others in order to get it.

The first time I met Nathaniel, at that party in Notting Hill, I felt he could see into my heart and that he didn't like what he saw. Maybe it was his training – most blokes don't have a clue; they are so gullible, easy to fool, especially when you're half-decent looking.

Rajpal saw inside me too, but by then I didn't resist. He was the only other person I confided in about the cancer. We didn't have sex; I lied about that too, to do what you would have expected of me. It would have been too painful by then. But I did learn about intimacy with a man, for the first time in my life – intimacy, without sex. We lay together for hours talking, touching, and I am so grateful for those precious hours. You were right to say I looked softer when we met up again, that's how I felt. He nurtured me like a mother, a brother, a lover, all the things I'd never had. I told him about my fear of dying, of pain, of nothingness. He didn't preach at me, but somehow I came away with faith, in something. Perhaps in life, in goodness, in Sunyata – emptiness or the open potential of being. I saw a bigger picture and started to let go of my bitterness. Whether a life lasts seven years or seventy doesn't really matter in the scheme of things; it is all much bigger than that. I found acceptance. I think I also felt the first tender budding of love. Perhaps he did too.

Shit, I'm not explaining myself very well; maybe it's just the drugs talking. I'm lying in this narrow bed in the worst room, in the worst hotel. The shower is dripping and I don't have the energy to drag myself out of bed to stop it. You've gone out to get water and probably to escape this sick room for a few hours while I pump myself full of morphine.

Each night we are kept awake by weird noises in this godforsaken hotel – I reckon Mr Sultan has a torture chamber in the basement, for all the guests who refuse to pay. I'm definitely going to investigate tonight, if I have the energy. Yet, I feel an odd contentment. For once in my life I have relinquished control. I am at your mercy, Marianne. I am allowing you to look after me, to bring me food and water. You won't let me down. I don't doubt that you will come back. You are the best friend I have ever had.

I could see how much Nathaniel loved you at that party and it scared me. You see, in some way I needed you already, although I hardly knew you at that point. I suspected that Nathaniel would tell you the truth about me, or the truth as he saw it, and I would lose you.

I'd had a bad day. I felt really scared about the cancer and really angry that it had chosen me. I didn't feel like being at the party. I went up to the bedroom to be on my own for a few minutes and found myself crying uncontrollably. I had learned not to cry at a young age; I never wanted to give Him the satisfaction. When Nathaniel came up to get your coats, I was thrown off-guard and felt embarrassed by my lack of control. It also pissed me off that you were leaving the party so early. I figured it was because Nathaniel didn't want to be there. I guess I was jealous of your relationship. If I'm honest, Nathaniel is the sort of guy I would have liked to meet one day but I knew then that I would never get the chance.

We were both fighting for you, to keep you – how pathetic is that? We both needed you in different ways, but I felt, at that moment, that I needed you more. I taunted him, told him he was suppressing you, holding you back, and he got really pissed off. Our anger kind of built up, irrationally, disproportionate to our knowledge of each other.

The sex was an act of anger, I guess, about all sorts of things, but not really about each other. I can't really explain it any better – you're the writer, Nathaniel's the shrink, you'll hopefully figure it out together.

I predicted Nathaniel wouldn't be able to carry on as if nothing had happened; he's too honest. He was deeply shocked and confused by what he'd done, but he didn't understand the power I have over men, the power that comes from a damaged psyche.

Rather than hurt you with the truth, he ended the relationship. I admire him for that, although I know it caused *you a great deal of pain. It left the way open for me to carry out my plan. I wanted to die in a strange country, on a new continent. I would have done it anyway, without you, but I didn't want to. See how selfish I am? Somewhere, I reasoned that I was also doing you a favour, that you needed the freedom to 'find yourself', or some bullshit like that. I also believe that you and Nathaniel will get back together one day, when you're ready. You belong with each other.*

I don't think I have very long to live. The pain is pretty bad most of the time. I am still scared of the end, Marianne. I have prayed that it will be quick; maybe that God or fate or whatever will intervene and end it quickly. Perhaps I'll get pushed in front of a train or be trampled by an elephant in the Bazaar. I don't want to die here, in this bed, with you having to tend to me, or in some crumbling Varanasi hospital. Strangely enough, I didn't think about the details of my death when I set off travelling.

It's funny what you come to value in these circumstances. Not money or beauty or cool friends, not even clever wit, love or comfort. The thing I value most is kindness. (I never thought I'd say something so crass.)

You are such a kind person Marianne, though you will probably hate me for saying it. You are a romantic soul; you like the idea of grand emotions, great passions, the agonies of unrequited love, but the thing I value most in you, in this moment, is your kindness; it's a quality that is greatly lacking in our world.

Maybe you should think about finding your mum, Mari; maybe she's not as bad as you think. Perhaps you're more like her than you realise – your bravery and sense of adventure. We are very harsh on women; we expect so much more of them in moral matters than of men. Men leave their families all the time and we hardly blink; women do it and they're seen as less than human. Perhaps it will help you just to know why. Perhaps I'm talking bollocks, I don't know.

I'll have to finish this letter; you're probably on your way back. I just want you to know these things, even if they put me in a bad light. I want you to know how much I love you and how much I have felt loved by you. I envy you all the years you have ahead of you, but I don't resent you for them. Remember, fear, not hate, is the opposite of love and in a world where fear is having its way, don't be afraid to love.

Sara x

Chapter 30

Death, in itself, is nothing; but we fear, to be we know not what, we know not where. John Dryden, *Aureng-Zebe*[16]

We attracted quite a crowd, both Indians and Westerners, their mouths open in question, eyes curious like small children on a school trip. We were no longer the voyeurs; we stood centre stage, fully involved in the action. Six solitary mourners accompanied the procession – Bert and Sam extended their stay in Varanasi and Rajpal, true to his word, made an appearance. He looked striking in a black headscarf, which contrasted with the white dress of Hindu mourners.

Mr Bakshi's friend, who was a pretty weighty official, had been very helpful in advising us on the proper procedure for a cremation, even authorising it to take place at Ghai Ghat; although it was not traditionally used as a burning ghat. It was surprisingly easy but then Varanasi is at home with death, and we had money. We were a godsend in our grief, willing to pay whatever price we were asked, all from Mrs F's guilt fund.

We paid over the odds for everything – the banyan wood used for the funeral pyre, the musicians who accompanied the procession with pipes and drums, and the untouchables who were experts in death. They weighed each log to calculate the price of the pyre, stacked it and then placed Sara's body, loosely wrapped in a white shroud, on top.

In the absence of a son, we asked Rajpal to remove the veil from Sara's face and expose it – for the last time – to the falling sun. He sprinkled purifying water from the Ganges, mixed with ghee, onto her face and then lit the pyre, coaxing the flames into life. The kindling wood shook heartbreakingly in his hand; his face was grey with grief. I wondered how deeply he had fallen in love with Sara.

The smell of sandalwood and lotus blossom masked less pleasant smells – the reminder that Sara's body had been slowly rotting in the ageing mortuary freezer for over a week. Yet her face now looked perfect, untouched by death, with no evidence of pain or fear etched upon it.

It was a particularly beautiful evening; the fragrance of magnolia inebriated the air so that I felt giddy with it, and the skies blushed like a love-struck virgin. The light died as the ceremony progressed and the day began to be replaced by night. The sky changed from deep to pale blue, bruised with purples and reds.

The onlookers seemed fascinated by a glimpse of a young white woman lying on the pyre, a virgin sacrifice with a rebellious strand of dark hair escaping the shroud to tangle with the flaming wood, and a straggle of disconnected mourners barely able to encircle her burning corpse. I'm sure they couldn't begin to imagine her story.

I was startled by a flash from above and felt an instant of anger as I looked up to see a tourist, a Western man, with a large camera. Then I smiled (as I thought Sara would have). I imagined a small, angry man approaching him…life goes on.

Everyone talks about how peaceful a person looks in death. I didn't think Sara looked peaceful; I thought she looked dead. Yet somehow that gave me comfort. As the flames licked her body, charring her once perfect skin and bones, singeing her glossy hair and melting her lascivious lips and eyes, I had a vision of her spirit rising from the shell that had housed it to find another home. Yes, it was a beautiful shell and had won her many things in life, but it had also brought her pain. It was just a shell. As she had once said of her ashes, "No bullshit, just burn them and scatter them in the river…"

It is difficult to completely reduce a body to ash and, as darkness fell and the sky changed to a brooding indigo, a few stubborn bones still remained intact. It is customary to leave a period of thirteen days between the burning of a body and scattering of the ashes, to give the mourners time to purify themselves. However, we didn't have this time and we completed our ritual immediately.

Sara had her wish – her remains were scattered with any further evidence destroyed forever. We each took handfuls of the ash and threw it into the air. For a few brief seconds, Sara filled the sky – she had been many things, but never small. Lighter particles were caught up by a breeze and continued to rise above our heads towards the city – off on another adventure – while the rest of her plunged into the sacred Ganga, into the arms of Lord Shiva.

The place where the Ganges leaves the mountains and enters the plains is called Har-ki-pairi (the footstep of God). It is considered to be the spot where the power of the river to wash away sins is superlative. Pilgrims hold onto chains so as not to get swept away as they immerse themselves in the waters and every evening, at sunset, priests perform a river worship ceremony in which floating lights are set on the water to drift downstream.

I pictured the long journey of the river from the mountains. I pictured it sweeping away the sins of all the pilgrims en route, taking their guilt and anger, their lust and lies, their prayers and sometimes their ashes, past towns, villages and rural plains. At Varanasi, the pure waters join with the filth of humanity to become a chai-brown soup. I imagined Sara leaving Varanasi and being carried through new and beautiful landscapes, before being released into the Bay of Bengal and perhaps, finally, into the vast expanse of the Indian Ocean.

It was dark when the six of us walked back up the steps of the ghat, heavy with our own reflections, past the indifferent stone cow, to the highest point. Rajpal had a flight to catch back to Agra and I had only a few minutes alone with him before he left. We stood away from the others.

"Sara loved you very much, you know." He held my hands between his.

I nodded, too choked to speak.

"You asked me a question, Mari, that night in Agra…about the way to find happiness. I think I was a little abrupt with you."

"No!" I protested, "I was being naïve." Raj didn't seem to hear me. His look was distant.

"I think I fell in love with Sara the first time I saw her. Not just because of her physical beauty, but because of something else, something I recognised in her; perhaps it was the cynicism, masking her vulnerability. When she told me she was dying I felt my one chance of happiness had been snatched from me, even before I had possession of it. I was angry.

"It was Sara who made me see the beauty of the few days we had together. She saw the fragile nature of relationships, that in themselves they don't bring certainty or happiness…"

"Marianne, are you coming?" Nathaniel was walking towards us.

"Marianne," Raj held my face between his hands and looked into my eyes with urgency. "Let go of your fear. Don't think too much about how to be happy; it is not complicated – remember the only way to happiness is happiness itself."

We waved goodbye to Raj and the remainder of our funeral party went to a nearby restaurant where we ate and drank in Sara's honour. My mind was still tingling with Rajpal's words. I slipped my hand into Nathaniel's; it was like the childish pleasure of fitting the last piece of the jigsaw.

"That was incredible," said Nathaniel, breaking the silence that had fallen over us all like soft ash.

"Awesome," said Bert, struggling with a large chapatti.

"Any closer to catching the culprit?" Sam asked Dave.

"We seem to have run out of leads," replied Dave, stubbing out his cigarette as the waiter brought his food. He examined his thali tray as if it was a crime scene, poking each portion with a spoon before digging in.

"I'm still waiting for a couple of calls."

"So what are your plans?" I asked Bert and Sam, partly to prevent them from interrupting Dave's pleasure.

"We're off to Nepal for a few days as planned," said Bert.

"Yeah, and then we fly home," added Sam.

"What will you do when you get back?" Nathaniel asked.

"I guess we'll have to work – been bumming about for too long."

"What kind of work?"

"Erm…we're both city bankers in New York," said Sam, almost apologetically.

I nearly choked on my dhal; even Dave looked up.

"You're joking!" I said. "I thought you were like college kids or west coast surf dudes."

Bert and Sam looked at each other and smiled as if they'd finally been rumbled, but were proud to have carried the joke on for so long.

"I'm like thirty; he's thirty-two," said Sam. "I guess you can be what you want when you're travelling."

I had the strange sensation that the play had finished and we were all taking a final bow.

After dinner, Dave said he wanted to walk the streets of Varanasi one last time. He seemed troubled and I felt he wanted to be alone. I, on the other hand, couldn't wait to get back to the hotel with Nathaniel. Despite my grief, I felt so alive after the funeral, so conscious of the joy of mere existence that my body was bursting with it. It was the first time we had made love since Nathaniel had confessed his liaison with Sara, and I felt an inexplicable happiness and freedom from fear.

Sara's letter had helped me in a way I could never have anticipated. It acted like a key unlocking a heavy shackle around my leg and I felt lighter, more hopeful. The letter also convinced me that Sara hadn't taken her own life and this was a great relief to me. However, her words had led me to ask myself some difficult questions and left me with the uncomfortable prickle of unfinished business.

At first, I reacted badly to Sara's suggestion that I might be more like my mother than I realised. I had always denied the maternal contribution to my genetic makeup and had even been ashamed of those characteristics that I had obviously inherited from someone other than my father. I modelled myself on my father, perhaps with some misguided sense of loyalty, despite my increasing frustration with his timid and fearful existence. It was as if Dad and I had held each other so close, wallowing in our mutual loss, that neither of us had had room to grow. Now, suddenly, the possibility that things could be different was strangely liberating.

It was Dave who suggested he could help me trace my mother. He had found birth parents for people who had been adopted and missing people for their desperate families. He said that in many cases the person wanted to be found, but was often too riddled with guilt, or fearful of rejection, to make the search themselves. For the first time I acknowledged the great void that had gaped in my life for years and which I had tried to fill with the wrong shaped things. I had been living with a thin bitterness, which had poisoned my life and caused inertia. The prospect of action now filled me with excitement.

I wanted to ask my dad a few straight questions, questions I had avoided for too long. I also wanted to help him eliminate signs of abandonment from every room, every corner of my childhood home. I wanted to replace beige with bright, contemporary colours, throw away dried flowers and replace them with living things. I couldn't believe I hadn't done it before.

"I've had an idea," said Nathaniel as we lay, side by side, in a state of soft contentment. "Why don't we carry on travelling the world together?"

"But we're due to fly home tomorrow." I felt excited by Nathaniel's spontaneity and the possibility of what he was proposing, but a little anxious about the implications for our respective careers.

"You've got nine months left on your ticket, Mari; it would be a waste not to use it. We can cancel our flights to London and I'll buy a round-the-world ticket. We'll fly to Delhi with Dave tomorrow and from there go anywhere we want – South America, New Zealand – the world's our oyster!"

"What about your placement, Nathaniel?" In the empty hours before the funeral, Nathaniel and I had talked at length about our career paths. I told him I'd made a decision to apply for the journalism course again – now that I had a bit more 'life experience'. I hoped I could one day put my training to good use in the pursuit of responsible journalism. I had also forced Nathaniel to talk about his psychotherapy training and I thought I'd convinced him to withdraw his resignation.

"I'll email my tutor, see if I can pick up the placement next autumn," said Nathaniel. "I'm sure it won't be a problem. You can apply for your course online…we can both start again next September." I had rarely heard so much excitement in Nathaniel's voice; his eyes gleamed with boyish delight. "Marianne, I need to push myself, the way you have. I realised it today at Sara's funeral. It just feels…right. Let's contact the airline now."

"Ok," I replied, enchanted by his enthusiasm, "but I've got something important to do first." I jumped from the bed and left the room before Nathaniel had a chance to say anything else.

The fear and fragility in my father's voice wounded my heart.

"Wouldn't it be better if you just came home, love? You'll be safer here."

"I'll be safe with Nathaniel, Dad; it's something I've always wanted to do with him."

I didn't give him a chance to put up any more objections. "Dad, I need to ask you something, it's important."

"Ok." His voice was hesitant.

"The photo...the one of Mum on the beach...she looked so happy, Dad. What was she laughing about? Please Dad, you must remember."

Another long sigh assaulted the earpiece. I wasn't sure if it was a sigh of exasperation, resignation or something else. I imagined his mind flooding with doubts and fears that would finally organise themselves into a decision: whether or not to tell me the truth.

His answer came out surprisingly quickly as if he had been waiting for my question for a long time.

"She was so happy, love, because...because she'd just found out she was pregnant...with you."

My father's words brought the past crashing into the present. The laugh was about me. She wanted me. In that exact moment, she wanted me, perhaps more than she had ever wanted anything.

"Why couldn't you tell me that, Dad? It would have made such a difference."

"I'm sorry love. I though it would make things worse. I thought it was better for you to believe she didn't care, that there was no hope of her coming back. I was wrong. She didn't leave because of you, sweetheart. She loved you more than you could possibly imagine...she left because...because she had to." His voice cracked like neglected leather.

"It's ok, Dad." I tried to soothe him with my voice. "I've got more questions, lots more, but I want to talk to you face-to-face; they can wait until I come back. Will you answer them?"

"Yes, love, I will....but I need to tell you something now."

"...Ok." I hadn't been prepared for this. It struck me forcefully, as it had with Nathaniel previously, that my Dad had a life that continued to evolve with or without me.

"I've met someone...a very nice lady from Red Rope." (This was a kind of Ramblers club with a socialist bent that my dad had been involved in for years.) "We want to get married... next September."

For a second I was too overwhelmed to speak. My first

reaction was one of shock that Dad hadn't told me sooner about this 'lady', we usually shared everything, and then came the desire to offer words of caution: Who is she? What does she want from my dad?

"Marianne love? I'm sorry if I've shocked you; I hope you don't mind…"

Then…happiness, bubbling up through rocks and soil, drenching parched earth.

"Dad, I couldn't be happier for you."

I put the phone down with a sense of something shifting into place.

Chapter 31

The following morning, we were interrupted at breakfast by a small boy waving a note frantically in our faces.

"It is most urgent sirs; you must read now; it cannot wait." Dave took the note and squinted at it, his eyes not able to focus at such an early hour on what appeared to be hastily scribbled words.

"Mr Bakshi wants us at the police station."

"But we have a flight at eleven," said Nathaniel.

"But it must be important; we can't not go," I said.

Dave studied his watch for a few seconds. "It's eight o'clock now. It takes about forty minutes to get to Babatpur Airport – let's say an hour to allow for Indian time. We need to check in forty minutes before the flight. I reckon if we load the car and leave in the next twenty minutes, we should have a good hour at the police station."

Nathaniel didn't look convinced, but we agreed to gather our belongings and meet at the car as soon as possible.

The atmosphere at breakfast had been stilted. Nathaniel and I told Dave about our plans to continue travelling and, while Dave seemed pleased for us, I thought I detected sadness in his eyes, as if our happiness showed up his own dissatisfaction. We were also battling with a strange mix of emotions. My passport had been released and I was no longer under suspicion of anything; therefore we were free and more than ready to leave Varanasi. However, there was a heavy sense of unfinished business that stirred uncomfortably and accusingly among us.

The police hadn't closed the case; they just didn't seem to be actively working on it. I felt they hadn't come up with anything of significance during the inquiry and concluded that they didn't care if Sara's killer was brought to justice or not. I felt disappointed. I wanted to believe that truth and justice are possible, even amid the chaos of India.

Dave was deeply frustrated that he hadn't managed to solve the mystery of Sara's death and, even on our last night in India, he pored over his extensive notes to see if he'd missed anything. While the funeral had helped me grieve for Sara and start to move on, I still wanted answers about her death and retribution for her killer.

"Sit down, sit down." Mr Bakshi waved his hands at the assortment of chairs in his office and smiled broadly. We followed his orders. We were dressed for air travel and I was already beginning to sweat in the airless room. I had the feeling once again that the play was over, and we were suddenly out of costume.

I looked around the room I had visited with trepidation each day for over a week; I felt a small thread of affection. The mountain of files on the floor looked even taller and I wondered how far down the pile was Sara's, how many new cases were stacked on top.

"We only have a short time; we have a plane to catch," said Dave, as we accepted probably the last cup of chai for some time – I would miss that too as I would miss many things about Varanasi. It surprised me that I could grow so fond of a place where I had experienced such trauma. Varanasi had held me in her arms, protected me, even nourished me with little signs of hope, despite the terrible events of the past week-and-a-half. I guess it is similar to the way we can feel exceptionally close to someone with whom we have shared great adversity, perhaps even mistake our affection for love. I looked over to Dave who was perched on the edge of his seat, his forehead furrowed in concentration. I felt heat rise over my chest and up my neck as I imagined what might have happened between us.

"Oh time, time!" said Mr Bakshi, leading me back into the present. "There is always more of it than we think." He continued to smile as he took a satisfied slug of his tea. "Where do you fly from?"

"From Babatpur Airport to Delhi." Nathaniel spoke with urgency, perhaps in the hope of forcing Mr Bakshi to his point.

"Then we're travelling on to Sidney," I said, "while Dave flies back home."

"Oh, home. How nice it is to go home." Mr Bakshi's eyes rolled up to the ceiling, as if remembering his own happy experience of returning to Mother India from colder English climes. "Back to your dreaming spires, hey?"

"What is it you have to tell us?" Nathaniel asked, distractedly cracking his fingers.

"Oh yes, you're in a hurry, aren't you." Mr Bakshi returned from whatever sweet recollection he was reliving and turned to face us. "I am happy to tell you the fabulous news…and I think we can accurately say that it is another feather in the cap of this police department…" he nodded at each of us in turn and adjusted his glasses. "I am happy to say that we have solved your case."

A garble of 'whats?' and 'hows?' merged together in the room. It was obvious from his expression that Mr Bakshi was enjoying the drama.

"You see…" He stood up and paced behind his desk like an officer planning an army manoeuvre. "You think you are so advanced in the West; you think we are ineffectual here in India, that we cannot possibly catch the villain." He came to standstill, his hands behind his back. He then scrutinised our three pairs of acutely attentive eyes. "Perhaps rather than rush around looking in every corner, behind every piece of furniture, we know how to stand still, let the frenzy pass; we wait for the mist to clear." He illustrated this with a majestic sweep of his arms. "We trust the gods that universal justice will be done, that truth will find its way to us." A hush fell in the room while we waited for this great truth to be revealed, but, after a slight pause, Mr Bakshi resumed his pacing.

"Yes, we use different methods to you; yes, we appear at times to be doing very little, but I assure you it is not always as it seems."

"Mr Bakshi! Who did it? Who killed Sara?" I had to restrain myself from jumping up and shaking him violently until he told us.

He slowly sat down and went through the familiar ritual of placing his glasses onto his rather fine nose. He then picked up several pieces of paper covered in the same beautiful Hindi flourishes as the post-mortem report. He banged them upright on the desk so that they fell into neat order and then placed them carefully in front of him. We pulled our chairs closer.

"Remember, my friends, it isn't *what* you find…" He leaned towards us. "It is *that* you find and I think you will be most surprised by what I am about to tell you."

Chapter 32

A statement taken by Officers Chaudhary and Gupta:

This evening, at approximately seven p.m., a man came into the police station. He gave his name as Mr Parag. He was a small, dark-skinned man who described himself as a devout Hindu. He appeared very perplexed and rubbed his hands together continuously, as if trying to warm them.

At first he did not make sense and we were about to dismiss him as yet another of the mad Dalit who frequent the station. However, he then claimed he had been present at the death of the Western woman, whose face he had since seen on posters by the ghat. We calmed his spirit and took him to the interview room.

Mr Bakshi looked up; he had a tantalising gleam in his eyes.

"There then follows the transcript of a taped conversation, which took place at seven-twenty-five. Shall I read it to you?"

"Yes, yes," we called in unison.

Officer 1: *Please confirm your name and address.*

Mr Parag: *My name is Mahesh Parag and I live in Chunar Village with my wife and seven children. Only three of them are boys... I didn't know she was dead; I am so sorry...*

Officer 2: *Can you please answer only the questions asked.*

Mr Parag: *So sorry.*

Officer 1: *Tell me the date to which you refer and what took place on that date.*

Mr Parag: *It was a Monday, the day of Govardhana Puja…*

"Are you aware of this festival?" Mr Bakshi looked over the top of his glasses.

"Yes," said Dave. "We know it honours the Sacred Cow."

Mr Parag: *I set off from Chunar at six o'clock in the morning to walk to Varanasi with my cow, as I do each year. I am not a wealthy man, sir; I think perhaps if I perform the ritual of Govardhana Puja, Lord Krishna, who is loved by milkmaids, will bless my family and give us prosperity. Perhaps Vishnu, from whose feet the great Ganga flows, will protect us… perhaps-*

Officer 2: *Yes, yes! How long did the walk take?*

Mr Parag: *She doesn't very much like walking…*

Officer 2: *Who?*

Mr Parag: *My cow, sir. I had to stop many times so that she could eat. She has a mind of her…*

Officer 2: *Just the facts. What time did you arrive in Varanasi?*

Mr Parag: *It was half-past one o'clock, or just after. I went straight to Ghai Ghat and ate roti and dhal, prepared by my good wife.*

Officer 1: *What happened next?*

Mr Parag: *I went to the mound at the side of the ghat, as always…*

Officer 2: *Which side?*

Mr Parag: *The right side, as you look at the Holy River. I began the ritual of Govardhana Puja.*

Officer 1: *And what did this involve, sir?*

Mr Parag: *I first placed some sweets – again made by my good wife – over the mound; this is to symbolise-*

Officer 2: *We know what it symbolises. Carry on.*

Mr Parag: *I then prayed to Lord Krishna for help to feed my children and to keep my cow healthy.*

Officer 1: *Did you see anybody else near the mound?*

Mr Parag: *Not at first, but then she came.*

Officer 1: *Who came?*

Mr Parag: *The beautiful girl.*

Officer 1: *At what time did she come?*

Mr Parag: *I am not sure...perhaps it was half-past-two.*

Officer 1: *Can you describe her?*

Mr Parag: *She was tall, with very pale skin...very beautiful, like the goddess Saraswati. She had long dark hair and she was dressed like many Westerners.*

Officer 1: *What did she do?*

Mr Parag: *At first she only watched me, and my cow. We walked around the mound seven times; each time I came round, she was there smiling at us, just looking and smiling. Nothing more.*

Officer 1: *Did she speak to you?*

Mr Parag: *No! I told you, nothing; she said nothing... I am so sorry.*

At this point the interview was interrupted. Mr Parag broke down; he sobbed loudly and his words were garbled. We suspended the interview for fifteen minutes, while Mr Parag had tea and the opportunity to calm his spirit. We then recommenced the interview.

Officer 1: *I am recommencing the interview after a break. It is now seven-fifty-five p.m. Mr Parag, can you tell me what happened after you completed your parkrama?*

"That means a circumambulation of the mound," Mr Bakshi explained.

Mr Parag: *I then led my cow to the top of the mound, where I stood for several minutes, contemplating the beauty of life and the goodness of Lord Krishna. I noticed that the girl had turned from me. She had her back towards me and was looking out across the Ganga.*

Officer 1: *Was there anybody else near the mound?*

Mr Parag: *No. There were many people in the middle of the ghat but no one by the mound-*

Officer 2: *So you had every opportunity to steal this young woman's money and murder her.*

Mr Parag: *No, no! I would never do such a thing. Why would you think-?*

Officer 2: *Continue with your story, Mr Parag.*

"Nice subtle interviewing technique!" Dave nudged me and raised his eyebrows. Mr Bakshi gave us a sharp glance as if we were children disrupting a class.

Mr Parag: *Suddenly, my cow lost her footing and fell... perhaps the heavy monsoon this year loosened the soil, I don't know, but I could not stop her; she just kept falling and falling. I tried to hold her rope, but I couldn't; she was dragging me with her. She fell onto her side and then rolled completely over. The girl didn't have time to move...I don't even know if she saw...oh my God...next thing I know, both my cow and the girl are in the Ganga. There is a great deal of thrashing about...many legs and arms...oh God...*

Officer 1: *Did you call out to warn the girl?*

Mr Parag: *I can't remember, I think so, Oh Lord Krishna, help me...*

Officer 2: *Mr Parag! What did you do?*

Mr Parag: *After some time, I managed to grab hold of the rope and pull my cow to the bank, where she scrambled to safety. I thought the girl would swim away, but by the time I had rescued my cow, she was gone...completely gone...oh dear, oh dear...*

Officer 2: *Mr Parag, please pull yourself together. Did anyone else witness this incident?*

Mr Parag: *I don't think so-*

Officer 2: *How convenient! So no one tried to help?*

Mr Parag: *Not at first, but then I called for help and many people came over. We could not find her. I should have helped her.*

Officer 2: *Why didn't you?*

Mr Parag: *I don't know. My cow is everything to me...I thought the girl would get out...*

"My God!" I rose from my chair, unable to contain my emotion any longer. "He chose to save a cow over a human being...over Sara!" Outrage was rising in me.

"Miss Taylor, before you make judgement, you must understand." Mr Bakshi looked at me with earnestness. "I'm not excusing his actions, but that cow is Mr Parag's livelihood and he had many mouths to feed. That animal is vital to his family's survival and is worth much more alive than dead!"

"And Sara isn't?"

"Perhaps you will allow me to finish the man's statement and then you can make up your own mind."

"Carry on," said Dave, pushing me gently back into my seat. Nathaniel placed his hand on mine. My legs were shaking uncontrollably.

Officer 2: *So why did you only come forward now, Mr Parag? I suppose it was for the reward, hey?*

Mr Parag: *No, no. I do not want a reward; you must believe me-*

Officer1: *Then why? It has been over a week since the girl died.*

Mr Parag: *I didn't know she was dead. I thought she must have swum down river and climbed to safety. I looked for a long time but it was getting late and I had to start my long journey back. When I arrived home, I told my wife what had happened. She was angry with me, saying I should have taken more time to look for the girl, that I should have informed the police. "Perhaps she was the beautiful goddess Saraswati, consort of Brahma," she said. "Perhaps she was setting you a challenge, which you have failed miserably." Each day, the guilt grew worse until I could bear it no more. I caught a bus back to Varanasi. When I saw the poster I thought my heart would fail. I came here immediately to confess. Oh my God, I am ruined.*

At this point Mr Parag broke down again and was inconsolable. The police officers ended the interview at eight-fifteen p.m.

Mr Bakshi removed his glasses.

"So, you see my friends, a cow did it; a cow killed Miss Fitzgerald, and we can hardly prosecute a cow, can we?"

We were stunned into a crackling silence, broken by Dave.

"Does the story add up?" He had regained his professional demeanour. "Could the blow to Sara's head have been made by a cow?"

"I checked with our forensic team in Delhi this morning," said Mr Bakshi, with a smug expression. "They say the measurement and shape of the wound to the head, as well as the force with which it was applied, is consistent with a blow from a cow's hoof."

"But what happened to the money?" Nathaniel asked. "Is it possible…"

"Shouldn't someone pay for Sara's death?" My voice rose towards hysteria, cutting through the emotionless exchanges of conversation. I don't think I really had a desire for revenge. Part of my anger was about Mr Bakshi's attitude, which seemed flippant, but also about the ridiculous nature of Sara's death, which deprived it of the great importance I felt it deserved. All three men turned to face me as if it had suddenly dawned on them how this news might affect me. Nathaniel quickly placed his arm around my shoulder but I shook him off.

"Don't any of you care?" I asked. A sob cracked the words.

"Of course we do." Nathaniel tried again to reach out to me, but I couldn't accept his comfort. At that moment I blamed him, in part, for Sara's death, for starting the rotten chain of events that had led us to this point.

"Miss Taylor." Mr Bakshi's authoritative voice silenced my sobs. "I have something very important to tell you." I was tempted to run from the room, feeling that I couldn't bear any more bad news. Mr Bakshi moved closer to me and his eyes softened into paternal concern. "Mr Parag has been detained here overnight…Miss Taylor, he has asked that you decide his fate."

Chapter 33

Fate, noun 1) The power beyond human control that determines events; destiny.
2a) An outcome or end, esp. one that is adverse and inevitable.
b) The expected result of normal development.
3a) A destiny apparently determined by fate. b) A disaster, esp. death. (Middle English via Italian from Latin fatum what has been spoken, neuter past part. of fari, to speak).
Fate. verb to destine (somebody or something) to doom (them or it).
Oxford English Dictionary[17]

Modern belief for the majority of the Western population seems to me to be: a weak blend of leftover pre-Christian superstition; fragments of childhood religion and ritual, only dragged out of a dusty cupboard for ceremonies around births, deaths and marriages, mixed with a smattering of new age belief and popular psychology.

If pushed, some will admit to holding a belief system but can rarely back it up with reference to religious texts, historical events or even show any evidence of devotion to their particular deity.

On the whole, even very intelligent and rational people appear to live their lives as if in the grip of a supernatural force that determines whether they will be sad or happy, whether they will win or lose, whether they will live or die.

This becomes most apparent after great catastrophes or when

people feel that their lives are under threat. We see news clips of bewildered people stumbling out of collapsed buildings or smoke-filled tunnels, uttering their ill-thought-out beliefs to a gullible world. "It's a miracle I avoided death..." "If it's meant to be..." "Everything happens for a reason..." "Touch wood, pray or fingers crossed..." And then always *that* word, with its irreproachable, unchangeable finality, sealed in those four frigid letters – 'fate'.

'All human things are subject to decay, And when fate summons, monarchs must obey.' (Dryden[18]).

Fate: cousin to that other unforgiving four-letter word, *'fear'*. Fate and fear hand-in-hand, take us to the Promised Land.

I had always believed that my fate was sealed at the age of three when my mother left. My choices, my actions, my thoughts had been negatively informed by that moment and all my future paths mapped by it. When Nathaniel left me and when Sara died, it only confirmed what I already believed about life and about myself: life is unpredictable and unsafe and I am the sort of person who is left by the people I love. My life had been about things happening to me, rather than about me making things happen. In consequence, I had trembled in the path of change, shuddered at the door of the unknown. A very slight shift in thinking could make all the difference in the world.

I had wondered over and over again since Sara's death why she hadn't fought harder to survive cancer, why she appeared to give in to it so easily. It didn't seem to be in character, especially in light of how courageously she had survived childhood abuse.

I talked to Nathaniel and Dave about this, in a desperate, grief-fuelled attempt to find some answers. Dave told me that he occasionally worked with survivors of catastrophe or terror attack and had been struck by the eerie similarity in the accounts of how these people survived against the odds, when others hadn't. This had prompted him to research the subject and through this he came across the concept of 'deep survival'.

Survival, they say, is determined by a person's beliefs about the world and about themselves; it is not dependant on physical strength but comes from deep within. Those who survive must first of all have the ability to admit that they're in trouble and reach a point of acceptance; then they must be able to act to do something about it. Those who freeze or remain in a state of denial are doomed. Survivors are not ruled by fear but are able to turn fear into anger – a sharper, more active emotion – that motivates rather than paralyses. Survivors must have the ability to think, analyse and plan, breaking large tasks down into small and attainable goals, so as not to be overwhelmed.

Lauren Elder was the sole survivor of a plane crash at 12,000 feet in the icy cliffs of the high sierra. She said she could see the San Joaquin Valley in California below her, but only survived by concentrating on the next task – getting to the next rock – handling what was within her power to deal with, rather than thinking about reaching ultimate safety. She had a broken arm, two-inch heels, a flimsy dress and no knickers on. She was even able to laugh at the idea of someone below looking up her skirt. Her journey took thirty-six hours. Most survivors say they were able to find contentment in their adversity and bizarrely could appreciate the beauty of their surroundings and even laugh aloud at certain aspects of their predicament.

It is important to survive for someone other than yourself – a greater cause – and to enjoy the survival journey, drawing on inner resources and believing you will succeed. Survivors lose the fear of dying and grow in the conviction that they can survive. However, they surrender to the reality that they might die – everyone does – but maybe not today.

A survivor must forget about rescue, everything you need is inside you already. One survivor of a sinking ship said, 'Rescue will come as a welcome interruption of the survival voyage'. He talked of how he actually enjoyed his awful journey.

It is about resignation without giving up, survival by surrender. Survivors do whatever is necessary to survive. If you're alive there's always one more thing you can do.

Nathaniel said that psychologists talk about meta-knowledge, which is a person's ability to know their strength without under or overestimating it. Survivors believe that anything is possible and act accordingly, never giving up. They keep their spirits up by developing an alternate world created from rich memories into which they can escape. We survive through a journey of transformation that doesn't miraculously appear, but comes from our deep inner core.

Dave told me about a guy called Gonzales who researched survival. He said that:

'A survival experience is an incomparable gift: It will tell you who you really are.'

I could see that in many ways Sara fitted the profile of a survivor. She could certainly turn fear into anger, as I had witnessed on several occasions during our travels, and she had been able to think on her feet and plan her escape with amazing clarity of thought, until she became too ill to do so. She had learned from an early age how to escape to other worlds and she never behaved like a victim, waiting to be rescued; she used her own inner resources to get her out of trouble and even to persuade me, through fair means or foul, to be her support network to the end of her journey.

So why hadn't she fought the cancer more ferociously? Perhaps she had made a positive choice to surrender to death; perhaps she didn't feel there was anyone or anything to live for, or perhaps the cancer was simply too strong to fight. I had to settle with not knowing. What I did know is that the incredibly short and electric time I spent with Sara had taught me many things about myself. It had forced me to get up from the floor and face my fear, rather than lie quivering at its feet. I couldn't change a thing about Sara's life, but I could change my own. I had found that I didn't have to be a victim of fate.

Chapter 34

'It is better to travel hopefully than to arrive.' Proverbs 604:12

"Me! What do you mean *'his fate'*? How can I decide another person's fate?" I looked from Nathaniel to Dave, hoping they would make sense of this nonsense, but they just stared back, mouths open like two dumb dogs.

"Mr Parag is guilty of negligence and of failing to report an accident." Mr Bakshi began his pacing again. "But it is not clear if he has committed a crime. He did not know it was a fatal accident at the time and he claims to have made some effort to find Miss Fitzgerald. However, he did not ensure she was safe and well before leaving the scene. You see, on the one hand, Mr Parag left the scene of an accident; on the other hand he eventually returned to report it, albeit a week-and-a-half later. I am certain we can find something to charge him with, Miss Taylor. Perhaps he can be given a large fine, although he is a very poor man, or he might even be given a short prison sentence."

My mouth had turned bone dry; I had been offered the role of God and felt I had no choice but to accept it. Mr Parag's fate was my fate.

"This is very unusual." Dave's sensible voice cut into my increasingly surreal world. "Why not just leave the matter to the legal system?"

"Yes, hon." (Nathaniel's concerned tones.) "You don't have to do anything; we'll leave now, go to the airport."

"It is your choice, Miss Taylor."

I pulled myself up straight and wiped my eyes. I was filled with a strong resolve.

"I want to meet him. I need to meet him. He was the last person to see Sara alive."

"Are you sure?" Nathaniel asked.

"Yes, I only need a few minutes."

"I'll come in with…"

"No, I'll see him alone."

Mr Bakshi escorted me through a dark maze of corridors at the back of the station. We arrived at a grey door.

"It is probably best if I come in with you, Miss Taylor."

"Please, can I see him alone?" I didn't want Mr Bakshi to take control of the situation or direct the questions. I wanted to take charge. "I'll call if I need you."

Mr Bakshi opened the door. A small man sat on a wooden stool, with his back to us. His dark, tightly-muscled legs poked out from beneath a loose white dhoti, which was wrapped around his waist. On top he wore a faded checked shirt that looked too big for his tiny frame. The back of his thin neck was darkened by the sun and looked vulnerable.

Mr Bakshi uttered a few words in Hindi and Mr Parag turned around. His eyes were unexpected; they were framed by dark circles and in them I saw sadness, hardship and humility; we held each other's stare for a few seconds.

"I will be right outside the door," said Mr Bakshi.

I sat opposite Mr Parag. The stools were the only pieces of furniture in the cell. A rush mat on the floor served as a bed and a crudely made clay pot as a toilet.

The first seconds were awkward. Mr Parag appeared to be grappling with his emotions, as was I. He then spoke in halting English.

"I am very, very sorry for what has happened, madam. You must decide my fate."

"Please, just tell me how she looked, the very last look?"

251

At first I thought he hadn't understood. His face twisted into what looked like puzzlement. I was considering how to re-phrase the question when, very suddenly, he plunged his hand into the folds of his dhoti. It crossed my mind that he had a weapon and I nearly called out to Mr Bakshi, but before I could he pulled out a parcel wrapped in old newspaper.

"I must return this to you." He handed me the parcel and I opened it cautiously. Inside was a huge wad of rupee notes. My blood ran cold.

"You…you killed her…for this?"

"No, no!" Mr Parag looked desperate and his hands flew to either side of his head, as if his brain might explode in the effort to convince me. "Your friend gave it to me. I could not tell the police; they would think I killed her for the money, but it isn't true."

"What *is* true, then?" I wanted to be convinced.

He lowered his voice to a whisper.

"I did not tell police the truth when I said I had not spoken to your friend."

"Why did you lie?"

"I will explain, madam. After I had completed my seven circles of the mound, she came over to me. She patted my cow and asked me many questions about what I was doing there and about my family. She seemed to be very interested. Then she gave me the money."

"Tell me exactly what she said…please."

"She said, "I no longer need this, spend it on your family." I nearly fell to the ground when I saw how much there was. I told her, "My family will be very happy indeed; we will not go hungry.""

"Anything else?"

"I asked her if I could do anything for her in return. She smiled and said, "Pray to your God that it will be quick." I do not know what she meant by that, madam, but in the name of Lord Krishna, I speak the truth, and I made the prayer."

My heart raced and I think I gasped aloud.

"I know what she meant, Mr Parag. She got what she needed." (Was it fate or did Sara determine what would happen?) "Tell me what happened next?" Mr Parag looked puzzled but I also saw relief spread across his face and soothe the lines, which I guessed had deepened in the past few weeks.

"She walked back to the edge of the Ganga and stared out, as if looking across to the other side. I climbed to the top of the mound with my cow, to thank Lord Krishna with all my heart for this good fortune and to ask him to answer the lady's prayer. That is when the terrible thing happened...oh my God, such a mishap."

"Did she cry out or struggle?"

"No. It was as if the river wrapped her up, made her invisible, so that I could not see her. I saw only her hair, for a very short time. It seemed to dance in the river like reeds, before it disappeared. I swear there was no struggle."

I swallowed hard, trying to hold back the flood, which I knew must come soon, but in that moment I felt calm and strong and as clear as I had ever been about what I must do.

"I forgive you for everything, Mr Parag. I want you to keep the money. Put it away, quickly; don't tell the police about it." I pushed it towards him just as I heard the door creak open. The envelope disappeared like magic into the folds of his dhoti.

"Is everything ok, Miss Taylor?" Mr Bakshi put his head around the door. "Your friends are eager to catch their flight."

"I want Mr Parag to be released. I don't want him to face any punishment."

"So be it, Miss Taylor." Mr Bakshi exchanged a few further words with him in Hindi and then Mr Parag jumped up, a broad grin on his face. He bowed to me several times and then flew out of the room.

"Thanks for everything, Mr Bakshi." I suddenly felt a great and unexpected fondness for him. I flung my arms around his neck and kissed his cheek. He laughed a kind of grandfatherly chuckle.

"Go on, go on," he said, with a little embarrassment. "The world awaits you."

I ran out of the police station to the gleaming Ambassador car, whose engine was revving impatiently. I jumped in next to Nathaniel.

"A man just flew out of the police station like the cat that caught the last bleeding mouse," said Dave. "Was that your Mr Parag?"

"Yes, he's gone home and we're leaving and everything's fine. I grabbed hold of Nathaniel's hand and squeezed it hard. "I'll tell you as we drive."

With a combination of luck and the expertise of the driver, we made it to the airport with only seconds to spare. The plane flew low over Varanasi, before making its turn towards Delhi. I glued my face to the window like a lover catching a last, desperate, glimpse of her beloved. At first, I could see only a small section of the city, but clearly, as if I could reach out and touch the tops of temples, mosques and churches, and run my finger along streets awash with golden light. From here my journey seemed small and insignificant, the tiny steps of a child, but what a journey it had been, both painful and terrifying. It had also been wonderful.

As we climbed, I saw a wider view. The streets and buildings were growing smaller, although I felt that it was I who was growing bigger: like Alice I had gulped down a magic potion and was filling the space around me. The desire to live a big life, a fearless life, coursed through my veins.

My last view, before the plane finally made its turn to Delhi, was of the whole city in miniature. Winding past it all was the River Ganges, looking as innocent as a silver ribbon dropped by a child at a birthday party.

Bibliography

[1]John Berryman, *A Point of Age*. Published by Faber & Faber (1942).

[2]Leon Bloy, *A Pilgrim of the Absolute*. Published by Arden Library (1977).

[3]*India (Lonely Planet Country Guide) 10th edition*. Published by Lonely Planet Publications (2003).

[4]Sogyal Rinpoche, *The Tibetan Book of Living and Dying*. Published by Rider (Random House) (1992).

[5]James Redfield, *The Celestine Prophecy – An Adventure*. Published by Bantam Books (Transworld) (1994).

[6]DH Lawrence, *Thought (Complete Poems of DH Lawrence)*. Published by Wordsworth Editions (1994).

[7]Marianne Williamson, *A Return To Love: Reflections on the Principles of A Course in Miracles*. Published by HarperCollins; New Ed edition (1996).

[8]Henry David Thoreau, *Walden: or, Life in the Woods*. Published by Dover Publications Inc; New Ed edition (1993).

[9]Don Miguel Ruiz , *The Four Agreements*. Published by Amber-Allen Publishing. Inc. California (1997).

[10]Edmund Spencer, *The Faerie Queen (Complete Works of Edmund Spencer, ed John Wesley Hales)*. Published by Macmillan (1870) (digitised 2006).

[11]Edmund Burke, *On Taste: On the Sublime and Beautiful; Reflections on the French Revolution*. Published by P.F. Collier (1909) (digitised 2006).

[12]T.S Elliot, *The Waste Land*. Published by E. Arnold (1973).

[13]Bertrand Russell, *Marriage and Morals*. Published by Routledge (Taylor & Francis Books Ltd) (2004).

[14]Robert Frost, *The Road Not Taken, The Road Not Taken and Other Poems*. Published by Dover Thrift Editions (Paperback), Dover Publications (1993).

[15]Morris Berman, *Coming to our Senses: Body & Spirit in the Hidden History of the West*. Published by Simon & Schuster (Bantam) (1989).

[16]John Dryden, *Aureng-Zebe (The Works of John Dryden: Plays – 'Amboyna', 'The State of Innocence', 'Aureng-Zebe')*. Published by University of California Press (1995).

[17]*Oxford English Dictionary (11Rev Ed Edition)*. Published by Oxford University Press (2006).

[18]John Dryden, *MacFlecknoe (The Major Works of John Dryden – Oxford World's Classics)*. Published by Oxford University Press (2003).

Note: where appropriate, all efforts have been made to receive permission for quotes published. Any queries, please contact info@legendpress.co.uk and additional credits can be added to future editions, if appropriate.